Hallmark
PUBLISHING

A GINGERBREAD Romance

Based on the Hallmark Channel Original Movie

LACEY BAKER

A Gingerbread Romance
Copyright @ 2019 to Crown Media Publishing, LLC

Print ISBN: 978-1-947892-43-9
eBook ISBN: 978-1-947892-58-3

www.hallmarkpublishing.com
For more about the movie visit:
https://www.hallmarkchannel.com/a-gingerbread-romance

Table of Contents

Prologue

EIGHT YEAR-OLD TAYLOR SCOTT BRUSHED small fingers over the soft fabric of her favorite red dress. Tears filled her eyes and the Christmas tree in front of her blurred. Her father had selected a great tree this year. It was taller than last year's, and so wide her mother had to move one of the end tables into the dining room so it would fit in the corner.

Taylor had hung most of the bulbs on the bottom half of the tree. Now, almost all of those were gone. She reached out to touch the only one that was still hanging. The white bulb that looked like it was frosted with snow was her favorite.

"Come on, Taylor. We're almost done packing," her mother said. She lifted the final white bulb off the tree and folded it into a piece of tissue paper.

Taylor was in awe of how her mother moved so gracefully in high-heeled shoes while carrying Taylor's favorite bulb across the room. The moment that bulb was stuffed into a box and that box was sealed with thick tape, Taylor wanted to sigh. Today was moving day.

Christmas was in one week, and instead of bubbling over with excitement for Santa's appearance and all the gifts she might receive, Taylor fought back tears. She shouldn't be sad. This wasn't new. Her parents were very busy with very important jobs. So what if that meant they had to travel a lot? It was for a very important reason. Even if it was right before Christmas.

Her mother closed the lid on the white box, and Taylor stared down at the word "Christmas" written in green marker.

So they were really leaving. All the wishes she'd sent up, on everything from the evening star to tossing at least a dollar's worth of pennies in the fountain at the mall, had been for nothing. The house was mostly packed. Everything in her room was boxed and waiting in the hallway for the movers to pick up.

They would not be in this house tomorrow. They were going to Washington...or France, or it might have been Australia. It didn't matter; they probably wouldn't stay in the next place very long, either.

Her steps were slow and heavy as she walked across the room to the mantel where her stocking was still hanging. She reached up and slipped it off the metal hook before carrying it to where her suitcase sat open on the coffee table. The memory of her mother folding clothes had her flipping the bottom half of the stocking up to meet the top and then stopping to rub her finger over the script letters that spelled her name. Her eyes blinked a few times. She was too old to cry. She slammed the top of the suitcase down and was about to zip it closed when she noticed her sketch pad, pencils, and crayons on the other side of the table. Taylor couldn't go anywhere without them.

Her latest picture wasn't complete, and since her mother had left the room, she knelt down to finish it quickly before they had to leave. This picture was just like her dream, the one she'd had about her future. She'd drawn the house from that dream, the stockings hanging for Santa and the family—a mother, father and a little girl—who lived happily ever after. Something felt heavy in her chest and she shook her head, concentrating more on what the picture still needed, rather than the dream. More red. The little girl's dress in the picture should be a deeper red, so she grabbed a crayon and pressed it harder to the paper.

"Taylor. It's time to go."

Hurrying to finish the dress and stay in the lines she'd drawn was tricky. But Mama was back in the room now, moving boxes, so she knew it was really time to leave. When the dress looked just the way she wanted it to, Taylor stuffed the crayons into a box and asked the question that had been weighing heavily on her mind.

"Mama, what if Santa doesn't find us this time?"

Carolyn Scott, wearing one of the nice business skirt suits she always wore, knelt down until she was eye level with her.

"Remember what I told you before our last move? Wherever you hang your stocking is where Santa will find you. And he did, didn't he?"

That was true. It was the year she'd received her first pair of ice skates. So she could believe her. Santa would find her in just a few days, and moving wouldn't be so bad. Maybe this time they'd stay in the next place long enough for her to make friends. That way Santa wouldn't always have to look for her stocking to find her; he would just remember her house.

"Oh, let's see today's creation." Her mother picked up the sketch pad, and that swishy feeling Taylor got in her stomach whenever somebody looked at her drawings began.

The bright smile on her mother's face as she set it back onto the table made Taylor smile, too.

"Sweetheart, I think it's your best yet!"

Still grinning, she fell into her mother's open arms and enjoyed the warm hug.

"Hey gang, the airport limo is here!" her father called into the living room.

Her mother pulled back from their hug. "So, you ready for our next adventure?"

"You bet!" Mama was right: Santa would find her, just like he always did.

She stood and put her sketch pad into her suitcase before grabbing her coat. In minutes, her parents had their coats on, too, and her father had zipped her suitcase. Taylor took the handle of the suitcase in one hand and walked beside her mother as they headed for the door.

That heaviness was no longer weighing on her chest. Her mother's smile and warm tone were reassuring. Maybe moving wasn't going to be so bad, after all. Maybe their new house would be like the one in her drawing: the one that the family stayed in forever.

Yeah, that's what was going to happen. This move was going to be their last, and they'd live happily ever after.

Chapter One

Twenty Years Later

CRISP WINTER AIR GREETED TAYLOR the moment she stepped out of the taxi and onto the sidewalk. A line of juniper shrubs alongside it served as the fence to her end-unit townhouse. The wheels of her hard shell suitcase rolled across the ground and she looked up to the driver who'd removed her bag from the trunk.

"Thank you," she said. Even bone-tired, she managed to smile and sound cheerful.

With a half bow and tip of his Santa Claus hat, he replied with a robust, "Merry Christmas!" and headed back to the car.

Of course she didn't want to seem lacking in holiday spirit, so Taylor called after him, "Merry Christmas!"

There was a quick beep of the car's horn and then the cab pulled away from the curb.

Taylor turned to grab the handle of her suitcase. This was definitely familiar: dragging a suitcase behind her as she walked either to a destination or from one. Tonight, it was from: her four-and-a-half month assignment was complete, and she was returning to her company's home base in Philadelphia.

After being with Ogilvy & Associates Architecture for seven years, Taylor figured it made sense to purchase a house here. At least that way, she had a familiar place to stay in between assignments. And she absolutely loved the upscale Northern Liberties neighborhood, conveniently located ten minutes from her office downtown. It was the closest she'd managed to settling down in one place. While she probably didn't sleep in the queen-sized bed in her large master bedroom more than ten times out of the year, her name was still on the deed, and owning the property gave her a deeper sense of meeting some of the goals she'd planned for her life.

At the moment, however, having this house was also a good thing because her feet were begging for mercy. She still wore the leopard-print pumps and navy suit she'd put on for her last meeting. There hadn't been time to change before she'd needed to be at the airport, so not only had she just taken a seven-hour flight which included a three-hour time difference, but her toes were screaming to be set free.

As she walked up to the front door, Taylor

couldn't help admiring her neighbor's endless strands of multi-colored twinkle lights and the cartoon Christmas family statutes adorning the yard. It had obviously snowed recently because the lawn was covered in a blanket of white, giving the statues a perfect winter wonderland backdrop. Her keys jingled as she pulled them out of her bag.

"Hey, stranger!"

Taylor jumped and almost dropped her keys as Wendy—one of the two friends she had, who also happened to be her neighbor—popped up from behind the bushes. It appeared she was stringing more lights.

With a wave, Taylor stepped away from the door. "Hi, Wendy."

"Merry Christmas. How was Tucson? Or was it Seattle? I'm sorry—with all the kids' activities and dates to remember, I don't know if I'm coming or going. But I did remember to grab all your mail from the box and any packages that came." Wendy was married to an advertising executive and had two children, a boy and a girl: the perfect pair.

She helped out tremendously when Taylor was away by keeping her up to date with all the drama from their home owners' association meetings and directing the landscaper to take care of her lawn.

"It was L.A. this time...I think," Taylor joked. "And thanks, I appreciate your help."

"Girl, don't worry about it. So you're in town for Christmas?" Wendy clapped her hands together hopefully. "You've got to come by."

Taylor had enjoyed a cookout and birthday party with Wendy and her family, but never a Christmas. A long time ago, that day had been designated for spending time with her parents. And once she'd become an adult, they'd tried to keep the tradition of celebrating together wherever they were in the world.

But lately, their schedules wouldn't even accommodate that. Case in point: Taylor couldn't travel to meet her parents this year because she had to return to Philly for a big meeting with her supervisor. A meeting she hoped would result in the promotion she'd been dreaming about.

"Um, I'm not sure yet, but I should know soon. And thanks for the offer."

"The standing offer," Wendy corrected. "Go on in and put your things down. As soon as I finish with this, I'll grab your mail and bring it over."

"Great. Thanks again, Wendy."

Taylor unlocked the door and rolled her bag into the foyer. She switched on the lights and sighed while stepping out of her shoes. In a few minutes, she'd carry them and her luggage up the stairs. She took her laptop to the dining room table and turned it on. She left it there because, right now, she really wanted to reacquaint herself with the place. Maybe it was silly, but for some reason she'd thought a lot about getting back here in the last couple of weeks, and now she had an urge to make sure it was everything she'd recalled.

It was. The clean, yet warm contemporary design of her personal space was a huge contrast from the bland corporate penthouse where she'd stayed while in L.A. Or anywhere else she'd been on business.

The artwork she'd selected during an impromptu trip to a gallery show hung in thick cherry wood frames on the wall. She'd been so impressed by the local up-and-coming artist that she'd purchased three of his portraits, which captured African-American families at different gatherings—Sunday morning church service, first day of school and a holiday dinner. Her fingers moved easily over the soft, bark-brown leather of the couch while she continued to stare at those paintings.

Growling from her stomach that sounded more painful than it actually felt echoed in the quiet room, and she frowned before heading to the kitchen. Her feet moved quietly over the glossy hardwood floors of the living room and onto the cool gray tile of the kitchen where she immediately opened the refrigerator.

"Well, that's helpful."

A lone bottle of water graced the top shelf, and as if in response to her blasé comment, her stomach grumbled again.

She grabbed the bottle just as there was a knock at the door. Wendy really didn't have to bring the mail to her tonight, but it was just as well; that way, Taylor could go straight to the office tomorrow morning.

"It's a lot." Wendy came through the door carrying a medium-sized box in one hand and two packages under the other arm.

"I see. Here, let me take that. You can set the box on the dining room table and I'll go through it later." Taylor grabbed the packages from under her arms, looking down at the return address as they walked into the dining room.

"Oh! This is from my parents." Giddiness bubbled inside Taylor as she tore into the first box.

"What is it? Your Christmas gift?"

"My Advent calendar," she announced after tearing off all the paper. "My mom makes sure to send me one every year." And this year, Taylor was so hungry she opened it and took out the first piece of chocolate.

Wendy chuckled. "Yeah, I thought you'd be hungry, and it's too late at night for you to be ordering food from any of those menus you have stuffed over there in your drawer. So I brought you some leftover spaghetti."

Taylor was already chewing the chocolate and reaching for another piece when she groaned. "Oh, Wendy, you are the best!"

That was the truth. In all her travels as a

child, Taylor hadn't been able to form many connections with girls her age. The bond she'd formed with Wendy had started as cordial and eventually turned into a real friendship.

Wendy pushed the box of mail closer to Taylor and went into the kitchen to set the bowl on the counter. The first level of Taylor's house had an open floor plan, so Wendy could still see and talk to her even though she was in another room.

"I'm just used to preparing three meals a day, and you're not used to grocery shopping on a regular basis. We match up well that way."

Taylor skimmed through some of the mail. "You're absolutely right. I've got to get better at basic things like that."

"Well, you could if you'd stay in one place long enough," Wendy said and then chuckled. "I know, I know what you're gonna say. But as your friend and neighbor whose kids would love to come over here for sleepovers and birthday parties too, I'm just tossing these things out there: get married, have some kids. They're wonderful at settling you down immediately and encouraging scheduled and unscheduled grocery store outings."

Taylor's first response was a grin because Wendy was always trying to get her to join the Mommy club. But Taylor was a realist.

"You know that's not in the cards for me right now. I'm still trying to get settled in my career."

"You're twenty-eight years old and a senior architect or something like that at one of the city's largest firms. How much more settled in your career can you be?"

That was a good question...with an even better answer.

"I'm a senior project manager, but my goal is to become a department head at Ogilvy. Hopefully in the international department. And I think I'm really close to claiming that. So to answer your question, I've got a little more settling to do."

Wendy was nodding as if she'd heard all this before. "Yeah, I know. And hey, you're entitled to your own dream. I'm probably just projecting, anyway, since my kids drive me crazy a good percentage of the time. But I wouldn't change a thing. For me, my family is my dream."

Those words replaced the giddiness Taylor had been feeling with a heaviness. Maybe it was just because she was tired and hungry. After Wendy had gone, she continued to stack her mail in organized piles and took the box over to the trash can. She knew she should warm up some of that spaghetti, but she was really tired. A hot bath to soak her feet and every other aching muscle in her body would help lift her spirits.

Her laptop buzzed. Taylor pulled out a chair, sat at the dining room table, and pushed a button on the screen to accept the incoming

Skype call from her mother. Then she grabbed a couple more pieces of chocolate from the Advent calendar.

"Hi, Mom," she said when Carolyn Scott's face came into view on the screen.

"Taylor, sweetheart. I hope it's not too late, but I wanted to catch you before we went to breakfast."

It would never be too late to talk to her parents. Since they always seemed to be in different time zones, Taylor looked forward to anytime they could link up. She missed them so much, especially around this time of year.

"Don't worry. I just got home." She unwrapped and popped another piece of chocolate into her mouth, enjoying the creamy taste.

"Hi, honey. Merry Christmas!" Her dad, Grant Scott, came onto the screen leaning in beside her mother.

They were still such a good-looking couple: her mother with her warm brown eyes and always-smiling face, and her dad with his stern but loving demeanor. In Taylor's eyes they were the standard for love and commitment. They were also the reason for her wanderlust, and for that she thanked them because otherwise she wouldn't be in a position to receive the greatest promotion of her life.

"Hi, Dad. Merry Christmas to you." Taylor quickly chewed her candy so she could speak better. "So how's Christmas in Singapore?"

"Hot and humid," he complained with a grin. "And this sweater isn't helping." Her father only wore Christmas sweaters once a year, and this was a nice red one. It had tiny wreaths all over and reminded her instantly of the early years when they each wore the craziest holiday sweater they could find and took lots of pictures. "So, now that you've seen it, I'm taking it off."

And as if to punctuate those words, her father walked away, leaving Taylor and her mother to chuckle.

"So how did things go in L.A.?" Carolyn asked.

Taylor was glad she'd asked. "Two sunny months and the new condo complex is almost built."

"And I see you've got the Advent calendar I sent. But is that tomorrow's chocolate you're eating today? Isn't it only December ninth for you there?"

Her mother knew her too well. Taylor never ate the chocolates chronologically. For her, a daily chocolate indulgence was nice, but lots of chocolate at once was never wrong.

"Hey, it's tomorrow in Singapore, right?" Another candy went into her mouth. "This one's for you."

Carolyn grinned. "Any chance you can join us here this Christmas?"

"Well, I'd love to, but I may be packing the moving boxes again. I'm meeting my boss tomorrow to talk about my next assignment."

"But honey, if you're not coming here for Christmas, what will you do? I really don't like the idea of you being by yourself at this time of year."

Why was everyone so suddenly worried about her being alone for Christmas? A good number of her adult Christmases had been spent alone, even if they'd been in a pretty nice location. Her mother was an international lawyer and her father was a diplomat, so their jobs had always taken a priority. Taylor had learned from the best.

The little girl who'd once dreamed of having a permanent home with a husband and kids where she could host large holiday gatherings for all her friends and family—her parents included—had grown up. Now she was content traveling the world and building her career. Christmas came and went each year, and she pulled out her stocking to hang wherever she was at the time.

"Well, Wendy's invited me over. I can hang my stocking there. Okay?" Hoping that would appease her mother and end this portion of the conversation, she continued, "Give Dad a big hug for me."

"That sounds good. Wendy's nice, and she has a beautiful family. When I see pictures of them, I can just imagine getting pictures of my future grandbabies at birthday parties."

Taylor vowed to never send her mother another photo of herself with Wendy and her family again.

"But I will definitely give your Dad that hug. Love you!" Carolyn blew a kiss and waved on screen as casually as if she hadn't just dropped that obvious hint.

"I love you too, Mom. And I'll let you know what my boss says tomorrow." She mimicked her mother's blow kiss and disconnected the call.

Lowering her head to the table, Taylor allowed herself a few seconds to miss her parents and remember the naïve dreams of the little girl she used to be. Then she stood. Her hot bath was calling, and pity-party time was up.

Chapter Two

THE NEXT MORNING, TAYLOR WALKED down the street looking at all the buildings in Center City, Philly's central business hub. A leather briefcase in the window of a supply store halted her steps. That would definitely hold her portfolio and laptop. It had a sturdy-looking strap and lots of side pockets where she could store things. She loved it. She leaned closer to look—and the purse and bag she was currently carrying slipped from her shoulder, making her stumble forward.

"Excuse me." A guy almost bumped into her. He wore tennis shoes with his suit and was obviously in a rush.

"And a Merry Christmas to you, too," she muttered to his retreating back as she readjusted her straps.

The city was decorated in full holiday regalia.

She'd already passed three sleighs, a humongous Santa, and too many twinkle lights to count. Even unlit, all those lights put Wendy's yard to shame, and made Taylor shake her head at how this time of year sent people into decorating overdrive. Taylor had nothing against decorations or the holiday. In fact there were parts of it she really enjoyed—namely, the chocolate in her Advent calendar she'd forced herself to ignore this morning. She loved Christmas carols and watching old holiday movies. The rest she'd left behind with her childhood.

Car horns and screeching tires blared through the chilly air. Taylor pulled the lapels of her beige wool coat closed. It definitely was not window-shopping weather. Besides, she needed to get to the office. Her meeting with Linda Woods, Senior Manager of Architecture & Design, was scheduled for nine-thirty.

Ogilvy was on the tenth floor of an eighty-five-year-old building with an industrial and contemporary style. It was one of the most iconic buildings in the city. That was one of the things she'd never forgotten about Philly. While the city wasn't as known for its notable buildings as New York or Chicago, there were plenty that spanned the spectrum of traditional and modern architecture.

She stepped off the elevator and walked down a short hall before going through a glass door. She'd just stripped off her gloves and was about to head toward her desk when her co-worker and another longtime friend, Josephine Lancaster, approached. Josephine had worked for Ogilvy the same amount of time as Taylor. With her ready smile and dark wavy hair, she was the one who kept Taylor informed of all the office gossip.

She was also the one who wanted Taylor's job. Not in a backstabbing type of way, but in the I-really-wish-I-could-move-up-in-this-office way. Taylor understood completely. Moving up was definitely on her mind this morning.

"Taylor!"

"Hey, Josephine. It's nice to see you."

"Welcome back. I'd say welcome home, but you spend more time on the road than here."

Taylor personally enjoyed her lifestyle but had always been amazed at how differently her friends felt about it. Where Wendy was all "settle down and have a family," Josephine openly envied Taylor's life of the single traveling archi-tect.

"Well, I might be on the road again. I'm sup-posed to talk to Linda right now, hopefully about the promotion to International Projects Depart-ment Head in Paris. How do I look?"

She'd carefully selected a beige pencil skirt—a classic favorite in her wardrobe—and a festive cranberry-red blouse for today's meeting. The coat she'd picked up during one of her few off days in L.A. matched perfectly. After a quick survey of said outfit, Josephine leaned in to attach a Christmas tree pin to the lapel.

Her co-worker stepped back with a proud smile and replied, "Very merry. And speaking of Linda, she's in a pretty good mood this morning. Not sure why because Del is late on his plans for the Links project. But you don't need to concern yourself with that. Just go in there and wow her!"

That's exactly what Taylor planned to do.

"Right. Thanks." She nodded and looked down at the pin. "I don't really know why you're carrying around extra Christmas pins, but it's perfect!" And definitely not something Taylor would have considered adding to her outfit. Not that she even owned a holiday pin to consider.

"I've been so busy planning this year's Christmas party, I've had decorating on my mind. But everyone's whispering about the Paris position. If you get it, then I can possibly slide into your position here. I'm more than ready to actually supervise a project outside of this city. " Josephine clapped her hands together, barely holding onto her glee.

Taylor knew Josephine's happiness was a mixture of promotion possibility and the office party. While Taylor loved her job, she wasn't a huge fan of office get-togethers, but since her goal was to impress enough to get this promotion she would make an exception.

"I'm looking forward to the party. But I should really get to this meeting. Don't want to be late."

Josephine nodded. "I hear ya. We'll catch up later and good luck!"

She crossed both sets of fingers and wagged them at Taylor.

"Thanks!" Taylor replied, anticipation giving way to a nervous excitement that followed her around the reception area and back to her desk, where she ditched her coat, briefcase, and purse.

This floor of the office was full of cubicles before branching off in the back to the conference room where she was scheduled to meet with Linda. She waved and spoke to other co-workers she hadn't seen for a while. The Christmas decoration explosion had hit this floor as well, and all the red and green cheer caused a dull ache in her chest she wasn't ready to examine.

Through the glass doors of the conference room, Taylor saw Linda, wearing a red blazer over a white blouse with black pants, on a phone call. Linda looked up as Taylor approached and waved her in.

In this spacious room, the walls were crisp white and floor-to-ceiling windows boasted a magnificent view of the city. Of course, there were more Christmas decorations. From a tree standing prominently next to the flat-screen television used for presentations, to the garland decorated with red and gold bulbs around the door and along the window frame, the space was extremely festive. An easy, but not totally genuine, smile touched Taylor's lips as she took a seat and waited for Linda to finish with her call.

"No, no, no. Yeah, we're excited too, and we promise not to disappoint. Thank you, Mr. Mayor. Goodbye." Linda's smile, however, was beaming as she disconnected the call. She leaned in before folding her hands onto the table.

One of the things Linda always mentioned loving about Taylor was her willingness to take initiative. True to form, Taylor spoke up without hesitation. "Wow. The mayor. What was that about?"

"Actually, it was partly about you." Linda was bursting with excitement.

And now, Taylor was too.

"Me?" She struggled to keep a tight rein on her emotions. Jumping up and yelling "Merry Christmas to me!" was probably a little premature and way over the top.

"Taylor, you've got a great eye. Your work is always cutting-edge, and your projects always come in on time and under budget."

She gave herself a mental pat on the back. "Thank you."

"And that's why the board is considering you to head up our new Paris office."

Yes! Yes! Yes!

The position in Paris would be a dream come true. One of the only dreams she'd be able to see to fruition. She'd been to the city twice before—once with her parents when she was a teenager, and the second time on a trip right after her college graduation. Even though that visit hadn't ended the way she'd planned and had put a serious damper on the whole "City of Love" vibe, Taylor still felt like Paris was the place of hope and possibilities for her.

"Wow. That would be terrific!" Being professional was slowly losing the battle to shouting for joy.

Linda appeared to like her enthusiastic response, but was very good at keeping her cool as well. "We'll see what happens," she said. "But in the meantime, there's this project I need your help on. A project I know the board will be watching closely because of its potential for more work with the city."

Taylor clasped her hands—because yeah, they were shaking just a little. "I'm totally open and excited. What's the project?"

"Ok, so you know that we submitted a proposal for the new downtown redevelopment project."

"Yes, but I thought Crestford had a lock on City Hall." Crestford was Ogilvy's biggest competitor in the city. They'd also recently moved their offices into this building which, she imagined, created a more competitive atmosphere.

"According to the mayor, we're currently his top choice."

Go Team Ogilvy! Her mood was apparently all about shouting this morning. "Great!"

"In the meantime, we need to do everything that we can to up our public profile." Linda's fingers drummed on the table as she spoke.

That made sense. Keeping Ogilvy in a positive public light would increase their visibility and gain more trust from the mayor, which would hopefully help the firm land his future projects.

"How can I help?"

"Well, the City's Christmas Marketplace is coming up, and they're doing a gingerbread house competition to raise money for an after-school program charity fund."

Christmas and charity went hand-in-hand, so Taylor could follow that part. She waited to hear the rest.

"We've got a spot in the contest and *I* need *you* to represent our firm as our designer."

And that's where Linda lost her. Confusion came like that chilly breeze blowing outside and Taylor stilled.

"You want me...to design a gingerbread house...as in gumdrops and candy canes?" Saying it out loud sounded just as odd as she thought it did in her mind.

Linda, on the other hand, was completely feeling this idea. "A life-sized one. I mean, we're talking big!"

Taylor was completely serious when she said, "Linda, I'm an architect. Not a baker. And besides, how does building this gingerbread house enhance our public perception and get us the city job?"

"Christmas is about love and giving. Just by entering this competition Ogilvy is showing how much it cares about the children. If we win, not only have we helped to raise money, but we'll also impress the mayor with our unlimited skills. In addition, the board will look kindly on the team player who is willing to get in there and help this company pull off a major victory. And yes, I know you're a very talented architect and not a baker. That's why I've already found you expert help."

Helping the mayor was one thing. Making an even better impression on the board was a big whopping thing that Taylor understood would seal the deal on her promotion.

"Have you ever heard of Annabelle Renard?" Linda asked the question as if she didn't need a response from Taylor.

Either that, or she knew what Taylor's response was going to be. "Ah, yes, doesn't she have a fancy restaurant downtown?"

The chic French restaurant sat on the corner across from the florist where she sometimes ordered flowers for her mother. How many times had Taylor thought about going in for dinner? And how often had she been pressed for time while she was between assignments and postponed that dinner?

"She happens to be the best pastry chef in the city. She's agreed to meet with you to discuss teaming up." Linda passed her a business card with the restaurant's name and address. "Taylor this is important. What do you say?" This was the somber Linda, asking for something she knew Taylor would not be able to decline.

And she was absolutely right.

This time Taylor's smile was genuine as thoughts of living in Paris played in her mind. "You had me at gumdrops. I'm in!"

"You're kidding me. A gingerbread house?" Josephine stood by Taylor's desk a half hour later and frowned while pinning poinsettias to the garland around the wall of Taylor's cubicle.

"I know. I thought I was getting Europe, but turns out I'm getting the North Pole." Taylor sighed. "But Linda wants me to do it, and it might convince the board to give me the Paris job."

And in the end, that was all that mattered. If she had to create a life-size gingerbread house to get the job of her dreams, that's exactly what she was going to do. But first, she had to make it to the meeting with the baker on time. Taylor grabbed her coat off the back of her chair.

Josephine still looked perplexed. "Hang on,

where are you going? The office Christmas party starts in a couple of hours." The party that Taylor hadn't wanted to attend in the first place.

"Oh, well, I'm scheduled to meet the baker Linda paired me with at noon. The competition starts the day after tomorrow. Which means I should have started yesterday. But I will try to be back in time for the party." Because despite their previous talk about Taylor's promotion hopefully leading to Josephine's, Josephine was looking crestfallen at the possibility that Taylor wouldn't be there for the festivities.

Josephine immediately perked up. "I'll save you a plate and some cake."

No matter the circumstances, Josephine always managed to make Taylor smile.

Only a couple of hours after she'd arrived at the office, Taylor was once again on the elevator. She put on her coat, hat, and gloves during the ride down and had just stepped off the elevator and was turning the corner to the lobby when a man on his cell phone bumped into her.

Their eyes met and they each turned. He slipped his phone into his pocket before saying, "Taylor Scott."

"Bradford? What brings you here?"

"Ah, Crestford just moved our offices here. We've got the top two floors now."

Josephine had already told her that, but Taylor didn't want him to think she was paying more attention to their firm than she needed to.

Taylor and Bradford Fleming had gone to college together. They'd each landed internships at Ogilvy and worked together for four years before Crestford made Bradford an offer that included more money, travel and the Director of Design title. Bradford accepted the offer. If she were in his shoes, Taylor probably would have done the same.

"Oh joy, we're back together again." That was a snide retort, but she had somewhere to be. She didn't have time to chat with Bradford.

But he apparently had more to say. "So...I hear you and I are going head-to-head, or should I say gingerbread-to-gingerbread."

Now that, Josephine hadn't told her.

"So you're doing the competition too?"

Because that would only be fair to make this promotion even harder for her to obtain. Bradford was a great architect, which was why Crestford had been so eager to steal him away.

"Yeah, what is it about Crestford and Ogilvy? They're always so competitive."

His tone was joking, but Taylor wasn't really feeling the laughter at the moment. "I don't know. Try asking your Crestford colleagues since they stole you away."

"Well, in one sense you already won this one. Snagging Annabelle Renard, I hear, as your partner. That was a lucky grab. You beat me to it."

Great—point one to Ogilvy. "Thanks. Well,

I'm actually late meeting her now. So I'll see you around."

"See you on the battlefield," he called after her.

Taylor walked out of the building feeling slightly less excited than she had when she walked in, but even more determined to once again do a great job.

LeCristal was a fine French restaurant on a corner in Rittenhouse Square. The outside of the building featured exposed brick and windows which were historic and created a unique feel. But the instant she stepped inside her mind soared back seven years to a sunny day in a Paris bistro.

"It's not you, it's me."

Shock from hearing the most clichéd break-up line ever had been the only thing that kept her from tossing her drink in Randall Kirby's face. That, and the fact she'd been dating him for the last nine months of her senior year. She'd thought at the time, *This has to be a mistake.*

"What?"

"I got that job with the start-up company I told you about. You know, the one in Alaska. I accepted it."

Was that all? "Okay, well, I'm the queen of

traveling. The only reason I've stayed put this long was because of school. You know I can live anywhere."

"But after you spent the summer working at Ogilvy they offered you a permanent position upon graduation. All you have to do is call them and you're off to Philadelphia."

He was right, and taking a paying position as an architect was the culmination of everything she'd worked for in college.

"I can't take your dream from you, and I don't want a long-distance relationship."

He'd said the words matter-of-factly. On the outside, Taylor had given the impression that she'd taken them the same way, but on the inside, a part of her had collapsed with sadness and disappointment. Her first long-term relationship—the one she'd thought, perhaps a bit naively, would lead to marriage—was over. But she'd been taught to always look on the bright side, and so she did. She was still in Paris, and her first job as an architect would be waiting when she returned to the States in a month.

She should've known it would turn out this way. That childish dream of home and family was no more. All that she had was her career, and she planned to make the best of that in every way possible.

"Can I help you?"

The server's deep voice interrupted her trip down memory lane.

"Ah, no. I actually think I see who I'm meeting with over there."

When he left she walked further into the dining area of the restaurant. The memory left her feeling a little lightheaded—and even more determined to do a good job in this competition.

Soft instrumental music played in the background while servers dressed in black moved to ensure each table was perfectly set with shiny silverware and pristine white napkins. Gold sconces hung on dark cherry wood walls and bathed the space in a soft golden light. White twinkle lights were neatly and strategically placed so as to provide a festive ambience without overwhelming the guests with the holiday, or taking attention away from their spectacular menu.

It felt just like Paris, which was why the memory had come so fast and fierce the moment Taylor walked in. If she believed in fate, this would definitely be it.

It was just about noon, which meant she was on time, and she walked on legs that were a little wobbly from the slap of nostalgia—not to mention her nervousness about the competition.

"Please, marzipan first, and then the piping." A woman dressed in black pants and a white chef's jacket was speaking to a man wearing the same ensemble.

The man was icing a Yule log cake to make it look as if it were surrounded by snow. "Get me the meringue from the kitchen," the woman directed him.

Earlier, Taylor had Googled the pastry chef. This woman with the air of authority was Annabelle Renard, the baker who was going to help her win this competition.

Taylor's steps grew a little more confident as she approached the table. "Excuse me, Annabelle?"

The woman looked up at Taylor, her gaze both assessing and questioning.

"Taylor Scott," she introduced herself and stopped directly across from where Annabelle stood.

Knowledge—at least of her name—registered on Annabelle's face. "Nice to meet you." The woman spoke with a frosty French accent.

"Wow, that looks amazing." She pointed to the items on the table: a Yule log, several smaller cakes, and one deliciously tempting cheesecake. The table was decorated to look like a winter wonderland, and the white frosting on each cake matched the tablecloth. A cute set-up that was definitely making her hungry.

"This?" Annabelle pointed down at the table before coming around to stand in front of Taylor. "No. This is a disaster, but I'll fix it. So tell me about this gingerbread competition."

They were going to get right down to business. That was fine—Taylor could definitely do that. "Oh, I would be honored to work on it with you," she began.

"Yes. Well, I do owe Linda a favor. But how much experience do you have in a kitchen?"

"Um, actually none." Honesty was her policy in life, including in business. "In fact, I'm pretty helpless except for microwave meals and simple things like cereal or boiled eggs." All of which were generally enough to survive on for long periods of time. Cooking was overrated, and while her mother had done a little more than Taylor could do, it was nothing she'd ever aspired to learning more about.

"Ah," Annabelle replied with a look that said she was definitely not impressed.

"But I have designed condos in Hong Kong and recreational parks in Seattle. I've lead teams of draftspeople and engineers. So don't worry, I know how to take charge. Every ship needs a captain and I am ready to lead."

Reciting the highlights of her resume in under a minute felt like a live Twitter pitch.

Annabelle folded her arms and pointed to Taylor. "So you would be in charge, huh?"

"Oh. Absolutely. I have been spearheading projects on my own for the last three years with Ogilvy. And while I've never participated in a giant gingerbread contest before, I'm certain I can design something that will produce a win for the company. I can do whatever I set my mind to." Her confidence was back. She could definitely do this job, and she would. She just needed Annabelle to join in by doing her part—the baking.

"Well, I see. Very impressive. But I just need to get in touch with Linda first." Annabelle looked away from her and then gave her attention to a man who appeared with a bowl of something white and frothy.

Was the meeting over? Weren't they going to talk about preliminary plans or something like that? Obviously not, since Annabelle was definitely engrossed in doing something else. It almost appeared as if she would've rather been doing anything else, which didn't make sense if Linda had already spoken to her about the project.

But what else was Taylor supposed to say—or do, for that matter? The woman was clearly finished talking about it for the moment. And Taylor was definitely hungry now.

"Okay. *Merci*." Her business smile was in place as she waited to see if she were at least going to get one last eye contact with Annabelle. Something to give some indication that the woman even knew she was still standing there.

"*Merci*," Annabelle said with absolutely zero enthusiasm.

She hadn't gotten the wrong vibe—Annabelle was just busy right now. Taylor could see that as she left the restaurant. All was well. She had her baker on board, and now all she needed to do was get some sketches together. Ideally, she would've liked more time to prepare, especially since it was so out of the norm from what she usually did, but it was fine. She could do this.

If she wanted that promotion, she didn't have much choice.

Chapter Three

Adam Dale was a perfectionist when it came to his baking. He'd spent hours making the fondant ornaments for the Christmas tree cake he'd been commissioned to create. The cake was a seven-tier masterpiece with several layers of his favorite vanilla cake and freshly made strawberry icing, all covered in Christmas-tree green.

He just had a few more ornaments to add and the gingerbread star to place on top, and he'd be finished. Unfortunately, that was ten minutes past the time that Ray DeLuth, his boss and the owner of Ray's Bakery, wanted him to be ready. But Adam refused to rush. Adrenaline pumped quickly in his veins yet his hands remained steady over the piping bag while he made the fondant ornament look like the real thing. He didn't get to work on cakes like this often, so when he did, he wanted to make sure to give it his very best.

One of his favorite memories as a child was watching his mother bake, and when he was tall enough to see over the countertop, Gloria Dale had allowed her son to assist with whatever she was doing in the kitchen. From the biscuits they often had for Sunday dinner after church, to specialty breads she made for the women on her various committees to school bake sales, Gloria was an expert at anything made in the kitchen. Her smile had been warm and validating when Adam had announced that he wanted to be a baker.

Unfortunately, Will Dale had a totally different idea for his son's future. In fact, Will was insistent that each of his four children get college degrees and secure themselves in a traditional, lasting career...in an office. Adam could accept that because his father had been raised by a single mother who'd worked three jobs just to keep food on their table. He'd stayed in Philadelphia after high school and gone to college, majoring in business management.

Culinary school had come later—after his marriage to Cheryl and Brooke's birth. His wife had encouraged him since day one to follow his heart. When that finally led him to register for part-time classes at the culinary school while Cheryl ran her in-home daycare and took care of Brooke, he'd finally started to feel like he was doing what he was meant to do.

That all ended three years ago with a car accident and Cheryl's death.

Adam had been devastated. And with only one income and a then-seven-year-old daughter to take care of, culinary school had no longer been a possibility. But Adam had never let go of the dream, and eventually he'd found a job that paid well and allowed him do what he enjoyed.

"Loading the other items in the truck, Adam," Ray bellowed.

Ray was a sixty-something year old man who'd spent his life building the reputation of his bakery. His scraggly beard and slow gait endeared him to customers, while his easy command of the bakery had taught Adam a lot about the business.

The final ornament was in place. It looked exactly like the vintage glass ornaments that always hung on his family's Christmas tree. They were brightly colored, with swirls, leaves, or pretty little snowflakes, like the one he'd just completed.

Now for the topper—the most important part of a tree. It was made of gingerbread, his mother's recipe with lots of molasses, and decorated with green, red and white piped icing.

"Perfect!"

Pride eased his lips into a huge grin and he pulled his phone out of his back pocket to snap pictures of the tree cake from all angles. It would go into his portfolio, just like the one he'd showed to the investors at the Brexley Group five months ago. They'd still decided not to back his bakery because he hadn't completed culinary school.

"You still back there playing with that cake? I'm starting the engine and pulling off in five seconds. You be there or be square!"

Nobody but Ray said that anymore. Adam shook his head and closed the box of red velvet cupcakes decorated in Santa hats and boots— his precocious and beautiful ten-year-old daughter's idea. Regardless how old the saying was, Ray wasn't known to kid around, especially about work. He would definitely leave without him.

Adam carefully loaded cupcakes and the Christmas tree cake into the back of the truck and, out of extreme precaution, sat in the back to make sure the cake didn't shift or fall during the drive. Ray chatted all the way from the bakery to downtown where they had a few orders of bagels and donuts to deliver as well.

An hour later, Ray was watching the clock again. "Adam, let's hurry. We have three more orders to drop off."

They were parked in the loading area behind a tall office building. Adam climbed out of the truck and focused on removing the Christmas tree cake as slowly as possible. It was a chilly day, but Adam had foregone the heavy coat, opting to wrap a festive red scarf around his neck instead. A red scarf that was threatening to slip off and onto the cake.

He frowned at the scarf and Ray's hoovering commands.

"You can't rush art, Ray."

The sound of Ray's raspy laughter echoed from the driver's seat. "Just move it along, Rembrandt!"

While beautiful and definitely tasty, this cake weighed a ton. He maneuvered it as best he could on the service elevator. Because of its height, the cake could not be packed in a traditional box; the best he could do was settle it into the bottom half of a large cake box and carry it that way. He'd memorized the floor number scribbled on the order form in his apron pocket, and he stepped off the elevator when it dinged at his location.

The place was a maze of cubicles with a surprising lack of people occupying them. Laughter and chatter came from a conference room at the end of the floor. He started in that direction but stopped when his phone chimed with Brooke's special ringtone from his pocket.

Adam took a few steps away from the entrance to the conference room and set the cake on a nearby desk so he could press the button on his Bluetooth to answer.

"Hi, honey." The only thing other than baking

that could make Adam smile on command was hearing his daughter's voice. "Just a few more deliveries and Daddy'll be home."

That wasn't exactly what Brooke wanted to hear.

"Aunt Jenny's cooking my favorite—mac 'n cheese! You can't miss that." Brooke was crazy about mac 'n cheese and ice skating. Everything else in her young life came in a dismal second place.

"I won't miss the mac 'n cheese."

"And then we're decorating the tree."

"Yes." Nodding was his way of reminding himself of what he'd forgotten during his busy day at work. "We're gonna decorate the tree right after dinner. So be sure to get all your homework done before I get there."

Adam was so lucky that his sister Jenny had also decided to stay in Philly for college. He'd promised his parents that he would keep an eye on Jenny while she was here, but after Cheryl's death, Jenny ended up being his lifesaver.

"I will. Now hurry up and make those deliveries!"

Brooke could also be a taskmaster. He blamed that on the time she spent at the bakery watching Ray.

Grinning and shaking his head, Adam ended the call and hefted the cake into his hands once more. He headed for the conference room and walked inside, stopping at the first edge of a table he could see around the cake.

"Ogilvy Associates?" Adam asked the moment he set the cake down.

"Ooh, yes!"

"Oh no!"

Two women spoke simultaneously, and he peered around the cake just in time to see one of them pulling at some papers that were on the table. Her actions made the cake wobble and Adam grabbed the base to keep it from toppling over.

"You're getting icing all over my plans!"

Alarm was clear in her voice. She had glossy black hair that fell past her shoulders, and she looked festive, wearing a Christmas tree pin and pretty skirt. But her frown was what concerned him.

"Sorry about that." He wasn't sure where the icing had come from. Possibly, some had been on the floor in the truck and had gotten onto the box.

Digging into his pocket, he found an old piece of tissue, which he used to wipe the icing away from the plans. She gasped at the larger smudge of green his efforts caused.

"It's ruined." She reached for his wrist, stopping him from wiping anymore.

He saw the mess his efforts were making and planned to stop before she touched him. It was too late: her hand was warm against his skin and a sweet aroma wafted through the air. The cake, no doubt. But no—there was something else, like flowers or sugar candy. Whatever it was it came from her; she was standing very close to him. And he liked it. Until she pulled her hand away and stepped back.

"But this must be the cake for our Christmas party. It's so beautiful."

The other woman said this—the one wearing holiday earrings. Up to this point, he hadn't paid that much attention to her because for some reason the sweet-smelling woman with the cognac brown eyes had kept him engaged.

"Thanks," he said, yanking his mind back to the moment. It was always good to hear that someone appreciated his efforts even before the cake had been tasted.

"What am I supposed to do now?" Brown Eyes asked the other woman.

"Can't you just reprint them?" It was the best suggestion Adam could offer even though she wasn't talking to him.

"Can't you just move your cake?" She leaned over to push the box away so she could gather up her papers.

He reached out to protect the cake and this time their hands collided against one side. They both pulled away with green icing on their fingers.

The other woman giggled. Brown Eyes stared

down at her hand and huffed. This wasn't getting better.

"Okay. On the count of three I'll lift the cake and you can get your plans," he instructed.

Their gazes held for what seemed like eons. A weird tugging sensation in the pit of his stomach made it seem as if he were somehow being drawn to her.

"Fine." Her teeth clenched and Adam knew she was really annoyed.

He was a little irritated that she was taking this so seriously, but he was more concerned with why he couldn't stop staring at her.

"One. Two. Three." He lifted the box.

She pulled the papers back. The papers were big and fanned back at her face causing a few curls of her hair to fall onto her forehead. She immediately reached up a hand to push them back...and smudged green icing over her forehead.

The other woman giggled again and Adam knew it was time to get a move on.

"I'll be back with your cupcakes."

When Adam turned to leave the room, he heard Brown Eyes mutter, "Unbelievable."

He repeated her declaration, but was certain it wasn't for the same reason she had. He couldn't believe that after all this time being single, the first woman to elicit any type of reaction in him was this one with her sacred plans and frowning—albeit, still quite lovely—face.

Two hours later, and just in time to avoid Brooke's classification of him being late, Adam checked the temperature on the oven and sat down at the table to enjoy his dinner. This is what he looked forward to each night. Working at the bakery had him up and out of the house pretty early in the morning, so Jenny usually arrived around six and was the one to get Brooke started for the day. After putting in about twelve hours at Ray's, Adam was usually the one to pick Brooke up from the aftercare program at school and they spent the evening together. The Christmas season had business booming at the bakery so his hours were a bit wonky, but this evening he was glad he'd made it in time.

As Brooke had told him, tonight they were having box mac 'n cheese along with chicken tenders. The moment he'd arrived home he'd put two trays of gingerbread cookies into the oven. They were cooling now. He'd already told them they could have one for dessert, but the rest were to finish decorating the tree—otherwise they'd attack him in the kitchen.

As strange as that may sound, the thought made him smile as they finished blessing their food and began to eat.

"It smells so good in here." Jenny inhaled

deeply and then forked mac 'n cheese into her mouth.

"Smells like being home for the holidays." He didn't know why he'd said that. Maybe because all the way home he'd been thinking about the fun and boisterous holiday celebrations his family had when he was young. Specifically, the Christmas Eve Adam and his siblings' pleas to open one of their gifts turned into an offer to sing one of their mother's favorite Christmas songs, "O Holy Night." That one song morphed into a full-blown Motown Christmas concert that ended when Jenny took her dance moves too far and slid into the Christmas tree. Jenny wasn't very fond of that memory, but to this day his parents brought it up every time the family was together.

Adam had been so fond of his childhood holiday memories that when he and Cheryl had Brooke they'd begun a few traditions of their own, such as reading *A Christmas Carol* to her on Christmas Eve and, when she was old enough, ice skating on Christmas morning.

Jenny made a groaning sound and nodded. "I know, right? Mommy would've definitely baked her homemade mac 'n cheese with all those different cheeses she adds. That's when a kitchen really smells divine."

She wasn't wrong. Their mother wasn't only a terrific baker, she could cook circles around all the women Adam had ever known.

"Grandma's mac 'n cheese is really good. But I like this kind too 'cause the cheese is so gooey when it first comes out of the pot." Brooke simply loved cheese.

His smile was genuine as he watched his daughter chew.

"There's fifteen days till Christmas," Brooke announced after a few moments. She'd been counting down the days since Thanksgiving.

"You're correct. So we've got to get this tree decorated tonight. Santa loves seeing all the different trees as he goes from house to house, so we have to make ours very special." He really wanted to make the tree special this year because he'd been late buying one. Their ritual had always been to visit the tree farm and find a tree to cut down the day after Thanksgiving. Brooke would wake up as early on that morning as she did on Christmas day, bouncing around and hurrying him and Cheryl to get ready so they'd be first at the farm and could get the best tree. This year had been the first year that he'd had to be at the bakery on that day to prepare for a huge order they needed to deliver. So he hadn't been able to get the tree until two days ago.

"Right! Me and Aunt Jenny already brought in all the boxes from the garage. So we're ready."

"Yes we are! I love Christmastime." Jenny loved any holidays that resulted in her receiving presents. As the youngest and only girl of the

Dale siblings, she'd received more than her fair share of gifts in her twenty-one years.

"Remember how we used to try and stay up and wait for Santa to arrive?" Jenny asked after eating another chicken tender.

The memory had Adam laughing. "I sure do! You would always make noise. You could never tiptoe back into your room, and Dad would hear you. We'd all worry the moment we heard his footsteps on the stairs."

"Yeah, but when he came up it was just to tickle each of us and warn once again that Santa wouldn't visit if we weren't sleeping." She laughed.

Adam did too, until he met Brooke's discerning gaze.

"You and Mommy never let me stay up to watch for Santa." Her normally cute forehead crinkled but there was a twinkle in her hazel brown eyes that never failed to touch his heart. Maybe because those eyes coupled with her tawny brown complexion made Brooke look just like her mother.

There were moments when Brooke talked about Cheryl as if she were still here. Those were the times that broke his heart, but he knew it was his job to make things better for his daughter. His tone remained light and cheerful even though the pain of their loss was still evident. "Just like my parents warned me not to, I do the same to you. And you see, it works. When you go to sleep, you wake up the next morning and Santa has been here. Isn't that right?"

His arm extended and his fingers tweaked her cute little nose. Her chubby cheeks lifted and the bubbly sound of her giggling erupted. "Yes, that's absolutely right!"

"I was thinking," Jenny said after a few moments of them enjoying their meal, "What if you put on your Christmas wish list this year that you would like to open your own bakery? Maybe that's what Santa will bring to you."

How had they gotten on that topic again? Oh wait, he knew, because Jenny had been obsessed with it lately. He shook his head, but Brooke jumped in for the tag-team.

"That's a great idea. We can write your list before we go to bed tonight, Daddy."

"You wanted double stories tonight, remember?" He brought that up even though he hadn't been late coming home after all, so he didn't owe her an extra story. But Adam really didn't want to put his wish in writing. That was almost as bad as making a plan. And one of his mother's staunchest warnings was, "life is what happens while you plan." He and Cheryl had planned a wonderful life of having more children that she would continue to take care of at her daycare while he ran his bakery. In one night, that plan had been destroyed. Now, he was focused on living life for every happy moment he and Brooke could claim in the present.

Brooke shook her head. "That's okay. Your list is more important. That way you can get everything you want for next year, just like me."

Adam didn't know what to say to that. If he told her there was a great possibility that he wouldn't get something he put on his list, then she may stop believing in the magic of Christmas. Yet, how could he make the list when he didn't believe in the dream he'd had most of his life?

The timer on the oven buzzed, saving him from further discussion.

"Gotta get the cookies." He jumped up. "You two get in there and finish adding the garland. You left a few spots empty last night."

In the kitchen, Adam took a tray out of the cabinet and found his spatula. He moved the cooled cookies from the cookie sheet to the tray. If seeing the perfect shapes and smelling the delicious scent of molasses made him long to bake his specialty cookies and cakes on a daily basis, it wasn't because of a dream, but simply because he was a baker. And as a baker, he was doing just fine working at Ray's.

Five minutes later, he joined Jenny and Brooke in the living room near the Christmas tree. Two stockings hung over the fireplace. Jenny insisted on hanging her stocking at her own apartment, even though she always met Adam and Brooke back at the house after they visited Santa's Landing and went ice skating on Christmas morning.

"All right folks, here they are. We have to put the hooks on them before we can hang them on the tree."

Brooke was just adding another candy cane to the tree, but immediately turned her attention to the tray of cookies when she finished.

"But they're good to eat," she said after grabbing one and biting into it.

"Hey. I left your cookie in the kitchen." Brooke continued to chew and he could only shake his head. "Every year we have this discussion. Gingerbread are for decorating. Not eating." He really did say this every year and nobody ever listened. There was a distinct joy in knowing that they never would.

"You can't blame us for liking them. They're too yummy. It's just more proof your talents are going to waste at Ray's." Jenny gave him that same look she'd been giving him since his meeting with the Brexley Group. It was the look that said she was tired of him not listening to her. Well, Adam was tired of explaining why he wasn't listening.

"Not all that again." It was the last thing he wanted to discuss right now.

"All what, Daddy? Your baking is always the best." And as if that compliment should serve as permission, Brooke snagged another cookie from the plate before running up the stairs. "Be right back!" she yelled.

Her ponytail bobbed up and down as she took to the stairs and grinned.

"The kid's right, Adam. You're an artist in the kitchen. But at Ray's you paint by numbers. It's high time you opened your own bakery." Jenny sighed at the exact moment his phone chirped with a text message.

"Thanks." He couldn't look at her while accepting the compliment because he was reading the message. "That's Ray and I've got a few thousand cookies to bake."

That meant he was going to be up late again tonight getting the dough ready at home to cut down on how early he needed to leave the house in the morning. He handed the tray of cookies to Jenny.

"Adam." She wanted to continue their discussion, or she wanted him to agree with her and collect recommendations from his satisfied customers to go along with his portfolio and meet with the Brexley Group again. Right now, Adam wasn't going to do either.

"Have a cookie," he told her and hurried back into the kitchen.

Chapter Four

𝒯HERE WAS NOTHING LIKE A lunchtime holiday shopping run. Especially when she didn't have to go alone. Taylor had done some shopping while she was in L.A., as she did whenever she traveled, but she really liked shopping with Josephine. And Josephine loved any reason she could get to visit the Shops at Liberty Place.

"So you never got a chance to tell me what happened during your meeting with Annabelle."

Taylor didn't have enough hands. Adding the bags she'd just received from the clerk in the department store to the ones she'd already had from the previous three stores they'd visited was like performing a juggling act.

"Ah, yeah, right. We were interrupted yesterday when I was about to tell you." And the last thing she wanted to think about was that interruption which had caused her to stay at the office until nine-thirty last night finishing the new drafts of her gingerbread house plans. Again, she recalled the baker who smudged green icing all over her original copies. His actions, coupled with his nonchalance about destroying her work, had infuriated her—so much so, she hadn't stopped thinking about the guy all night.

"Yeah, that was too bad about your designs. But the Christmas tree cake and those cupcakes tasted awesome!"

Leave it to Josephine to be more concerned with the food.

"Anyway, the meeting with Annabelle went very well," Taylor said, wanting to believe it was true. "I watched her work a little and she seems like a perfectionist."

"I've seen her on TV before and she was pretty tough. Do you think you'll be able to work with her?"

"We're a great match. Annabelle is a consummate professional and only puts out the best product." Unlike the delivery guy yesterday. He obviously had no idea how to properly deliver a cake, let alone bake one. He did, however, have a certain appeal... "Annabelle Renard!" Josephine marveled. "I cannot believe you're going to be working with her. And that design you did for the gingerbread house was fantastic. I've never seen anything like it."

"Yeah, well, I had to start all over again, but I

was able to copy it pretty accurately. I still can't believe that guy."

A sly expression flitted across Josephine's face. "Wait, you mean the cute bakery guy who couldn't stop staring at you?"

He definitely hadn't been staring at her.

"Probably wondering if I was angry enough to smash his precious cake," Taylor said. "Which I was, by the way."

They turned toward the exit and Josephine shook her head. "I don't know. He couldn't stop looking at you, and he was nowhere near as upset as you were. In fact, I think he looked besotted."

Taylor laughed. "Nobody uses that word in everyday conversation."

Josephine shrugged as they walked through the door. "They do if they just watched the 1940s version of *Pride and Prejudice*."

That was one thing Taylor and Josephine had in common: they both loved old movies. While Taylor preferred the holiday classics, Josephine was all into the vintage romances.

"Anyway," Taylor said, "this project may not have been my first choice, but I intend to make the best of it."

She glanced up, hoping it wasn't about to start raining; she'd left her umbrella at the office. The sky looked as if it might open up and let out a downpour at any moment.

"That's the spirit." Josephine's positive attitude continued. "And who knows? You may actually end up really enjoying the work. I mean, it's so different from anything else you've ever done."

The best way to avoid getting wet in a downpour was to walk faster. "True. I just never thought after all of my studying that I would be designing a large gingerbread house. But hey, opportunities come in different places at different times. That's what my mother used to say."

"That makes sense. And this is a great opportunity, especially if it makes you a frontrunner for the Paris position."

"And if I get Paris, I'm recommending you to Linda to take my job."

"Oh, my goodness!"

Again with the words nobody used, except maybe the children who starred in the *Annie* movie. Josephine was definitely one of a kind, and Taylor found her uniqueness endearing.

"You're a great architect, and it's time you got the chance to spread your wings."

Josephine was no doubt about to gush with excitement, but Taylor's ringing phone put a loose lid on it. She glanced down at the screen. "Oh. It's Linda right now."

She answered. "Hi, Linda. I'm out doing some Christmas shopping. What's up?"

"My blood pressure, if you must know," Linda snapped. She was clearly not in as good a mood as Taylor was.

"Why? What's wrong?" Taylor asked.

"Oh, nothing much. Crestford poached our talent again. They got Annabelle."

Taylor stopped walking and Josephine looked at her questioningly. "What?" A sick sensation began swirling in the pit of her stomach. "How? She seemed so excited about the project when I met with her yesterday." Annabelle had actually seemed a tad disinterested, but Taylor had chalked that up to her being busy with that winter wonderland table. Not that she hadn't wanted to work with her or that she was entertaining another offer to be in the competition.

"Well, apparently, she was even more excited when Crestford offered her top billing on all of their promotional items for the competition, and to feature her house in a separate ad campaign later." The irritation in Linda's voice said she was more upset that she hadn't thought to offer Annabelle the same things.

"She can't...well, I suppose she can, but... where does that leave us?" Taylor didn't know what else to say. This project had come out of the blue and was as far from what she'd been trained to do as she could imagine, but that didn't mean she still didn't want to win.

"Chefless," Linda quipped. "Any ideas?"

"No," Taylor admitted. "But you know what, don't worry. I'll figure out something."

"Keep me posted," Linda said before hanging up.

Taylor was stuffing her phone back into her pocket when Josephine asked, "Taylor what happened?"

"Annabelle dropped me. The competition starts tomorrow. I need to find another baker, fast."

That was all the explanation Taylor gave before hurrying back to the office.

At almost four in the afternoon Taylor was on her tenth call.

"Look, I totally understand it's a busy time of year for bakers, but it's for a good cause." She paused briefly to remember the pitch she'd been reciting all afternoon to one baker after another. "And a giant gingerbread house. I mean, come on. Doesn't that sound like fun?"

Rubbing the back of her neck, she tried to keep her smile in place and prayed her tone was still upbeat and personable.

The baker turned her down, anyway.

"Of course," she replied, disappointment like a familiar slap in the face at this point. "I'm sorry to bother you. Merry Christmas."

Time to scratch another name off the list. After hanging up the phone, she did just that, with more gusto than was probably necessary.

But she would not be defeated. Taking a deep

breath, she picked up the phone and dialed another number. Her gaze went to the cherub-like Santa on the edge of her desk.

"Hello? Le Gateau? Hi! Yes. This is Taylor Scott again, um, I was wondering if you'd reconsider... Hello?" Did he just hang up on her? "Hello?"

Are you kidding? Was that what people did at Christmastime? Hang up on other people because they happen to call back to ask a question they'd asked—more like begged—an hour ago? How could that be possible?

Taylor frowned and hung up the phone seconds before Linda walked by.

"Any leads?" she asked hopefully.

Taylor gave her a thumbs up, because again, she was not going to admit defeat. There was a way to fix this and she was determined to find it.

She was a troubleshooter by nature; that was what made her good at supervising projects. If there was an issue, Taylor could evaluate it and find a solution. There was never any doubt in her mind about that...when she was on a normal architecture project. But this gingerbread house contest was anything but normal. And it was the biggest obstacle in her career at the moment.

Sitting back in her chair and moving so that it started to spin slightly could be a way to spark an idea. Or not. But then the Santa on her desk once again caught her eye. She stared at him a few seconds, wondering if she were being childish or silly. This was no time for games. Then again, what did she have to lose?

"Come on, Santa, can't you grant me an early wish this year?"

She tried not to take the non-response personally.

"Any luck?" Josephine asked from her desk on the other side of the cubicle.

Taylor turned in her seat. "Not yet. And I've already called half the bakeries in town."

Josephine frowned. "So what will you do?"

Glancing back at her desk, she saw the wrapper to the cupcake she'd eaten while she was making her list of bakeries to call. She picked it up.

"Josephine, what bakery did you use for the Christmas party?" Yes, the delivery guy had been rude, but the red velvet cake had tasted delicious.

Josephine left her desk and now stood at the entrance of Taylor's cubicle. "Ray's Bakery. Why?"

She had an idea. Dangling the cupcake holder between her fingers she grinned. "'Cause desperate times call for desperate measuring cups."

Josephine stared blankly. "Did you just make a baking joke?"

"Never mind." Taylor stood to grab her coat. "I'll call you later."

The first thing Taylor noticed when she walked into Ray's Bakery were the delectable scents. Fresh baked bread, cinnamon, and sugar aromas wafted through the air. It was like a preamble to the picture-perfect line-up in the display case. While chocolate was her favorite decadence, the iced pastries looked divine. Huge muffins stood in straight lines while rows of cupcakes in a rainbow of icing colors marched up and down the row beneath. On the other side of the case were cookies and cakes and in seconds Taylor could feel herself gaining weight from simply staring at all the treats.

But she wasn't here to purchase anything to eat. She had an agenda and she remained focused on that alone.

"Be out in a minute!" someone from the back yelled.

There was no one in line, just a little girl sitting at a white table who appeared to be doing schoolwork. It was a nice-looking bakery with five sets of table and chairs and a glass storefront with *Ray's Bakery* in frosted white letters on the window. She'd used every bit of her control to not become mesmerized by the contents of the display case.

Instrumental Christmas carols played lightly, and she hummed along with "We Wish You A

Merry Christmas." Her humming was apparently so loud the little girl sitting at the table looked up at her. She was a pretty child with chubby cheeks and thick brown hair styled in two afro puffs. Caught, Taylor covered her mouth and whispered "Sorry!"

The little girl chuckled and shook her head before going back to her work. Taylor returned her attention to the display—this time a little more quietly—and admired the poinsettia-themed design scheme that started with a few bulbs and a bunch of the holiday flowers twined into a thick thatch of fresh garland. Even if Christmas decorations weren't so much her thing, she loved flowers, and poinsettias were among her favorites.

The delivery guy came out carrying a tray of cookies. He immediately leaned over to slide them into the display case, so he didn't see her until he stood up.

"Yes," he said. "How can I help you?"

The words seemed to slow as his lips dipped into a frown, telling her he wasn't happy to see her. To tell the truth, she wasn't all that thrilled to see him, either.

"Oh no, it's you," was his follow-up line before he glanced over at the little girl. "Brooke, hide the cakes."

Taylor pasted on her best smile.

"Are you Ray?" She really hoped he wasn't the baker she needed to help her win this competition. This guy, as annoying as he still seemed, was actually more alluring than she'd recalled. He had wary yet kind root-beer-colored eyes, which she'd glimpsed when he talked to the little girl, and a rich sepia brown complexion. But his looks didn't matter. What mattered was talking to Ray and getting him to help her.

Clearly she had to go through this guy first. "Look, I know we got off on the wrong foot the other day."

"That's putting it mildly," he said and walked around the display case until they were standing in front of each other.

Taylor frowned, but before she could reply, the little girl, Brooke, was up from her seat and coming to stand next to them.

"Daddy, you told me to always be nice to customers," she said.

Taylor couldn't help but smile at how cute she was with her two puffed ponytails. She was equally impressed with her when Brooke extended a hand for Taylor to shake and said, "Hi. I'm Brooke. Welcome to Ray's."

Taylor happily accepted her hand for a shake. "Nice to meet you, Brooke. I'm Taylor."

Satisfied that introduction may have changed his attitude toward her, Taylor turned her attention back to him.

He was still frowning, but he did say, "How can I help you?"

"I need to speak with Ray."

"I'm Adam. I work for Ray. He's not here."

So if you're looking for him, you can be on your way. He didn't say those words, but definitely looked like he wanted to.

It just dawned on her that he was putting cookies and cupcakes onto the shelves, not carrying boxes out of the bakery to be delivered. "Did you make that Christmas tree cake? And those amazing red velvet cupcakes? Or did Ray?"

"Yeah, that's all me," he said nodding his head.

That wasn't good. Or rather, it was, since he was here for her to speak to about the competition. She'd just have to try and get him to forget about what happened yesterday.

Even though she wasn't totally sure *she* could. It had been a very long time since a guy stayed on her mind all night.

"And obviously you have a lot of experience with baking. Cookies. Icing. Decorating." Her practiced pitch began to roll smoothly off her tongue.

"My dad can make anything." Brooke spoke up as if she were a live commercial.

"Ever make a gingerbread house?"

Brooke was ready with another answer. "Dad made a whole gingerbread village one year."

Encouraged, she pressed on. *This has to work!* "And what about a giant gingerbread house? Big enough to stand in? Could you make one of those?"

"I'm not sure I understand." As he peered at her, she couldn't help but think about Josephine's words. Had he been staring at her yesterday? Because he certainly didn't look besotted now.

"Look, I'm an architect, and I'm representing my firm in the City's Giant Gingerbread House Competition. Seeing that it needs to be at least eighty percent edible, I need a baker to team up with. And I'm thinking that should be you."

His smile was slow, but genuine...and sort of sweet.

The fact that he was also shaking his head in the negative was *not* so cool.

"I'm flattered." He looked at Brooke and then up to Taylor again. "But I don't have a lot of spare time."

"But, Dad, it sounds so fun," Brooke insisted.

Please listen to Brooke!

"Don't you have homework to do?" Adam asked, not really swayed by his daughter's comments. "That table right there has got your name on it. And keep your paws off the Christmas cupcakes. I got eyes in the back of my head," he warned with just the slightest tinge of humor.

Brooke giggled and hurried away. Taylor liked the sound of the little girl's laughter, but immediately pressed on.

"Look, you have a gift. That cake was amazing and obviously you're a great pastry chef."

"I'm just a baker."

He was sweet to his daughter, *and* modest.

"'Just a baker' could not make that amazing Christmas tree cake." It took a few seconds to realize she meant those words. Despite the mess he'd made of her plans, the cake had been spectacular in taste and design.

"That was just a passion project my boss lets me do every now and then. This doesn't really fit our clientele. I'm here to crank out the donuts and the muffins."

Those last words sounded like a pledge he recited to himself every day.

He looked over Taylor's shoulder to the line that had formed while they were talking. "And speaking of which... I'll be with you folks in just a few seconds."

She looked back then turned her attention to him once more.

"But you have to do it." She was pleading—very close to begging, but whatever, it was what needed to be done. "There'll be prestige. Christmas spirit. Something for your free time."

He laughed. "Free time? That's something I don't have."

Desperate beyond measure at this point, she leaned in and whispered. "But I'll be in a terrible situation if you say no."

Again, that not-impressed look crossed his face. It was followed by a lift of his brow and a hint of amusement. None of which should have been appealing to her in any way.

"Are you trying to guilt me?"

"I don't know." She actually contemplated that question for a second. Guilt hadn't been part of her original pitch, but... "Is it working?"

"To guilt someone you have to know them and ah...well, we don't—"

"Fine. I'm a Sagittarius and I love peppermint bark." This was taking too long and she didn't have time to waste.

"Still no." He looked around her again. "Ms. Mason. Cherry Danish as usual?"

Taylor glanced over her shoulder to see the woman nod.

She tried again because there was no other option. What was she going to do if he didn't agree? Bake her own gingerbread? "Ah, but it would be great exposure. I mean everyone around the world could see your talents. Our local news will definitely be there, and you know people are constantly recording on their phones. Who knows? It could go viral."

"I have a line," he insisted.

She made the mistake of looking back to see that the line was getting longer. Desperate as she was, she still didn't want to cost the bakery any business. She pulled off her glove and handed him her card. "Here. In case you change your mind."

Adam took the card. She couldn't tell if he was just being polite or if he was actually going to consider her offer. But she'd given her pitch, so it was time to go. She walked away from the counter, offering the people in line an apologetic smile as she moved toward the table where Brooke was sitting. The girl had just snagged a red velvet cupcake from a stand behind her.

"Nice to meet you, Brooke. Merry Christmas."

"Merry Christmas," Brooke replied.

Taylor left Ray's Bakery without a baker.

Chapter Five

*I*T WAS AN INSANE OFFER.

And she was a persistent and unpredictable woman.

Brooke said she had a pretty smile.

Those thoughts and many more competed for attention throughout the remainder of the day. When he gave a customer a red velvet cupcake instead of the blueberry bagel she'd ordered, Adam knew he was in trouble.

Was he really considering this? He couldn't. He was a simple baker, working the job that paid the bills while allowing him to do the two most important things in his life—take care of his daughter and bake.

"The idea is totally ridiculous."

He was leaning against the counter in his kitchen with the woman's business card in had.

That proved the conflicting thoughts had followed him home.

"You've been twirling that card all evening."
Jenny looked up from where she stood on the
other side of the island. "And Brooke can't stop
talking about the Giant Gingerbread Competition."

He hadn't meant to speak his thoughts aloud.
Especially not after he'd officially put an end to
the family discussion of the gingerbread competition during dinner. Jenny was right; Brooke
couldn't stop talking about it. The excitement
in her voice when she relayed the entire scene
from the bakery to Jenny had caused Adam even
more indecision. What parent didn't want to do
whatever made their child appear so eager and
excited?

"I can't. I got a job. I've got responsibilities."

"You also have a life. One which you've been
neglecting since Cheryl died."

His fingers stilled on the card at the sound
of her name, lips setting in a line while the rem-
nants of grief tugged at his soul. "I'm taking care
of our daughter."

Jenny nodded, her chin-length black hair
swishing with the motion.

"You used to do that when Cheryl was here,
too. And you still invited all the family over
during the summer to eat tons of barbeque and
fresh biscuits and visit. You were on a bowling
league with those guys from the barber shop,

and you used to go for a jog every night after dinner."

"Are you trying to tell me I'm out of shape?" The question was meant to take the serious edge off this conversation. Instead, it solidified the lump forming in his throat. There was no lie in what she said.

With a tilt of her head and quirk of her lips Jenny gave the perfect "I'm serious" look, and his fingers tightened on the card. He glanced down at it again seeing her name in bold black letters. TAYLOR SCOTT.

Pretty. Determined. Courageous.

"Brooke said this architect told you that the competition would be great exposure. That it would show the world your talents. What if it also showed those investors?" His sister had a pinch of determination as well.

"You know that meeting did not go well. I could never go back to them without a culinary degree."

"Why would you need a degree if you had a gigantic gingerbread house under your belt?"

It made sense, from a very basic point of view. If he could make a giant gingerbread house, didn't it stand to reason he had superior baking skills, which could translate into big sales for a bakery he owned? The instinctive answer would be yes. But Adam wasn't certain Nick Brexley and his partners would feel the same way.

"Adam, don't you want Brooke to see you doing something that makes you happy, the way you used to be?"

"How would I find the time to do this? Business at the bakery is crazy busy with the holidays coming up and all these orders for office parties to fill."

"Ray's sons are in town to help him through the holidays. And you do have weeks of unused vacation," she told him. "I really think you should take this opportunity, Adam."

He couldn't believe he was even considering this. But looking at Jenny right now, listening to her very convincing pitch, reminded him a lot of their mother.

There was no way Gloria would allow him to pass up an opportunity like this. And if she was here instead of in North Carolina where his parents currently lived, his mother would probably call Taylor and accept the job for him if she had to. The thought made him chuckle. He tapped the card in the palm of his other hand before heading into the living room to grab the phone.

Quickly dialing the number before his mind could shift again, he listened while it rang, heart thumping with each droning sound.

"This is Taylor." She answered the second he contemplated hanging up.

"Hey. This is Adam. The Christmas tree cake guy." *Yeah, that sounded very professional.*

"Oh. *That* Adam. The one who turned me down. How could I forget?" She didn't sound excited to hear from him.

He supposed he could chalk that up to how nonchalant he'd been with her earlier today. A direct result of their very first encounter. But this was a new conversation, a fresh start for him—in more ways than one.

"I'm calling about your offer. Look, I'm ah..." The fresh start would go a lot better if he could figure out how exactly to say "yes." But then the look on Brooke's face as she had talked about this competition earlier today flashed in his mind.

"Hello? Are you still there?" She was saying through the phone signaling his silence had stretched on.

He cleared his throat. "As difficult as it was for you to ask, it's just as difficult for me to—"

"To accept my offer?" she prompted.

Adam nodded with relief. "Yes. That."

"So you'll do it?" Was that excitement he heard in her voice?

"Yes."

"Great! In that case we'll start tomorrow."

"Sounds good." She rattled off an address before hanging up and Adam stood for a few startled moments.

He was going to bake and build a giant gingerbread house. His smile spread as quickly as

the ideas about how to construct this gingerbread house popped into his mind.

Now he was excited, too.

Christmas Village was an annual event in Philadelphia that ran from Thanksgiving to Christmas Eve in LOVE Park, located near City Hall.
The predominantly outdoor event was fashioned
to give the city a taste of an authentic German
Christmas market. Dozens of vendor booths
sold genuine European foods, ornaments, and
arts and crafts from all over the world, while an
indoor facility called the Marketplace had been
constructed to keep Santa and his elves warm
while picture-taking. In addition to the jolly old
guy, there were more vendors inside, as well as
a main exhibit stage.

Of course, no Christmas market would be
complete without holiday sweets—cakes, cookies, brownies, gingerbread and candies. Those
were Adam's favorite parts. Each year, he came
with Brooke and Jenny at least once throughout
the month of December.

The gingerbread competition was being held
inside the Marketplace on the main exhibit
stage this year. Last year they'd held a themed
Christmas tree decorating contest. A tree featuring superheroes had won, and Adam and Jenny

had been split on whether they thought it had been the best. Brooke had been clear in the fact that she'd thought the pink themed tree was the hands-down winner.

Today, Adam wasn't here as a spectator. He was a participant in the competition. The thought still made him a little nervous, but seeing the smile on Brooke's face last night when he told her, and then again this morning when she'd happily finished cleaning her bedroom so they could get dressed and come down here, was the best reward.

They'd already walked the rows of outdoor vendor booths, visiting each one to ogle over the new and unique items on display. Now, they were inside where lovely aromas wafted through the air. The strong earthy scent of fresh pine from the stand with homemade wreaths and centerpieces. Sweet and tangy smelling candles in fragrances such as cranberry soufflé and evergreens. The nutty scent of roasting chestnuts and more.

There was also music: loud and cheerful Christmas carols piped through overhead speakers. These carols had the lyrics, which Adam actually preferred to the instrumental station Ray insisted they play in the bakery.

Adam held Brooke's hand as they walked through, glancing at the stalls. Jenny was going to meet him here after her study group at the library. That would give Adam time to meet with Taylor to discuss the competition.

"Look! Candy!" Brooke could barely hold her excitement while pointing at the stand. That was just a prelude before she tugged him in that direction.

The display at this stand was festive and creative. Mason jars full of everything imaginable, from Christmas tree and Santa gummy bears to old-fashioned peppermints. There were lollipops, handmade chocolates, and what had really caught Brooke's attention: gourmet candy apples.

"These look delicious!" If she hadn't spoken the words, Adam would've still known she liked them by how wide her eyes opened the second she saw them.

"They look like you'll be at the dentist every week for a month."

Her excitement immediately ebbed. "I don't like the dentist."

Adam chuckled and nodded. "I know you don't." They moved on to a stall selling hot chocolate with mountains of whipped cream.

"Mine is better," Brooke said a few minutes later after they'd ordered their drinks and were playing the same game they played each year— best whipped cream mustache.

"Are you kidding? Look how thick mine is." He checked his out using the mirror function on his phone which Brooke was currently holding.

"Nah, I think mine is better because I even have a whipped cream beard," she proudly announced and handed the phone back to him.

She wasn't joking. He had no idea how she'd managed to get the whipped cream on her upper lip, the tip of her nose and her chin, but she looked absolutely adorable.

"Okay, you win this year." He conceded and pulled a napkin out of his pocket to clean her face.

She accepted another napkin from him and returned the favor.

After finishing their drinks and dropping the cups into the trash can, they were on the move again. Brooke smiled at the huge Rudolph blow-up they passed, and Adam promised a visit to Santa later because the line to take pictures with the giant red-nosed reindeer was long already. She looked a little disappointed, but Adam immediately spotted something else he knew would catch her attention.

"Pies. Wanna go look?"

She nodded and they headed over to the stall. Once there, Adam had to lift Brooke up to see all the pies in the top of the display case.

"Oooooh those pies smell good," Brooke said.

Adam chuckled and set her down. "They do, but you need to get some lunch before you have any sweets. I'll tell Jenny to bring you back to the pie stand later."

"Look, ice sculptures!" Brooke said as they walked a little further.

He didn't mind being pulled through the crowd by his young daughter so that she could admire the sculpture of an eagle.

"It's beautiful. Just like the one in Mom's office."

Brooke may have been amazed by the sculpture, but she would forever recall every detail she could about her mother.

"You're right. She loved birds. That's why she collected all those pictures and statues." That were now in a box in their basement. Cheryl's office was now an exercise room that Adam rarely used.

He looked up. "Oh, there's Taylor!" She was setting up a red and white sign with "Ogilvy Architecture In Partnership with Ray's Bakery" written in bold print. He and Brooke made their way through the crowd and came to a stop right behind where Taylor was standing.

"Hey," he called to her.

She was just finishing with the sign and smiled when she turned to say, "Hi."

Brooke had been right—she did have a pretty smile. Adam wasn't sure he'd noticed that before, and figured he should probably brush it off now.

"You got that sign up quick," he said.

Taylor nodded. "Our design team is pretty on the ball."

From beside him, Brooke pointed at the sign. "Daddy why isn't your name on it?"

"It's fine, honey." He'd noticed that too, but wasn't going to bring it up. Ray's Bakery was on the sign and that's where he worked, so that was good enough.

"But, Daddy, you need the bublicity," Brooke insisted. Taylor frowned as she looked from Brooke to Adam. He knew she probably didn't understand what Brooke was trying to say. If Jenny didn't talk about *her* plan for *his* new bakery in front of Brooke all the time, this wouldn't be an issue.

"Oh! *Pub*licity," Taylor corrected.

Brooke's head bobbed in agreement. "Right. Publicity. To help when he opens his own bakery."

Taylor looked surprised while Adam begged for a hole to open up in the floor and swallow him. "Seriously? You're opening your own bakery?"

"My daughter has an ah, big imagination." He hugged Brooke close to him. "But I already have a job."

Thankfully at that moment, the mayor began to speak from a podium in the center of the exhibit stage. The podium had been painted a festive green and was decorated with red ribbon and cardboard peppermint candies.

"Ladies and gentlemen, boys and girls, may I have your attention please?" he began. "As your mayor, I am thrilled to welcome you to our Christmas Marketplace and our first ever Giant Gingerbread Competition."

All the people who'd gathered around at the sound of the mayor's voice clapped, including Adam, Taylor and Brooke.

As the mayor continued, Adam noticed Taylor looking at a couple standing a few feet from them. "Friends of yours?"

Taylor shrugged. "More like a former colleague. Bradford, he used to work at the firm. You can say we have a friendly rivalry going on."

Last time Adam had checked, rivalries were rarely friendly, but he kept that comment to himself.

"And Annabelle Renard, she's the best pastry chef in the state," he whispered to Taylor about the woman standing with Bradford. Annabelle caught them staring at her and nodded.

"Okay, truth is, she and I were talking about working together on this."

That made sense. Taylor was obviously very good at her job or her bosses wouldn't have let her be in this contest. She'd want to have the best pastry chef she could find working with her.

"But your colleague over there made a more convincing sales pitch." What had that guy done to get Annabelle Renard?

Taylor pointed to another group standing a few feet away from Annabelle. "That team over there is a combination of students from the local culinary and high school. They're being financed by one of the banks in the area." She was leaning close to him, whispering as if they were working on some type of heist instead of a gingerbread contest.

"Amateurs," he quipped.

She nodded her agreement. "And as for the final team, their sign's not up, but I saw them bringing it in. They're a church group that I heard have won regional baking contests. Their designer is an architecture student."

Adam digested all that information. "Bradford/Renard is definitely the team to beat."

"I agree," she said seconds before the mayor continued.

"Now each team has twelve days to build their masterpiece for final judging on December 24th . So without further ado, let the Giant Gingerbread Competition begin!"

The mayor lifted a huge brass bell, ringing it with the crowd's boisterous applause.

"Looks like we've got our work cut out for us," he told Taylor the minute the crowd disbursed.

"That you do," came a quick reply.

They both turned to look at the smiling blonde-haired woman who approached. Taylor flashed a grin. "Linda, this is Adam, our baker. And Adam, this is my boss, Linda."

Ah, the boss was here as well as an ex-coworker. Questions about the significance of these variables roamed through Adam's mind, even though he figured it was none of his business.

"Nice to meet you," he said.

"Likewise." Linda turned her attention back to Taylor. "We're counting on you. So think cutting-edge and be bold with your designs, and we can win this." Linda pointed at Taylor and gave her a nod before leaving.

"No pressure, right?" Adam asked when Linda was gone.

"Tell me about it," Taylor replied with a huff. "Okay. Let's get started."

"Sure. " He pulled out his phone that had just vibrated. "Just let me drop Brooke off and I'll meet you, say over by the food court?"

Taylor nodded. "Yeah, sure. I'll go find us a table. It was nice seeing you again, Brooke."

"Nice seeing you too, Ms. Taylor," Brooke replied and instead of shaking her hand like she'd done at the bakery, Brooke leaned in to give Taylor a quick hug. A quick tug of intrigue hit him as Taylor grinned down at Brooke.

"Come on, Brooke, we have to get going." He held his hand out to take his daughter's and told Taylor, "I'll be over in a few minutes."

Adam brought Brooke to Jenny and hurried to meet up with Taylor again. Now that he'd seen Annabelle Renard was in the competition, he was anxious to get to work. How great would it be if he could boast about beating *the* Annabelle Renard in a competition? Not that he knew who he would boast to. Just because he'd decided to do this didn't mean he was ready to re-visit the idea of opening his own bakery.

Taylor was already sitting at a small table on the edge of the food court where it was a little quieter. She had her plans spread out on the table and a pencil in hand as he approached. She looked like a woman about her business, which at the moment was this gingerbread contest.

Adam had thought about her a lot the night before. That was new to him, and he wasn't ready to try and figure out why it was *this* woman and *this* time. Getting to work made more sense than overthinking this, so he sat at the table beside her.

She barely looked up at him but spoke as she continued making notations at the bottom of the page. It was another large sheet of paper like the one she'd fussed at him for getting icing on.

"What's that?" he asked.

"Plans for our gingerbread house." Her tone coupled with the look she finally gave him indicated she thought that was self-explanatory.

He only glanced briefly at what was drawn on the paper. "I assumed the design was something we would come up with together."

He'd had some ideas and was expecting to run them by her to see how she felt about them. And now that he'd seen their competition, he'd already begun thinking of ways they could possibly go in order to win. He hadn't expected her to come up with a complete plan on her own.

"Well, I am a professional architect. I think I know what I'm doing."

So they were back to her brisk tone again? This sounded like the Taylor he'd first met at Ogilvy, not the one who'd come to Ray's practically begging for his help. But her company was the one entered in the contest, so Adam figured he should at least look at what she had planned. He glanced down at the paper and immediately frowned.

"Really? Because that house doesn't look very Christmassy." Looking at her work didn't mean he planned to sugarcoat how he felt about it.

She frowned. "Not Christmassy? What is that supposed to mean?"

Good. Maybe she was at least open to his explanations. "Well, it's so modern. It looks like a twenty-first century gingerbread condo. I had some thoughts on things we could do to give a new flair to an old theme." He was all set to expound on that idea when she tapped the pencil on the paper.

They both looked down at the plans this time, and Adam hoped that meant she was at least considering what he'd said. That hope was quickly dashed as she shook her head. "Well, you heard my boss. It needs to be sophisticated.

Cutting-edge." Those words seemed to cheer her up as she said them with a toss of her head.

"Christmas isn't about cutting-edge. Christmas is about warmth and tradition."

Her lips pressed into a thin line. "Thank you for your input. But I think there's been a little misunderstanding. In a construction project, an architect oversees all creative choices."

"And in a baking project, typically the head chef is in charge." Adam pointed to her plans because he had some expertise to be considered as well.

"Of building materials," she said.

If he was willing to give up any spare time he had to work on this project, the least he could expect to receive was a little fun and the opportunity to create something.

"Look, all day long I'm stuck making blueberry muffins. Okay? My fingers are stained blue. This is my chance to get out and do something artistic." Something that might even get noticed.

Taylor was not persuaded.

"Ok, how 'bout you stay out of design decisions and help with building materials."

"I need to be involved with design decisions so I can advise on which gingerbread to use for the building material," he countered.

"How 'bout we agree to disagree. But at least get started in the meantime."

"Are you always this stubborn?" he asked,

frustration ebbing out the excitement he'd been feeling when he first sat down at the table.

"I was going to say the same of you."

So she wasn't budging on her design, and he wasn't the type to argue over things he couldn't change. Besides, this was her company's project, and he was just here to show Brooke he wasn't afraid to have a little fun. "Fine. But we better head back. We gotta start baking. First step is coming up with a gingerbread dense enough not to crumble, and that's going to take some experimentation."

"Great idea," she said and seemed to relax into his suggestion.

She was definitely intense about her work and Adam really couldn't blame her. He was the same way about his baking.

"So let's go," he told her.

For the first time since they'd started this conversation Taylor looked puzzled. "Let's?" she asked with an arched brow.

"Didn't you just agree to be my baking assistant?"

She didn't answer and he knew she was thinking that she'd been tricked into that agreement—which she definitely had, but it served her right for being so obstinate.

"Fine. I'll go back to the bakery with you, but these plans are final."

"We're not going back to the bakery. We're going to my house to do some trial runs."

"Oh. Is that why you want to open your own bakery? Because you're not allowed to do things like this at Ray's?"

He'd been doing so well taking this conversation in the direction he wanted it to go. He hadn't expected this question.

"I've always wanted to own a bakery. But when my wife passed away a few years ago I had other priorities to tend to." He stood up then because he had no intention of going any further with this subject. This was just a holiday competition. They would work together to get it done and then they'd go their separate ways. No point in getting too personal.

Especially now since her gaze had softened into a look of sympathy.

"Oh, Adam, I'm so sorry. That must have been hard for you and Brooke."

"We're doing fine now. We should get going. We have to mix and bake gingerbread and I don't want to keep you out too late."

"Oh, I think I'm old enough to stay up late, and I'm up for being a baking assistant."

She was standing now, folding her paper. When one of the cups on the table wobbled, Adam hurried to catch it just before it could spill.

"Got it!" He looked up at her with a grin. "Wouldn't want your plans to be destroyed again."

She narrowed her eyes at him, but if she was

about to make a sarcastic remark she quickly changed her mind and instead responded with a smile that sucked the air right out of his lungs.

"Thanks for saving my plans, Adam."

He muttered something he thought might have been a thank-you, but really his mind was trying to wrap itself around that punch of attraction he'd just felt.

Chapter Six

WHEN ADAM HAD LEFT HIS house that morning, he'd had no idea he'd be bringing someone home with him. Especially not a woman. And it wasn't until he'd unlocked the door and they'd walked inside that he'd felt the tiniest tendrils of doubt over whether or not it was a good idea.

This is not personal.

On the ride from the marketplace those words had played in his mind. It was the truth: there was nothing personal here, so this was not a date, and therefore he had no need to worry about how she might react to his home—the one he used to share with his wife.

Brooke led Taylor further into the house while Adam closed and locked the door. He took those moments to focus.

He wished Jenny hadn't had other plans after keeping Brooke while he and Taylor met earlier today. Having his daughter around Taylor—who she seemed to warm up to quickly—might not be such a good idea. In the years since Cheryl's passing, he'd been very careful about Brooke's feelings. Limiting both his and Brooke's emotional attachment to anyone other than family had been his way of keeping them both safe from experiencing such a tremendous loss again.

"Where do you live, Taylor? Is it a big house or a small house?" Brooke's chatter continued from the truck to the house. She looked up at Taylor expecting an answer while taking off her coat and handing it to Adam to hang up.

"I live in a townhouse," Taylor replied. "It's sort of big, definitely more than enough room for me."

"You live alone?" Brooke asked.

After Adam had hung up Brooke's coat and his own, he extended a hand to Taylor for hers. She took it off while answering Brooke again.

"Yes. I've lived alone since I graduated from college."

"Did you like college? Because I'm not sure I'm going to like it. Daddy won't be there to bake his famous chocolate chip cookies when I pass a test. If you do something good at work maybe he'll bake you cookies, too." Brooke told her.

He knew he should intervene, but he was way more interested in the impromptu Q&A because it was giving him more information about Taylor Scott—the woman, not the architect.

Not that he needed it to work with her. His mind was a jumble of contradictions right now. It had been since Taylor had walked into the bakery yesterday. The quicker they got this lesson over with, the better.

The front door led to an open foyer with tiled floor. The closet he'd hung their coats in was to the left, the stairs to the right. Straight ahead was the living room with its dark hard wood floors and warm beige painted walls. That's where Taylor and Brooke were headed.

"Wow. That's a huge Christmas tree." Taylor looked up to the angel topper they'd finally managed to put in place the other night.

"Actually, we got the smaller one this year."

Brooke's inquisition continued. "What kind of Christmas tree do you have, Taylor?"

She glanced at Adam briefly before returning her attention to Brooke.

"I don't usually have one. You see, I travel a lot, and they don't fit too well in carry-on luggage."

"Why do you travel so much?"

A light came into Taylor's eyes as she clasped her hands in front of her.

"As part of my job I get to travel to different places and design special buildings and houses. It works out really well for me because I've always loved to travel."

Which meant this competition thing was just a pit stop for her as well. That was a relief.

He didn't need any further reminder that this wasn't personal. It couldn't be, with Taylor, the pretty, work-focused jetsetter.

"But still, everyone should have a Christmas tree," Brooke insisted.

"Everyone has their own Christmas traditions, Brooke." The Q&A session was over. "I'll just get the oven turned on and gather all the ingredients we'll need, Taylor. It'll only take a few seconds."

"Sure. It's no problem. Brooke is great company."

Loving the compliment, Brooke grabbed Taylor's hand. "I'll show you around."

He moved to the kitchen but could still see and hear them. They'd only taken a few steps when Taylor spoke next.

"Brooke, did you make that? It's beautiful."

Brooke replied with a nod and then led the way over to the table so Taylor could have a closer look. She climbed onto a chair and leaned over the table. "It's a school project. I'm supposed to be making a Christmas diorama, but I'm kinda stuck on making the trees."

Adam moved to the double ovens and turned each one on. Eager to get started with the plans he'd come up with last night, he'd prepared gingerbread dough and rolled it out before leaving the house earlier. Once the ovens warmed, he'd slip the two trays inside to get them started while working on a new batch of dough with Taylor.

But when he looked up again, he saw Taylor standing over Brooke's school project with her and offering suggestions.

"Do you want a little hint? You can make great tree trunks by wrapping sandwich twists in parchment paper. I made a lot of models when I was in architecture school."

"Thanks." Brooke nodded as if processing Taylor's suggestion.

With their heads together now, they both studied the project. Warmth spread in his chest as scenes of his wife helping Brooke with something flashed through his mind. Grief and longing overcame him and he flattened his palms against the marble top when his knees threatened to buckle.

"Oh, sous-chef, you're needed." He told himself he was calling Taylor away because it was time for them to get started, not because seeing her in such an intimate and touching position with his daughter made him uncomfortable.

"I think that's me," Taylor said and smiled at Brooke.

Brooke nodded. "And I have a hint for you, too," she told Taylor conspiratorially. "When you cook with my dad, wear an apron. Cause a lot of things splash."

He'd started to move around the kitchen again, but the sound of their laughter caught his attention. When was the last time he heard

Brooke laughing with anyone other than him or Jenny?

"Wish me luck," he heard Taylor say as he purposely opened a cabinet to avoid looking at them together again.

"Okay, I'm ready to help," she announced when she arrived in the kitchen with him. Adam handed her an apron.

"Thank you," she said as she accepted it from him and started to unfold it.

"Gingerbread batch number one is in the oven already. Just needs two more minutes. Each batch cooks in six minutes. Your job is to keep track of time."

"Oh, I'm doing the job of an egg timer," she quipped.

He ignored the sarcasm, even though she'd followed it with a grin.

"Gingerbread batch number two I'm making with butter instead of margarine. And for our third experiment, I'm substituting corn syrup for molasses. This keeps the pastry from puffing out and maintains its shape. These are all variations of my mom's gingerbread recipe. Hers used lots of butter. Stir this," he instructed.

"Oh really? Did your mother do a lot of baking?" Taylor asked as she began stirring another bowl of a mixture he'd previously started.

The question caught him a little off guard, but Adam rebounded quickly. "She did. My Mom loved to cook and bake, and I enjoyed spending time in the kitchen with her."

"My mother wasn't much of a cook, but we didn't starve," she said and used the whisk to scrape along the side of the bowl. "My refrigerator is rarely stocked."

"A good home-cooked meal can soothe the soul. My mother used to say that," he added. She was quiet now, either focused on stirring or not really interested in talking about personal matters. He could understand that.

"Well, once you finish with this competition you'll know how to make great gingerbread," he offered optimistically.

"Something to add to my resume," she said with a smile.

He didn't look away when she smiled this time. Earlier that day, he'd told himself not to stare too long or read too much into the light feeling in the pit of his stomach when he'd seen the pretty tilt of her lips. It was no big deal. And yet, right at this moment he couldn't look away. And neither did she. That warmth in his chest just moments ago was now spreading, moving slowly like pouring molasses.

He dropped a few chunks of butter into the bowl she was stirring.

"A little trick they don't teach you in culinary school: butter improves the taste of everything. You'll have to use the mixer for this part." He nodded toward the mixer at the other end of the counter.

"But no one will taste it. You should be concerned with durability." Oh boy, the boss tone was back as she attempted to correct him.

But this was not only his kitchen, his domain, but baking was a huge chunk of his life. "I've never compromised on taste and I'm not about to start now." He could let Taylor take the lead on what she felt was her area of expertise, but not here, not in the kitchen.

"And you went to culinary school?" Her skeptical tone was not lost on him.

He frowned and figured they'd had enough of the personal discussions for tonight. "Long story. Keep mixing."

He picked up the grater and began pushing the stalk of ginger along its sharp prongs.

"Ah, you do know they have powdered ginger," she said after a few seconds of silence. When he looked over at her she nodded down at the grater.

"Creativity and inspiration can't be rushed, okay? Rome wasn't built in a day, and our gingerbread house won't be either." Okay, he did sound a little fanatical when talking about baking, but he couldn't help it: this was his passion, and if he was going to be in this competition, he was going to give it one hundred and ten percent.

"Clearly not if you're involved." She stopped

the mixer and looked at him with earnest concern. "Wouldn't working with a recipe be more efficient?"

"I like to take my time. Let my creativity flow." His tone was almost wistful as they continued the semi-joking banter that seemed to be their favored form of conversation.

She shrugged. "Sounds risky."

"Maybe, but for every fallen soufflé there's a perfect profiterole tower."

They couldn't seem to agree on anything. Whether it was her design for the gingerbread house or now, the recipe.

"You know, I'm really glad you're not an architect, because that approach would not pass inspection. Now remember, we don't want bricks. We need thin rectangles of gingerbread."

"Why so thin?" he asked.

"Well, remember my design? It calls for thin pieces of gingerbread. I need for my design to be ultra-sleek and modern." She was clearly pumped by the idea; he could see it in the way her eyes lit up.

Again with the getting off track. He really needed to get it together.

"But that'll make it more likely to crack."

She frowned. "Maybe use less butter."

Blasphemy!

"And compromise taste and texture? What do you say we stop the backseat baking? Remember our deal: in the kitchen I'm in charge."

"Yeah, but I'm the arc..." She stopped mid-sentence and sniffed the air. "Do you smell smoke?"

He followed suit, sniffing as well. Without missing a beat he ran over to the oven and yanked the door open. Smoke poured out and he grabbed his oven mitts. Slipping them onto his hands quickly he pulled the tray of burned gingerbread out. He set it on the counter and stared at her.

She looked contrite—for about ten seconds. "Okay. So our first collaboration could've gone slightly better."

Chapter Seven

Eleven Days Until Judging

TAYLOR WAS UP SUPER EARLY the next morning. She'd actually been up most of the night. When she hadn't been thinking about the competition, her mind had been full of the baker working with her.

It was ridiculous. She no longer dreamed of a big house with a cute daughter and a handsome husband. That had been her fantasy a long time ago, when she was a little girl who believed in that pot of gold at the end of every rainbow.

That wasn't who she was now or what she wanted for her life.

Then why had it felt so warm and cozy when she'd been at Adam's house last night? The heat worked just fine in her townhouse. And why had helping Brooke with her project and standing in Adam's kitchen debating over how best to bake gingerbread feel so natural? When she'd left his house thoughts of the competition hadn't been on her mind. Instead she'd wondered if Brooke had gotten the Christmas trees for the project finished, and if she'd been tucked in.

When Taylor's alarm clock had finally blared, she'd rolled out of bed and headed to the shower. Then she'd gone to her bedroom and did something she normally didn't do while getting dressed—turned on the TV. Her heart had leaped with joy when she saw one of her favorite holiday movies was on. It was a classic that she remembered watching with her mother almost every season—*Miracle on 34th Street*.

Unfortunately, it was already close to the end. Climbing back onto her bed and folding her legs under her the way she used to when she was young, Taylor watched like this was her first time seeing the movie. They were at the scene where Susan, the little girl in the movie, was trying to convince herself to continue believing in Santa when he obviously had not brought her what she'd asked for. This part felt like fingers wrapping around Taylor's heart and squeezing tightly every time because she'd felt the same burn of disappointment that Susan did.

When she was eleven, her parents announced they were moving from Australia to Milan. They'd been in Australia for almost a whole year, and the children at school had just stopped teasing her about her American accent. And they were going to move again. That year when Taylor wrote her list for Santa, she'd asked for a house to live in for the rest of her life, a place where she wouldn't have to worry about moving ever again. Her parents' jobs required them to move five more times after that.

In the movie, Susan didn't get her house, and neither had Taylor, at least not in the years that she'd wanted it most. So there was no use thinking about having such things now at this point in her life. She had a great job and had developed a love of traveling. That was enough.

After the movie, Taylor made a point of searching the guide to see when it would be airing again. She set it to record so she could watch when she was ready. It occurred to her that she could also purchase the DVD. Half an hour after the movie ended, she was dressed and in the backseat of a taxi on her way to the Marketplace.

Adam had a nice house, she recalled. It had an open concept similar to hers, but it was much wider and his ceilings were higher. Where her townhouse was stylish and accommodating, Adam's house had a distinctly homey feel. That was especially true with the homemade orna-ments that adorned his tree and the cute gin-gerbread men sitting on some of the branches. There were ropes of garland and twinkle lights draping almost every surface with Santa, the reindeer and the North Pole knickknacks on the tables. She'd enjoyed it from the moment she entered until she'd left. At least, when she ignored the part where she let the gingerbread burn.

By the time she climbed out of the taxi and walked into the Marketplace, she'd promised to herself to keep Adam and his daughter out of her mind. At least to the extent that she was wondering how Brooke's school project was coming along. That was too personal, and her connection to Adam Dale was strictly professional.

"Hey," she called to him when she turned into the area of the exhibit stage and saw that Adam was already there working. A few times throughout the night she'd been concerned that he might bail on the competition after their squabbles yesterday—and then the scorched gingerbread. She hoped he'd been able to get rid of that awful burnt smell in his kitchen.

"Morning." He spoke while holding up a strip of lumber and standing on the platform where they would be building their gingerbread house.

"I, ah, wasn't expecting to see you here so early," she said standing a distance behind him.

He set the lumber down and looked up at her. "And why not? Bakers always get up early."

"Well, after yesterday's fiasco I wasn't sure..." Her words trailed off. She didn't really want to say what she'd been thinking.

He finished the sentence for her. "I'd show

up? Well, I always finish what I start. Besides, we've got a frame to build. But first, coffee."

She watched as he casually moved away from her to a table where coffee had already been brewed. He poured the liquid into two white mugs and brought one back to her.

"Thank you," she said before accepting the mug. "So you always make your own coffee?"

Adam nodded and watched her take a sip. "It's the most important tool we've got. And we may have a bunch of sleepy volunteers arriving this morning."

Taylor sipped the coffee and was surprised at how good it tasted. "Mmmmm." She looked down at the mug and then up to him. "Okay. I see your point."

She also saw how kind he was. When he'd first met her—at the Ogilvy offices—she'd snapped at him. And here he was, helping her out of a bind, anyway. Sure, she'd sold him on the fact that the competition would gain him some exposure, and that would certainly help him if he were truly looking to start his own bakery. But at the same time, he'd owed her nothing. He wasn't being paid to do it, and there was a possibility that they would lose. In that case, the exposure for him might not be that good.

Well, she wasn't about to let that happen. Taylor wanted to win, and she wanted that win to boost both their careers.

"Now, let's finish the base. Then we can start

shopping for ingredients if we want to start baking," he said.

They were standing much closer than they had been before. His dark brown eyes seemed a little darker, and maybe a touch warmer, than she remembered them being yesterday.

Talk about work. Winning this competition is important for both of you. The rest is foolish nonsense.

"I assume you have a shopping list," she said while fully intending to listen to that voice in her head.

"Sure I do." He pointed to his temple. "It's right up here."

Taylor looked at him skeptically. Lists are what kept her repeatedly on budget in her projects. "No list? Doesn't that seem a little off the cuff?"

"I got a couple things written down, but you gotta leave room for inspiration."

He sounded so convinced that his way was the right way. "Inspiration sounds expensive." She walked over to the table and set her mug down. "I think I'll tag along."

Because she wanted to make sure he didn't overspend on his inspiration. Not because she'd liked standing that close to him.

The restaurant supply store they went to looked like a warehouse that was stocked from the top shelves, at least fifty feet off the floor, to the bottom. Blue signs with white numbers identified the aisles, while a map Taylor had snagged from the basket when they first entered helped them navigate.

"Aisle 12 row E; that's where we should find the baking items," she said while looking down at the map. Adam had secured one of those flat-bed carts and was maneuvering it expertly while they walked.

"We'll start at the beginning of aisle 10 and work our way down. There are different items I need and some aren't specifically geared toward baking."

She followed his lead because shopping for food items was not on the top of her things-perfected list. In fact, since she'd returned from L.A., she'd been telling herself she was going to get to the grocery store to grab a few things. After her conversation with Adam last night, she'd felt the need to make that trip a little sooner. She could prepare a home-cooked meal if she had the time. Or if she made the time.

"If you employ this 'wander around' type of strategy you're more likely to overspend. Let's just focus on what we need to get the batter made." She purposely changed her tone to give more of a suggestion instead of a command.

"You cannot plan everything. Sometimes it's best to let things flow and see where they lead you." He turned down aisle 9 instead of 10 and Taylor frowned.

"I like plans. I like order, and I like the predicted results that come when I've done exactly what I set out to do."

"And do you ever manage to have fun in between all those plans and goals?"

He stopped, reached up onto a shelf she would have never been able to get to on her own because he was a good bit taller than her, and grabbed two large white tubs.

"I have plenty of fun." Taylor tried to ignore the slight sting of his very accurate words. In the last couple of months her idea of fun had been the few hours she'd managed to step away from the project in L.A. to go shopping. "But I also know the value of hard work."

"So do I." He turned the corner to go down the next aisle. "Watch!"

Never in a million years would she have guessed what was about to happen. But in the next few seconds Adam took a couple steps and then broke out into a run, his hands firmly on the handle of the cart. When he stepped up onto the back bar of the cart and proceeded to take a ride along the coasting wagon, Taylor held her breath. Then she covered her mouth to stifle a grin as the store manager turned the corner just in time to scowl at him when he almost crashed into a display. By the time she came to the other end of the aisle, he was jumping down off the cart.

"Now that was fun! My friends and I used to do that in the supermarket parking lot when we were kids. Until our mothers caught us one day and made us come back to the store during closing to make sure all the carts were neatly stacked for customers the next day." He laughed and stepped away from the cart. "You wanna try it?"

Taylor couldn't help but laugh, too, because she could imagine a younger Adam doing exactly what he'd just done but going much faster outside in a parking lot. "Oh no," she replied with a brisk shake of her head. "That's a little too much fun for me."

She felt a twinge of admiration at how easily he'd been able to let go and do exactly what he'd wanted, when he wanted to...but that would remain her secret. Did that make her dull or too uptight? It probably meant he was right: she didn't make the time to stop and just have fun. She hadn't realized how much she wanted to until that very moment.

"Okay, back to work," he announced and they made their way down the remaining aisles.

Forty-five minutes and a completely full cart later, they were standing in the check-out line.

"You must come here often," she said. Adam had known exactly where to go in this mammoth store. He was also very familiar with the check-out process because he'd bypassed the self-checkout stating the machines at that end didn't allow businesses to use their discount card without calling a staff member to assist.

He figured it made more sense to just get in a clerk-assisted line and enjoy a little cordial conversation while he made his purchases.

The self-checkout lines were shorter, but she didn't say that.

"I'm here at least twice a month. Ray's getting a little older so I like to do as much as I can to help out."

Fun. Helpful, compassionate.

It hadn't occurred to her that there were men like this around. Not like her ex, with his careless, callous breakup talk.

It was finally their turn and they stepped up to the register. The clerk came from around the little area where he'd been standing with a scan gun in hand.

"Hello. Nice day for shopping," he said cheerfully.

"It's a better day for Christmas shopping, but sometimes work overrules." Adam jokingly thrust a thumb over his shoulder in Taylor's direction and the clerk looked over to her and grinned.

"I see. Taking care of what your wife wants to do first. That's a smart man," the clerk added with a chuckle.

Wife? What? *No!*

"Ah, no, we're um, we're not married." That correction needed to be made immediately.

"Oh." The clerk looked from her to Adam and

then back to her again. "My fault. You two look like the perfect couple."

With that comment, Adam glanced at her and Taylor stared back.

Did they look like the perfect couple?

Of course not. She'd been part of a couple before and that had blown up in her face. Even thoughts of trying again over the years ended with work coming to save the day.

Clearing her throat she looked away first. "We're working together on a *fun* project."

When she chanced another glance at Adam, he'd stopped staring at her but was grinning. "Yeah, she says it's fun, but I'm the one doing all the heavy lifting."

She dug into her purse for her wallet. "But I'm the one paying." She pulled out her company credit card and waved it in the air.

The clerk looked at Adam and they both laughed. "She wins!"

They rode back to the bakery in Adam's company truck, their purchases stacked in the back. After he parked, Taylor stepped out and met him around the back of the truck where she opened one of the doors. Adam ran into the bakery and came out with a smaller version of the flatbed cart they'd used in the store. He positioned it on the curb right across from the open doors and they began unloading their haul.

"Imported honey?" Taylor asked when she

had the chance to read the label on those first tubs he'd put on the cart in the store.

"I'm known for not skimping when it comes to quality." He reached into the truck for one of the large bags of flour.

"Well, I'm known for coming in under budget." The tub was heavier than she'd anticipated so it took a bit of her rarely used muscle to get it off the truck and onto the cart.

"I'll get those and you can get some of the lighter stuff."

Turning her lips up she shook her head. "I'm good. They're not too heavy for me. But thanks."

"You say thanks, but you look like you're thinking 'oh please, stand back and watch me work.'"

Laughter came in a quick unexpected burst— the way every emotion she'd been experiencing around this guy had in the past few days.

Adam placed a second bag of flour on the cart and stood to stare at her. He had been doing that a lot, especially since that wife remark back at the store. Had that made him as uncomfortable as it did her? He hadn't corrected the clerk. Maybe because she'd jumped to do that so quickly. With a shake of her head she told herself for the billionth time that none of this mattered. She only wanted them to be the perfect team to win this competition.

"So did you pick up all your fancy baking skills during the time you were at culinary school?" She had to say something because this stare-off they had going wasn't ceasing.

"A few, but I wasn't there long," he replied. "Maybe six months before Cheryl's accident."

Her heart immediately sank. She hadn't meant to bring up his wife's death. "Oh Adam I'm sorry. We don't have to talk about that."

He stopped and looked as if he were really contemplating her words before shaking his head.

"No. It was a long time ago. Well, three years ago. My father was big on what he thought were good long term careers for his children. Becoming a baker wasn't exactly what he had in mind for his son, so I went to college here in Philly and graduated with a business degree. That's where Cheryl and I met. We were married right after graduation and had Brooke months later. My dad always taught his sons especially, the importance of taking care of their responsibilities above all else. So I worked two jobs to support my family until Cheryl was able to start her in-home daycare. About a year after that Brooke started school, and we were finally in a good financial position where I could work only one job. So I went to school at night."

She hadn't imagined she'd have to fight back tears hearing his story, but her mood had suddenly gone melancholy at the thought of what he'd gone through.

"And then Cheryl died." She finished for him

because saying those words had to be hard for him.

"A car accident."

"Oh, Adam." She forgot about the supplies in the back of that truck and stepped closer to him but then stopped. Should she touch him? Just a consoling hand to his arm or shoulder? Would that be appropriate? Would he think she was overstepping their professional boundaries?

He stood a little straighter, holding his head a bit higher. "It's been a challenge raising my baby on my own, but baking is something that always seems to put a smile on my face. And on Brooke's. So, where'd you get your passion for architecture?"

She never thought she'd be so glad to see a smile on someone's face. How wonderful was it that even through the midst of all that loss and sorrow, that he could still find some happiness.

"Seeing amazing buildings all around the world when I was growing up." Feeling a bit lighter now, she grabbed another tub from the truck and he picked up a box. They met at the cart, both putting their items down as she continued. "I was born in Philly and mostly lived here until I was six. My mom's an international lawyer and my dad's a diplomat. We moved every couple of years."

He looked surprised. "That's a lot of moving."

"Oh no, I loved it. Well...at least I learned to love it. Being so young and having to be uprooted so much was hard in the beginning, but as I got older I learned to find the best in every move. I mean some kids collect dolls. I collected passport stamps."

And she really loved looking at her old passport books to see all the different places she'd been. It gave her a sense of accomplishment.

Adam chuckled. "Don't ever say that to Brooke. She loves her doll collection above all else."

"I'll bet she does. But you know, being single and loving travel is why the firm sees me as the go-to girl for faraway projects."

"Is that what you want to do forever? I mean, travel to faraway places to do these special projects? And where do you go for Christmas?"

It had been a long time since she'd thought about forever. One project at a time had been her motto these past years.

"I planned on forever once. It didn't work out. But for Christmas I usually visit my parents. Unfortunately, this year they're in Singapore. And I have a gingerbread house to build here." A fact which she was actually very excited about, and not just because of the possibility of a promotion. She was actually enjoying working on this project so far.

"So you don't miss hosting your own traditional Christmas?"

A traditional Christmas – like the ones she'd seen in Christmas movies with a family in their house, a Christmas tree with lots of presents underneath, stockings hanging by the fireplace, a big home-cooked meal. She hadn't thought about it in a long time, but yeah, she missed it because it had once been her only dream in life.

"Life doesn't always turn out the way we plan. So wherever I hang my stocking, it's Christmas." For the first time in all the years she'd been saying that, it sounded hollow.

"See, that I understand because I was going to be a world famous pastry chef. But sometimes plans just don't work out."

"It's never too late." For him, at least, she believed that.

They finished unpacking the supplies and she moved to stand closer to the cart while Adam closed the doors of the truck.

When the truck was locked he came to stand on the other side of the cart. The air today was brisk but the sun shined brightly while people moved about going to and from, but for just a few moments it seemed as if it were just her and Adam. A breeze blew lifting her hair on the sides where her hat did not cover. He extended his hand, brushing back the few strands that flew into her face.

"Thanks for saying that and for your help with the shopping today."

His fingers brushed over her chin and every word in her vocabulary was lost. A familiar voice broke through the haze of...what exactly had she been feeling in that moment?

"Taylor. I thought that was you. You know Annabelle, I believe." Bradford and Annabelle walked up to them and Taylor was only half grateful for the interruption.

Before she could wonder what the odds were that they'd run into their rival teammates on the street like this, she remembered Annabelle's restaurant was just around the corner. Bradford was wearing his usual charismatic smile and wool dress coat. Beside him Annabelle was casually dressed and effortlessly pretty. Taylor summoned her best professional smile.

"Yes. We've met."

Annabelle gave Taylor a cordial nod and then turned her attention to Adam to introduce herself, "Annabelle Renard."

Bradford pointed to Annabelle. "Gold medalist in last year's European Pastry Panache Competition."

Adam nodded and extended his hand to Annabelle. "Adam Dale, voted best personality in high school," he said proudly and with a smile.

"Oh?" Annabelle replied while shaking his hand.

Bradford continued his very obvious display of showing off by pointing at Adam. "Wait, you're ah...you're the donut guy from Ray's." He looked toward the bakery window. "Right here. Man, you make the best jelly donuts."

"Yeah, that's me," Adam nodded and looked like he accepted the compliment.

But Taylor wasn't satisfied. "And that's just his day job. Adam is a very talented patisserie," she announced.

"Oh?" Annabelle replied once more. "How nice. May the best team win, huh?"

"Absolutely," Taylor replied and watched happily as Annabelle and Bradford walked away.

"Talented patisserie? I like the sound of that," Adam told her when they were once again alone.

She grinned at him. But was now more determined than ever to stay focused and win this competition. "Don't let it go to your head. Let's hurry back, we gotta meet the volunteers."

Chapter Eight

B ACK AT THE MARKETPLACE, ADAM immediately jumped into work. He'd assembled a tool belt which made Taylor chuckle.

"Are you a baker or a construction worker?"

"I'm a jack of all trades," he replied with a hand on the side of the tool belt as he posed like a cowboy.

"Okay, well as long as you master the baking on this one, sir, I'll respect that," she replied easily.

There was a level of comfort with them now, one she hadn't realized she needed but was glad it existed. While he measured and cut, she reviewed her notes to make sure she was totally satisfied with the design. Since he was cutting out the frame, it was a little late to turn back, but she could check anyway.

They worked in companionable silence for

about twenty minutes before their volunteers arrived. Taylor stood to greet them and saw that while they'd been working the Marketplace had begun to get a little more crowded—and not just with visitors. The other three teams had arrived to work on their gingerbread houses as well. She avoided looking at their progress and instead smiled as the volunteers stepped onto the platform.

She began the introductions. "Adam, this is David, our new intern at the firm."

"Nice to meet you." Adam gave him a cordial nod. "You can, ah, lose the jacket."

"Yes, sir," David replied and immediately removed it.

David was in his last year of college. He looked nervous and a bit uncomfortable as he no doubt assumed all his work would take place in the office. Most of hers did the summer she'd interned at Ogilvy. Appearance was next to doing a fabulous job, so she could see why David had worn the jacket. But she did agree with Adam; he could take it off.

"And this is my friend and co-worker, Josephine," Taylor continued. Josephine was all smiles with her Christmas tree earrings and festive green sweater.

"Hi," Josephine said and added a wave.

Adam replied with a friendly, "Hi."

"And this is my friend and neighbor, Wendy."

Wendy smiled, but immediately apologized.

"I'm sorry I couldn't draft my kids, Taylor. But it's for the best because they would have devoured the gingerbread."

Taylor and Adam chuckled.

"Just like my daughter," Adam said.

"Thanks for volunteering everyone," Taylor began. "We have a big project ahead of us. So first, we put up the frame. Next we bake and cover the frame with gingerbread. And then, the final phase, decorating. We can make this amazing, if," Taylor said while glancing at Adam, "we stay on schedule, that is."

"Is that comment directed at me?" Adam stared at her.

"Well, I'm simply reminding everyone that we're on a strict time limit." Keeping her tone even she glanced at Adam but then looked at the volunteers.

Adam also kept his eyes on the volunteers this time. "But we want everyone to feel free to follow their creativity."

Taylor's smile remained in place. "As long as we meet certain benchmarks and construction timetables." Her tone was a little pinched at the end, but that was because she wanted to make sure Adam was getting her point. They did not have time for him to linger with his creativity.

She tried to ignore how Josephine and Wendy were watching the exchange with amusement. Poor David simply continued to smile while holding his sports jacket.

"While making the most colorful and delicious gingerbread house we can," Adam insisted with a smile.

At this point, David looked at Wendy and Josephine, who by this time were grinning conspiratorially.

Taylor felt her frustration with Adam returning. And just when she'd thought they'd found a comfortable common ground. "Okay do you remember what we agreed on? Staying on our own side of the street."

Adam looked at her. "Yes, but—"

"You're driving on my sidewalk," she said speaking through the side of her mouth while looking at David.

David nodded and grinned at her in return.

When Adam and Taylor realized the volunteers were not only staring at them, but were also waiting for them to give instructions, they both stopped to take a deep breath.

"So, shall we begin?" Taylor asked.

The volunteers looked at each other and stifled another grin but immediately disbursed to begin working.

After all assignments were given out the team fell into an easy flow of getting the frame assembled. Taylor had finished reviewing her plans, and she came over to help Adam with attaching the beams. He hadn't been joking when he'd said he was a jack of all trades. His father had not been a fan of Adam spending so much time in the kitchen learning from his mother, so it wasn't unusual for Will to draft his son to help him on a worksite.

"This takes a little more precision than baking a cake," Will would say in his gruff tone. "If you miss an ingredient in the cake, it doesn't taste good. You toss it out." He'd shrug his wide shoulders and turn his thick lips down in a frown. "But if you put these beams up and don't make sure they're level, or you haven't secured these nails into measured intervals along the base here, then this entire house could come tumbling down. Get what I'm sayin'?"

Adam would nod because it was always easier to agree with his father. And truth be told, he enjoyed building things because it also allowed him to flex his creative muscles.

"I get it and I'll make sure I'm measuring precisely. The last thing I want is for Jenny and this treehouse to crash to the ground. Mama would kill both of us."

Then Will had chuckled. A rich booming sound that never failed to make Adam smile. His father was a good man with stern – sometimes rigid – rules and thoughts, but he'd taught Adam many things; most importantly, how to take care of his own family. Which was exactly what he was doing now. He only hoped joining this competition would continue to work in his family's favor.

Taylor was standing on the other side of the frame, checking the half that Adam had just nailed into place. He was trying not to notice the soft floral scent of her perfume or how her long hair brushed lightly over her shoulders when she tilted her head. That's when he caught her frowning at the corner beam. Adam shook his head and bent down to pick up the leveler. He handed it to her and she accepted it.

"How did you do that?" she asked.

"Do what?"

She looked at him skeptically. "Give me what I needed before I asked."

"In the kitchen you get good at predicting who needs what. And you made a face," he replied.

She looked at the leveler and then pressed it to the beam she'd been surveying. "And obviously you still want our house to have a traditional roof."

"How do you know that?" he asked.

She smiled. "Because you made a face."

Adam grinned. How was it they could be scratching against each other in disagreement one minute, but then existing in such easy friendliness the next?

That question wouldn't be answered today as Adam glimpsed a familiar face heading toward the exhibit stage. Was that Nick Brexley? He was dressed in a dark colored suit, crisp white dress shirt and a festive red tie. For a slither of a moment Adam felt excitement at the possibility that somehow Nick had heard he'd entered this competition and wanted to let him know he'd be looking out for his work. As quickly as the giddy sensation appeared, it was gone. Annabelle stepped down from the stage to walk away with Brexley.

"Hey. You okay?"

Taylor had come to stand beside him and when he noticed she'd followed his gaze and was now watching Annabelle walk away with Nick, he put on the best smile he could muster.

"Sure am. Just taking a little break. But now that's over. Back to work, ma'am."

His tone was playful and Taylor immediately added, "I was going to tell you to get back to work."

She'd looked back over her shoulder and he knew she wanted to ask more questions.

He decided to continue with the friendly rapport they'd had going before the interruption. "So, how did you get caught up in this project anyway?"

She went back to her measuring and shrugged. "My boss asked me to do it. Last month I was crafting a ten-story condo, and this week I'm in charge of gumdrops."

He detected an edge in her voice and was quick to declare, "There's no shame in designing a gingerbread house."

She didn't admit or deny. "Well, I like a challenge – besides just working with you."

Adam chuckled. "Very funny."

They exchanged glances and in a blink, easy friendliness shifted to something else. Something strange and decidedly uncomfortable.

"And I'm in charge of gumdrops, by the way," he announced and effectively broke the spell.

By the end of the day Adam had decided it was definitely getting worse. He'd found himself gazing at her more times than he should have. Watching her do simple things such as pick up a hammer or toss her head back in laughter at something Josephine and Wendy said. Even when they were both entrenched in the building process, Adam could still sense when she was close to him and searched for her when she wasn't.

It was enough to annoy him but he'd pressed on anyway. Now that their workday was over, he felt a little relief. The volunteers had left an hour ago so it was just him and Taylor walking out the door. He held it open for her and she walked out into the early evening air.

"Why thank you." She rubbed her hands together after she'd slipped on her gloves.

It was a cold, breezy day. Adam zipped his coat as they began to walk.

"I'd say we made pretty good progress today. The frame's nearly done." He looked around enjoying the atmosphere.

Lighted snowflakes danced on wire hung high above the street while ribbons and huge red bows wrapped around lamp posts. The area was full of people either going into the market-place or coming out. Classical versions of holiday songs were being played inside and outside, so that the entire area was wrapped in holiday cheer.

"So, is it true what Brooke said before? Do you want to open your own bakery?" Taylor asked while they walked toward the parking garage.

He couldn't help but admit how timely her question was, considering who he'd seen earlier.

"I wanted to," he admitted. "I tried a while back, but no investors wanted to fund a culinary school drop out."

Adam noticed earlier that Taylor hadn't re-acted in a negative way toward him telling her that he dropped out of school. That probably had more to do with the reason he left school rather than her actually thinking of him as a quitter. Still, he'd hoped the admission did not put him in a bad light in her eyes. Apparently it hadn't.

"Well, if we win, maybe you should reach out to them again," she continued.

Jenny had that same thought. But Adam wasn't sure. "I'm doing this for one reason only, and that's to make Brooke happy."

Because thinking of it any other way was simply opening the door for disappointment.

He'd had enough of that in his lifetime and had no intention of putting himself in line for more.

She nodded, but did not respond. They walked a little further until he couldn't take it anymore. He had to ask.

"You think that means I lack ambition?"

Taylor stopped walking to look up at him. "Absolutely not. I think it makes you guilty of being a great dad."

Adam had heard people say something was music to their ears before, but this was the first time he could actually relate to the saying. He couldn't explain why it meant so much for her to understand where he was coming from and to not negatively judge him for it, but he actually felt like dancing to the tune of her compliment.

"Speaking of Brooke, she wanted me to give you something," he said after they'd resumed walking and then stopped at the corner to wait for the traffic light to change.

Taylor tilted her head in question.

"An invitation for dinner tonight. And if those instant noodle cups you snuck in with the supplies are what you're calling dinner, you have no choice but to accept our invitation."

She thought about it a moment, but Adam knew her answer when he saw her lip lifting in a smile.

"Okay, sure. Anything for Brooke," she replied.

Chapter Nine

TAYLOR STEPPED INTO ADAM'S HOUSE and felt all of those thoughts she had last night come flooding back. For starters, it was very warm inside. It was extremely cold outside, so the heat was welcome. But stepping into a warm house always reminded Taylor of coming home after school before her parents had started traveling so much. Her mother had always bundled her up good with coat, hat, scarf and gloves, but when Taylor came home after unwrapping all of that stuff, she used to sit on the bottom step and just get warm.

They'd stopped at Brooke's friend's house to pick her up on the way and now they both stood in the same spot as last night removing their coats. But this time when Adam went to hang them up, he said, "You two can set the table.

Dinner is a quick preparation that I'll take care of."

Brooke immediately grabbed Taylor's hand. "Come on, Taylor. I'll show you where everything is."

Adam looked at her and they shared a grin before Taylor was whisked away.

"Daddy keeps all the knives on the back part of the counter so I can't reach them," Brooke said as they entered the kitchen.

"That's a good idea. So why don't we just get plates, napkins, forks and cups," Taylor suggested.

She hesitated because even though she'd worked in this kitchen with Adam last night while baking, she wasn't going in his cabinets and drawers. Sure, he'd given her permission by telling her to help Brooke, but it still felt a little odd.

"Over here in this drawer," Brooke told her and moved to the other side of the kitchen.

Taylor decided not to overthink this. She was having dinner with her partner in a competition she was only in because of work. So he was like a co-worker. Yes, that was it. Dinner with a co-worker. No harm, no foul.

"Plates are up there," Brooke said while she was selecting and counting the silverware.

Taylor took a slow breath and released it before opening the cabinet and taking out three plates. She closed the cabinet door and almost jumped when Adam was standing right there on the other side.

"Sorry," he said and moved around her to grab something out of one of the lower cabinets.

Was he taller than she originally thought? Oh no, she'd changed out of the heeled boots she was wearing earlier and now had on flats. Still, he'd seemed really tall and really close to her just a few seconds ago.

"Come on Taylor, I have the napkins and the forks all set."

Right. She was supposed to be setting the table with Brooke, not acting as if she'd lost her mind over her co-worker who had been nice enough to offer to feed her. Shaking her head and hopefully dismissing those crazy thoughts she'd been having for good, Taylor moved to the table to help Brooke.

Half an hour later they were sitting at the table enjoying the best pizza Taylor had ever tasted.

"That was delicious. Thank you both for inviting me. So what's in the pizza anyway?" she asked just in case she'd like to try making it herself.

Adam sat back in his chair and folded his arms over his chest before giving her a smug look. "Just my special recipe," he replied.

Taylor narrowed her gaze at him. "Except you don't use recipes."

Brooke chimed in, "Pecorino cheese, fennel sausage and truffle oil."

"Hey, honey! Those are trade secrets," Adam leaned over to say to Brooke who gave him a guilty shrug. "Guess Taylor's now in our circle of trust."

Taylor enjoyed watching them together. It was obvious how close they were. Even without Adam's admission earlier today, she knew that he was the type of guy that would do anything and everything he could for his daughter. The sight made her respect him even more.

"Well, anyway," she told them, "that was delicious. Seriously, the best dinner I've had in months."

"I'm going to work on my diorama. Do you want to help?" Brooke asked Taylor.

And because Taylor had been wondering about Brooke's progress, she quickly replied, "Sure."

They left Adam to clear the table and moved over to the second island between the kitchen and the dining room, occupied by Brooke's class project.

"Oh, your Christmas diorama is looking better and better. You clearly have your dad's gift for decorating." Taylor was excited to see how much Brooke had gotten done. There were houses and people, snowmen and a piece of white felt covering the cardboard base representing snow.

Brooke did not look happy about the project. "It just takes so long though. I need a herd of reindeer and each reindeer takes forever to draw."

"I see. Well, it doesn't have to," Taylor told her and reached over to grab a sheet of paper from the stack at the end of the table.

"All you need is a template. Just think of it as a Christmas cookie cutter but for art projects," she continued.

Brooke smiled at her and a part of Taylor melted inside. This little girl was looking at her as if everything she were saying was the gospel. Taylor had only offered to help with the project, she hadn't performed some great miracle. Actually, she'd done nothing to garner that gracious, appreciative and cute-as-a-button look from Brooke. But she liked it just the same.

"Here, let me show you," Taylor said. "Let's draw our reindeer."

Taylor was used to drawing, even though it was normally buildings, houses, etc. She used to draw other things when she was a little girl, and while that had been a long time ago, she discovered it was just like riding a bike. Once she started, it all came back to her. And when it was done she looked down at the reindeer and thought she'd done a mighty fine job.

"Now, all we need to do is cut it out," she told Brooke and reached for the scissors. She cut out the reindeer and held it up. "And we've got a master stencil to create all the reindeer we need. Viola!"

"Wow, thanks Taylor." Brooke's tone was incredulous as Taylor gave her another sheet of paper and placed the stencil on top for her to trace.

"Well, like I said, you have a great eye for decorating. So I propose we make you chief decorating officer for the gingerbread house. That is, if that doesn't step on anyone's toes?"

She'd caught sight of Adam walking into the room and decided to include him in the conversation.

"I'd be more than happy to share the glory," he announced.

Brooke smiled. "Yes! And after I finish cutting out all the reindeer, we should watch a movie. That'll be the best night ever!"

Oh, no. Taylor was certain she should be leaving now. She'd been with Adam all day—at the store, the marketplace and now at his home. She should leave. This had surpassed co-worker cordiality.

"Sounds like a plan," Adam answered and looked pointedly at Taylor.

What was she supposed to say now? *No, Brooke, I can't stay and watch an innocent movie with you because my mind keeps wandering to not-so-normal thoughts about your dad.* That was not going to go over well at all.

"Sure!" Taylor heard her answer and tried to

smile. She was staying to watch a movie with this very nice little girl and her very nice father.

Taylor was already in the living room when Adam joined her. She'd been hoping that Brooke would finish and come in first, but nope.

"So we're watching a movie," he said rubbing his hands together. He moved to a shelf that was lined with a number of DVDs. "What should we watch? Something with action or maybe super-heroes?"

"Superheroes? Really? How old are you?" she quipped.

He looked over his shoulder at her with a mock frown. "Hey, I happen to be as serious about my superheroes as I am about my baking. Come see for yourself."

Taylor crossed the carpeted floor to a stand near the window and leaned over slightly to look at the DVDs on display. He was right, there was an entire row of superhero movies. She shook her head. "This is pitiful, you know,"she teased, though she was sure he could tell that she didn't really mean it.

"What? Why? What type of movies do you like?"

Taylor stood to answer and they were once again face-to-face. How did this keep happening?

"I um...I like," she cleared her throat. "I like..."

"Christmas movies!" Brooke announced when she came running into the living room.

Taylor had instantly backed away from Adam at the sound of her voice, so Brooke easily slipped between them and selected a movie off one of the lower shelves.

"This one. I like it, but Jordan said it was old the last time I took it to her house. It's not old because it's in color. I tried to tell her that," Brooke explained.

"Oh, that's actually my favorite holiday movie," Taylor admitted when she glanced at the case. "Well, I like the older black and white version. But this one was good too."

Adam shrugged. "Then I guess I'm outnumbered. We're watching *Miracle on 34th Street*."

He took the case from Brooke and moved over to the television. Taylor gave Brooke a high-five and the two of them made their way to the couch to take a seat.

Almost two hours later, Brooke was asleep between Adam and Taylor and the movie was near the end.

Once again Taylor watched the little girl Susan experience the heartbreaking discovery that Kris Kringle had not gotten what she'd asked him for. It didn't matter how many times she saw this part, or in which movie version; the heaviness in Taylor's chest was just the same. Longing burned in the pit of her stomach as she thought of the house and family she'd wanted, just like Susan.

Minutes passed in the movie before Susan was riding in the car with her mother and soon-to-be step-father when she saw the house she'd dreamed of and asked for. Susan's elation upon seeing that house was exactly how Taylor wanted to feel. That moment of completion when Susan is in the house running up to her bedroom and the mother and father are standing in the living room trying to figure out what's going on—it was precisely what Taylor wanted. What she'd had to accept she might never have.

She twisted her fingers together and finally had to look away from the television. "Aww." Brooke's head had fallen on her chest. "She didn't even make it to the end of the movie."

"It's been a long day for her," Adam said looking down at his daughter.

They'd turned off the main light, and the glow from the Christmas tree in addition to the television illuminated the room. It had been a comfy and cozy movie night.

"I should go." Or rather, she really needed to go. She couldn't take much more of the emotional rollercoaster she was on at the moment. "I can call a taxi and be gone in a matter of minutes. Then you can properly put her to bed."

"No, it's late, I'll take you home," Adam said.

"But Brooke's asleep. I don't want to disturb

her. I've interrupted your routine enough to-night."

"Nonsense," he told her. "She's a heavy sleeper and will probably sleep the whole way. Besides, I'm not letting you catch a cab home. I'll just get her coat."

Adam was up before Taylor could say another word and a few minutes later they were all piled into his truck.

"Thanks for the ride," she said when they pulled up in front of her house.

"I had to. You're the only adult I know in Philly who doesn't own a car," he joked.

They'd already discussed her reasons for not having a car—because it didn't make sense if the car would spend most of the time parked in her garage while she traveled. So she only offered him a smirk before turning to look at Brooke who was, as he'd predicted, still asleep in the back seat.

"Cute," she whispered and then looked at Adam. "She's a great kid."

He nodded. "Well, she certainly seems to have taken a liking to you."

And she liked Brooke. She just didn't want to like Brooke's dad.

"Hmmm," she said in another attempt to change the subject in her mind. "So um, you even decorate your truck for Christmas." She motioned toward the Santa bobble head dancing on the dashboard.

Adam laughed.

"Our house is all decorated, my truck got a little jealous."

She chuckled too and then they were staring at each other. Smiling and staring. Staring and smiling. Like two silly teenagers in love...

"That your house?" he asked and Taylor could not have been more relieved.

"The one on the end there? You don't have any decorations up," he continued.

"Who's got the time?" she asked with a shrug.

Adam looked shocked or maybe he was offended, or both? She wasn't sure. "No Christmas decorations?"

She didn't have a reply. Decorations had not been a part of her Christmas routine in so long she didn't think anything of it anymore. But now that he'd said something, the fact that every other house on her street was heavily decorated made hers appear dark and lonely. Perhaps even unlived in, or unloved.

Boy, she was really having an emotional night.

"You know if one of the gingerbread judges saw this we'd be disqualified for lack of Christmas spirit. No wonder you don't know what a real gingerbread house should look like."

"Ah, please,"she said with a wave of her hand. He was really taking this seriously.

"It should be colorful and inviting. It should

be decorated to the hilt but with love. It should make you think of your grandma's house."

"Well, my grandmother lives in a high rise... in Tampa," she informed him with a chuckle.

Then she unsnapped her seat belt because it really was time for her to go. "Goodnight."

"Hey," Adam called before she could get out. He reached for the Santa bobble head and gave it to her. "The first item in your Christmas decoration kit."

She accepted the weird-looking Santa and stared at it a few seconds. "This?"

"What can I say? It's a start."

They both laughed and Taylor opened the door. "Thanks again for dinner, the ride, and the Santa." She was smiling as she climbed out of the truck and closed the door.

And as she walked up her driveway the Santa had her grinning again, so she turned around and waved it at Adam. She could see him smiling in the front seat and her chest tightened. Taylor turned and hurried into her house. She closed the door behind her and fell back against it, thinking that she was glad to have survived the night. Now she could stop having weird thoughts about Adam.

But as Taylor walked further into her house, the silence seemed louder. At Adam's house there'd been the sounds of the TV when they were watching the movie and their chatter during dinner. It was also a bit chilly. She moved to the thermostat to check the temperature, but realized the chilliness came from her stark white walls and the bare rungs of the banister going up the steps. Even her paintings didn't make her house nearly as warm as Adam's home felt. Brooke had explained that she'd wrapped the garland around each rung on the banister at their house and she'd put the big red bow at the very end.

Now Taylor felt like a Scrooge for not putting up Christmas decorations, and more than a little homesick for the dream she'd once had.

"Thanks, Adam," she muttered and then sighed as she went up the stairs.

Chapter Ten

𝒯HE NEXT DAY TAYLOR GOT a call she never thought she would receive.

"I can't make it to the Marketplace to work on the gingerbread house today. Brooke's sick. I had to keep her home from school."

She stopped what she was doing—looking over a draft of an apartment building for Josephine to submit to Linda for approval. Her hand immediately went to her chest as beneath the pale blue sweater she wore her heart began to thump wildly.

"Oh no, Adam. Is she okay? Do you think you should take her to the hospital instead?"

His response was a light chuckle which had her staring at the phone receiver as if he could see that she was giving him the "are you crazy?" look.

"I don't think it's that serious. Probably some

type of twenty-four hour virus. The school sent a letter out last week that several students had fallen ill. She's not running a fever, but she's not able to keep any food down. I've already put a call in to her pediatrician, and his advice is to continue to force liquids and as long as no fever develops, the virus has to run its course. If she's not better in the morning I'll take her into his office. But I wanted to let you know because losing a day will set us back."

Her pulse calmed a bit after the full explanation and now that the vision of an ambulance or Brooke lying on a stretcher had dissipated.

"Well, you were going to speak to your boss about us using his kitchen to bake the gingerbread faster today. So maybe I'll just come over and we can work in your kitchen and that way you can still keep an eye on Brooke."

And she wanted to see her. Of course, she couldn't say that. Because how would it sound that she—Adam's co-worker of sorts—would want to see that his daughter was okay? Crazy. She knew because that's what she'd told herself when she'd lay in her bed last night, trying to fall asleep, but instead thinking of Brooke and how happy she'd been watching the first part of that movie last night.

"You don't have to do that. Using the professional kitchen at Ray's would be better and cut some of our time, so I'll call him as soon as I hang up with you. And if Brooke's feeling better tomorrow I can get in there early and make up for lost time."

She opened her bottom desk drawer and pulled out her purse. "Nonsense. Then we'd lose an entire day and have nothing to show for it. If I come over we can at least get some of the batches done. Just let me wrap up here and I'll be right over."

"Okay. If you're sure this is what you want to do. I'll see you when you get here."

"I'm sure. I'll see you in a little bit."

She hung up the phone just in time to see Josephine leaning over the ledge of her cubicle staring directly at her.

"What's going on?"

"Brooke's sick. She can't go to school today. I have to go."

Standing she pulled her coat off the back of her chair and was about to walk out of the cubicle but she noticed Josephine's quizzical look.

"Oh, I was almost finished with your plans anyway. I made some notes in the margin. Once you address those, it should be good to go to Linda." And as far as Linda was concerned, Taylor's prime assignment right now was winning this competition, so she hadn't been given any other projects to work on.

Josephine tilted her head. Today's bell-shaped earrings jingled with the motion. "I'm not thinking about those plans right now. I'm kinda wondering what's going on with you."

Taylor frowned because she didn't understand what Josephine was trying to get at, not because Josephine was almost blocking her way and she needed to get going. She wanted to stop by the store to get some things for Brooke—orange juice, ginger ale and popsicles. Taylor's mom always gave her popsicles when she was sick.

"What do you mean?"

"Taylor Scott doesn't do house calls for sick kids. The Taylor I know works her butt off on every project even when a team member is down."

Since she was still standing there, Taylor pushed her arms into her coat. "We're going to work at Adam's place."

"Oh, right. Adam, the very good-looking baker who had you just slightly off your game yesterday."

"What? I'm never off my game."

Josephine stood up straight and folding her arms over her chest. "You two were verbally sparring in front of us, and for the rest of the day you worked almost side-by-side. And if you think Wendy and I, your closest friends in the whole world, didn't notice that, you might be further gone than we thought."

She pushed her purse onto her shoulder and shook her head. This time of year Josephine's mind was normally somewhere between Christmasland and the office, but this might be the worst she's ever been. She was obviously confused.

"We got a lot of the preliminary set up done yesterday. After today we have nine days left until judging. Between work and everybody's holiday shopping, that doesn't give us a lot of time."

"Uh huh. Right. If that's the excuse you want to go with. But I'm thinking you might be looking at the hot baker a little closer than just his gingerbread skills. And it's cool because he was certainly checking for you."

"Stop." The one word wasn't spoken with as much force as she thought would have been more successful with Josephine. The woman's wide grin in response was proof. "I gotta go."

Josephine stepped aside. "Okay. Yeah, you definitely gotta go. Tell Adam I said hello."

Taylor was already walking away by the time Josephine yelled that last part. Her giggling could be heard even as Taylor steadily moved away.

She was still shaking her head by the time she stepped into the elevator. "I just want to check to make sure she's all right. That does not mean I want to get closer to the hot baker. Does it?"

"It's all right, sweetie. It's okay to be interested in a hot baker."

The older woman standing in the opposite corner of the elevator and holding two big shopping bags startled Taylor. She hadn't even noticed there was someone else in the elevator when she boarded.

"Oh my, did I say that out loud? I'm sorry. Just have so much going on in my head right now."

The woman smiled, her thin brightly painted lips spreading slowly. Her silver-white hair was styled in tight curls and wise brown eyes twinkled. "My advice? Slow down and let love find you. It shouldn't be a race, but a gentle glide into your destiny."

The elevator bell dinged before the doors opened. Taylor waited while the woman stepped off and walked through the lobby never looking back at her. She hurried outside to get a cab, all the while wondering how strangely eventful this morning was turning out to be.

Five hours later Adam had baked most of the gingerbread on his own while Taylor spent the bulk of her time going in and out of the bedroom with Brooke. About half an hour after she arrived at his house and they'd gotten settled in the kitchen, he'd gone in to check on Brooke and mentioned that Taylor was there. From that point on Brooke's requests had been for Taylor.

During the few times in the past that Brooke

had been home sick, Jenny was able to stay with her. But today Jenny had classes she could not miss. She was only one semester away from graduating with her marketing degree and winter finals were beginning. Adam was used to sharing his daughter's attention when she didn't feel well, but he wasn't used to sharing it with another woman—or at least, one who wasn't a family member.

Right now she sat on the edge of Brooke's bed leaning forward to wipe her face with a cool cloth. He'd told her that was something he did to keep the fever away and because it comforted Brooke, something his mother had told him to do when she was a baby. Watching Taylor do it now stirred something inside Adam.

"Do you want to try another cracker?" Taylor asked Brooke in a voice so soft Adam barely heard her.

"No," Brooke replied. "I'm tired now."

"Okay, honey, well you just take a little nap, and when you wake up maybe you'll be ready for some nice warm soup." Taylor finished with the cloth and set it on Brooke's nightstand right beside her princess-themed lamp.

"And after soup we can watch another movie," Brooke told Taylor. "I already picked one out— *Home Alone*, the one where the little boy is home sick by himself."

Taylor's smile—the one Adam was getting very used to seeing—spread fast as she agreed.

Adam couldn't believe this woman was here in his house, with his daughter. A few days ago he had no idea who Taylor Scott was, and now she not only had him participating in a giant gingerbread contest, but she was helping to take care of his sick daughter. What was going on?

"She's feeling much better," Taylor announced when she stepped out of Brooke's room to see him standing in the hallway.

They were treating his daughter's bedroom like a hospital room, heading into Brooke's bathroom once they came out to wash their hands and do a secondary coating of hand sanitizer since they were also working in the kitchen.

"Good. Then the doctor was right." He walked down the short end of the hallway with her as she entered Brooke's aqua blue-colored bathroom.

He leaned against the doorway as she stepped inside and turned on the water at the sink.

"I don't know how you do it," she told him when she reached for the soap.

"Do what? You're doing everything for me today." And that wasn't totally a bad thing. He hadn't realized how much he'd missed the tag-team of two parents working with a child. Again, Jenny had been doing a great job helping out for the past few years, but this was different. He'd been seeing how throughout the day.

"How do you stay so calm?" Taylor asked. "Each time she calls for me, I'm a nervous wreck wondering if she's getting worse or not. And I really don't know what I'm doing. I only remember a little bit of what my mom used to do when I was sick. I knew you were doing all of the baking, so I've been texting back and forth with Wendy to see what she does for her kids when they're sick."

"I'd say you're doing a pretty good job."

She'd pulled her hair back from her face, holding it with a black band at the nape of her neck. It made her seem more relaxed, at home. He wondered what he could do to keep her looking that way.

"Ah, I made us some sandwiches. Come on down when you're ready." He quickly got away from her because his thoughts were all over the place.

He was sitting at the table when she entered the dining room and took the seat across from him.

"Why don't you have a boyfriend, Taylor?" The question tumbled out of his mouth before he could think to stop it.

It clearly startled her too, because she stopped chewing to stare at him.

"Sorry. I was just wondering why a smart, beautiful woman would not have someone. I mean, you don't have a boyfriend, right? Not that it matters, I was just wondering." And now he was babbling. He shoved a chip into his mouth.

She cleared her throat when she was finished

chewing and then picked up a napkin to wipe her mouth.

"Well, ah, yeah, no there's no need to apologize. I guess it's a fair question since I've been here all day playing house." She quickly looked up at him with a mortified expression.

"What I meant to say was, I've been here working, but not really, since I've been taking care of Brooke. And I really like doing that, even though it's my first time. But—"

She stopped talking, and Adam could only nod because he'd just been through that same babbling spurt.

Taylor took a deep breath and released it slowly while Adam took a drink of the soda in front of him and then wiped his hands on a napkin.

"I had a boyfriend a long time ago. It didn't work out. Since then there's been nothing long term."

He accepted that, as if there was something to actually accept.

"What about you?"

"What about me?"

Her lips twisted into a smirk. "Girlfriend?"

"Oh, yeah. That. No. Um, my sister tried a blind date thing about a year ago. Crashed and burned within the first five minutes. Apparently, I'm out of practice. My conversation consists mainly of baking muffins and taking my daughter to dance class or ice skating."

Taylor rested her elbows on the table and leaned forward. "That's not bad conversation. I'd probably talk about building specs or how valuable it is to sign up for TSA pre-check. That is, if I ever stayed put long enough to go on a blind date."

"Huh. We're a pair aren't we?"

"Yeah, I guess so. You know, I thought I wanted all this at one time. The house, kids, dance classes, Little League games."

Intrigued, he decided to press on, besides he was already all-in with the questions now.

"You don't want it now?"

Her smile wavered and she did this really cute thing where her nose crinkled.

"Not really. I mean, it's nice, but dating's time consuming and I've got work and travel. And actually, the more time passes, the less I think about it."

She paused after those words and Adam thought she might be questioning them. Only because he'd been doing a lot of that himself lately. Saying something and then wondering if what he'd said was actually true, or if he'd just been so used to saying it that the words had naturally come out.

"Yeah. Me too. Right now for me, Brooke is the priority. I don't really have time for anything else."

Way to prove his own point.

"She's really great, Adam. And you do such a wonderful job with her."

"She misses her mother." Now that was totally honest. "I see it sometimes when I pick her up from school and her friends are being picked up by their moms and talking about doing things with their moms. It's hard for her, but she's such a trouper. She tries to act like it doesn't bother her as much. She likes to say she's older now so she can't act like a baby."

"Awww, that's so sad. But doesn't your sister fill in?"

He nodded. "Yes. Jenny has been great and Brooke really loves her. But she also knows that Jenny is almost finished with school. Depending where she gets a job, she may not be here with us much longer, and I would never ask her to stay."

"No. You wouldn't."

She was looking at him differently. Adam hoped she wasn't pitying him, but he couldn't blame her if she was. He was really giving her enough ammunition for those thoughts.

"So. I managed to get a lot done today," he said, changing the subject. "Ray said we're a go to use the bakery kitchen whenever we need to, so we can go there tomorrow. You're still set on your plans?"

She sat up straight then and he could see her shifting from the relaxed Taylor to the professional Taylor. He liked that there were two sides to her.

"Yes. I think they're good. We just need to finish getting the frame up and transport the gingerbread to the Marketplace, and we'll be all set to start assembling."

"Well then, we'd better get to work on baking more gingerbread." He stood from the table and picked up his plate.

She stood too. "Look at you trying to stay on schedule. I think I'm rubbing off on you, Adam Dale."

He walked behind her into the kitchen thinking she had no idea how true her words actually were.

Chapter Eleven

"OKAY, CAN YOU, UM—" ADAM said, but Taylor quickly finished the sentence for him.

"Take the last tray out of the oven," she replied with a nod. "I'm on it."

Three days after Brooke's stomach virus, they were in the kitchen at Ray's. Over his shoulder, Adam could see her slipping the oven mitts on and moving to take the tray out of the oven.

"Hot! Hot! Hot!" she whispered. Immediately, he turned from putting the already cooled trays on a shelf and helped her move this new tray to rest on the racks he'd positioned on the counter.

When the tray was out of her hands he started to ask, "Can you ah, pass me the—"

"Spatula." She finished his sentence again and reached over to the utensil holder to get one for him. "Here," she said, handing it to him.

Adam couldn't help but smile at how at

ease she now looked in the kitchen. She was a really fast learner and all the baking tips and kitchen etiquette he'd been dishing out had not only been well-received, but were now being implemented. And by such a talented woman, to boot. The gingerbread smelled delicious and was cooking exactly as they'd planned. There was good reason for him to continue smiling.

"We need to wait until these are nice and dry so that...?" She hesitated this time.

He looked over to her and noticed the soft yellow sweater she was wearing today. It was a nice color on her that made her eyes light up. "The frosting adheres." Adam finished for her this time.

"Hmmm," she said with a nod.

"Hey, did you notice?" he asked and leaned in slightly as if sharing some great secret.

"What?" The question held just a hint of concern.

"The smell of nothing burning," he replied with a grin.

She chuckled. "Amazing, right? I'd say our current collaboration is a teeny bit better than our first."

"Well, that isn't saying much," Adam quipped. And yet, he knew it was.

It said they were becoming a great team. Just like the night when he'd watched her and Brooke setting the table for dinner, and then how the two of them not only worked together on Brooke's project but talked about that movie as if they'd seen it a billion times.

The entire arrangement was turning out to be cozier and more comfortable than Adam would have ever imagined.

They'd gotten off to a rocky start, but this morning Adam had awakened knowing that he was going to see Taylor at the bakery today, and that thought had made him happy.

"Well, well, well. It looks like the elves have taken over my kitchen," Ray said as he walked in.

"Tired elves," Adam replied. "Taylor, meet my boss, Ray."

"It's nice to meet you, Ray. Thank you so much for letting us use your kitchen," Taylor said.

"No problem," Ray told her. "Adam, can I talk to you for a minute?"

Oh, that didn't sound good. Ray had given Adam permission to use the kitchen at the bakery and to have some time off to work on the competition, but Adam had insisted on still doing some of the baking for the bakery as well. He wouldn't have felt comfortable leaving Ray totally in the lurch while he did the competition.

When they'd walked over to the other side of the kitchen, Ray leaned in and whispered to Adam. "That's quite a project you two have going."

"Hey, don't worry about it. I can keep up with the muffins and the bagels." Adam immediately assured him.

Ray nodded. "I know. And look, Adam, I know I've got you baking below your potential."

He immediately interjected. "I like working here, okay. You're a good boss."

Ray clasped his hands behind his back and nodded before continuing, "You know I'd let you bake the fancy stuff full-time, but this is an old family bakery. I've had customers here for the last twenty years—" he started to explain.

"And our customers only want the basics." Adam finished Ray's statement. "I know, Ray. And I won't forget that."

"You read my mind," Ray told him with a chuckle. "Anyway, this week the sky's the limit. My kitchen is at your command."

The fact that Ray acknowledged Adam's passion as a pastry chef and was granting him this opportunity meant the world to Adam. He tapped Ray on the arm and smiled giving him a silent thanks.

"You know I'd offer to help, but it looks like you two have the situation in hand," Ray said, his voice intentionally louder as he began walking back to the counter where Taylor stood.

She was cleaning up the area they'd been

working in, gathering the utensils and wiping down the counters.

"Aww, thanks again for letting us bake here." She gave Ray one of her amazing smiles.

Ray beamed. "My pleasure, lovely lady. And I'll be at the competition cheering for you. Good luck!"

He'd already begun to walk away when Adam said, "Our gingerbread needs to cool. So can I suggest a break?" He hesitated when it occurred to him that a break might mean she would go and take care of some other business she had. "You busy?"

Taylor stopped what she was doing and looked up at him skeptically. "Why?"

"I gotta get some stocking stuffers for Brooke, and since you're a Philly native maybe it's time you get reacquainted with how your hometown celebrates Christmas." After noting how much he liked seeing the relaxed Taylor the other day, he'd been thinking of a way to reinforce his "Taylor needs to learn to enjoy herself more" idea. She was always so focused on work, this competition in particular, and she traveled so much, he thought it would be a good idea for her to get to know Philly again. Maybe if she did, she would be more willing to stay here instead of traveling all the time.

"Okay," she replied with a shrug.

He smiled more on the inside than he let show. "Okay, let's do it!"

"I can't believe you're not cold," Taylor said half an hour later when they were walking around the outside portion of the Christmas Market.

She had on her coat, a very fashionable beret that matched, and gloves. She looked chic and beautiful and Adam found himself staring at her even more. He, on the other hand, had been so eager to get out of the bakery and to be with her in a scenery other than a kitchen or the work site, that he'd forgotten his coat. Luckily he'd worn a long sleeve flannel shirt today, so that helped fight off the chill a little.

"It feels good after being near the ovens all day." That seemed like a much more viable excuse than the truth: that he'd been so focused on her that he'd forgotten his coat.

Night had fallen and there was a light crowd of people milling about. The music was still playing and lights from all of the vendor booths added to the festive atmosphere.

"Is this really your first Christmas in Philadelphia since you were little?" He talked while they walked.

"As an adult, yeah."

"Wow. So you have no Christmas memories here as a kid either, huh?"

She tilted her head and squinted as if trying to recall right at this moment. "Well, it feels familiar but cloudy. Kind of like in a snow globe. I remember going shopping at the Reading Market, the neighborhoods with lights and yummy food, of course."

"Hmmm, so you remember the most important things. Food."

"Ahh, yeah," she chuckled.

Adam smiled along with her. "Ah, here's what I came for." He spotted the stand and jogged over to it. Checking the sign to get a price before reaching into his pocket, he pulled out some money.

He handed the bills to the salesperson. "Can I get a pound of your bark, please?"

Taylor joined him at the stand just as the woman was handing him a red and white tin wrapped in a green striped bow. He turned to her and opened the tin.

"I heard you like peppermint bark, and this company is known for theirs," he said, extending the tin in her direction.

She blinked. "Oh! Thanks." She reached in to select a piece. "It looks delicious."

She'd told him that the first day she'd come into the bakery. Maybe she hadn't expected him to remember. But there wasn't much he'd forgotten about Taylor since then.

"It is. I buy some every year because when I make it, mine never turns out as good."

She took a bite and chewed. "Mmmmmm, yes. This is delicious, Adam."

He chewed a piece as well and they continued walking until something caught her attention. She walked over to one of many toy stalls along this aisle.

"Oh, that tiny train set would look great in Brooke's Christmas diorama," she said when she turned to look at him.

And before he could reply, she was telling the salesperson, "I'll take one of those."

They waited while the small train was placed into a box and wrapped. Taylor paid for it and took another bite of her peppermint bark.

"She'll love it," Adam said when they started walking again. "What about you? You want anything special for Christmas?"

"Not really. I don't wish for specific things anymore."

"Why? Oh, let me guess, you wished for something before and didn't get it." He'd actually been joking but her reply came quick.

"Well, if you can believe it, I wished for an Easy-Bake Oven one year." She grinned.

"Really?" He couldn't help looking at her skeptically. "Was it broken or—"

She laughed. "It turns out I didn't have much use for it. Kind of like you and a cookbook."

"Oooh, touché," he replied with another chuckle.

It was very easy to laugh when he was with her. Easy to relax and, for a little while, not be a dad or a baker but to just be Adam. He hadn't realized he missed that.

"Ahhh," she said, the sound and the fact that she'd walked in a different direction pulling him from his thought.

"I always wanted a chandelier in my imaginary house," she continued.

Adam followed her gaze to a chandelier with white frosted sconces and black iron arms. It was decorated with real pine branches tied with red and green ribbons.

"Imaginary house?" he asked.

She stood back from the stall and looked up to him with what he could only describe as a starry look in her eyes.

"When I was a kid, I had a vision of a perfect house. I sketched it out and everything. I even drew Santa on top of the roof because I was worried that when we moved he wouldn't find us. But my mom always said, wherever we were, if I hung my stocking, Santa would find me. And he always did."

The story was charming and touching and he wished he weren't being interrupted now with an incoming text message. He pulled his phone out of his pocket and read the message.

"Is something wrong? What's that about?"

Taylor asked when he'd stuffed the phone back into his pocket.

"Ah, just checking on my Christmas planning," he said. "Let's get out of here. It's getting a bit cold."

She glanced at his no-coat status and shook her head. "Okay, I'll bet it is," she replied.

Adam didn't take them back to the bakery, and when he pulled up in front of her house, he half expected Taylor to go off about their strict timeline again. She didn't. But after he parked and they got out of the truck, she did look over at him in question because Jenny and Brooke were standing on the sidewalk.

Brooke was already giggling as they walked toward her, and for the first time since he'd put this plan into play Adam felt a twinge of nervousness. This could either go perfectly right or horribly wrong. The possibility of the latter was making him a bit nauseous. After she'd spent that day taking care of Brooke, he'd wanted so badly to do something nice for her. He'd thought about it and planned for the last few days and couldn't wait to get out of bed this morning to see that it all fell into place.

"What's going on here?" Taylor asked as they

came to a stop in front of Brooke and Jenny, but he didn't answer right away.

"Hi, Taylor, I'm Jenny, Adam's younger sister." Jenny extended her hand to Taylor because while they each knew of the other, this was their first time actually meeting face-to-face.

Taylor shook Jenny's hand. "Hi. Nice to meet you." There was still a very skeptical look on her face. "Um, what are you guys doing here?"

"Just delivering Brooke to her dad," Jenny stated.

Adam would swear he'd seen a look of relief flash across Taylor's face at that moment. She nodded to Jenny and was about to speak again when she caught sight of something near the car parked in front of Adam's truck.

"Nice Christmas tree," she said. "Is that yours, Jenny?"

Jenny looked at Brooke, who giggled again and Adam continued to stare at Taylor, whose expression was now bordering on worry.

"What is everyone smiling about?" Her tone was still light, a tentative smile was in place, but she was clearly ready to know what was going on.

"Follow me, Taylor," Brooke finally said, but couldn't help giggling again.

It was a wonder his daughter was managing to keep the secret for this long. Brooke was ecstatic when Adam discussed the idea with her. They all walked through the gates leading toward the houses on Taylor's row. Because Taylor's was an end-of-the-row house, they headed to the side of the house where Brooke flicked a switch before yelling, "Ta-da!"

When all of the lights that had been strung around the outside of Taylor's house lit up, Taylor stared in awe.

"What in the world?" She sounded incredulous as she looked around at all the lights: her front door, the front windows and the bushes in front of the house. There was a wreath filled with red, gold and green bulbs on her door and one in the center of the large window next to it. Along the gate of her tiny yard were red and white lights.

Relief and extreme pleasure washed over him the moment he saw her look turn from shock to sheer pleasure. He leaned over to whisper to her. "I told you, your house needed decorating."

She looked over her shoulder to him and then back to the house. "But I—"

"And don't you worry, we had tons of leftover decorations," he interrupted.

"And the tree's for you," Brooke added.

"Oh, you didn't have to do all of this." Taylor turned to him. She was shaking her head as if she really could not believe what she was seeing. If he could describe the way her eyes danced and her voice wavered on that last word, he would call it joy—Christmas joy.

"Sure we did! You needed to have Christmas at your house, too!"

Brooke was absolutely right: this was something they had to do as a special thank-you for what she'd done for them. Jenny smiled at Taylor, but then looked at him. "Okay, Adam, can you please help me get the tree off my car?"

"Sure," Adam replied.

"You have fun, kids, I'm heading out to a Christmas party," Jenny told Brooke and Taylor.

"Enjoy the party, and thanks so much, Jenny," Taylor told her.

When Adam returned with the tree, Taylor and Brooke were holding hands while still staring at the lights. If the tree hadn't been so heavy, he might've paused to enjoy the sight. Instead, he pressed on until Taylor unlocked her front door. The three of them managed to get the massive tree through the doorway and inside Taylor's living room.

"It looks perfect right here," Brooke pronounced.

"I have a stand in the basement," Taylor said and immediately left the room.

"Do you think she really likes it?" Brooke asked Adam when Taylor was gone.

He'd been taking the opportunity to look around her place and answered, "Yeah, I think she really likes it."

And she definitely needed it. If Adam thought the outside of her house lacked any Christmas spirit, the inside was totally dying. Sure everything was neat and clean, but it was all white, brown, beige or some otherwise bland color. It was a good space with a clear view from the living room to the dining room and kitchen: ultra-modern and sleek, just the way she'd designed the gingerbread house. But there was no Christmas, no photos, no treasured items, and definitely nothing out of place as there often was at his house. Only a few paintings, which were lovely, but they didn't do much to warm the place up.

Taylor was single, neat and orderly. All good traits that may not exactly work with a child and a baker.

"We need popcorn and Christmas carols," Adam stated when Taylor returned with the tree stand. "You two take care of that while I get the tree set up."

Brooke pulled the packets of popcorn she'd brought from home out of her coat and asked, "What about bulbs? We only have lights and garland left."

"I have a couple of boxes in the basement with ornaments and stuff," she replied. "You wanna help me bring them up?"

"Sure!"

Adam worked on getting the tree stabilized while Taylor and Brooke disappeared. He had a little trouble because the trunk needed to be cut to fit properly into the base. He went out to his truck to see if he had a hand saw. By the time he'd returned, there were two boxes in the center of the living room floor with the word "Christmas" written in green magic marker on top.

"This is a great Christmas playlist," Taylor was saying from the other side of the room where she had an entertainment center. "My co-worker Josephine plays it all day at the office."

"Rudolph the Red Nosed Reindeer," the version by the Temptations, began playing and Brooke immediately started singing. They both headed to the kitchen and Adam hummed along with the music as he finally got the tree situated in the stand. He started going through the boxes, finding some things that he could use to liven up the place while the popcorn popped.

Minutes later when they joined him in the living room again, "It's Beginning To Look A Lot Like Christmas" began to play and Taylor smiled. "This song is so appropriate," she said as she looked around the room.

"Glad you like it," Adam said, because he was genuinely happy to be here doing this for her.

She stood in front of the tree looking at him, and Adam continued to stare at her. It occurred to him that this felt very real and extremely normal.

"Let's decorate the tree," Taylor said abruptly.

Adam was grateful for the reprieve. He went

to the bowl that Brooke was holding and took a few pieces of popcorn.

"We won't have enough to string if you eat it all, Dad," she told him, repeating the same words he told her when they were decorating their tree.

Adam popped it into his mouth and grinned.

"All right, I knew they were down there somewhere," Taylor said as she came back into the room with another box.

She opened the box and removed a hunk of red tissue paper, unwrapping it slowly before lifting the white frosted bulb into her hand.

"It's beautiful," Brooke whispered.

Taylor twirled the white bulb in her hand. "It's hand blown crystal from Prague. My parents lived there for two years. They have an amazing Christmas Market in the old town square with giant trees and vendors. There's people and music and lots and lots of Christmas."

"Oh, look at this one," Brooke said to him when she very gingerly lifted a red bulb from the box.

"Be careful with it, sweetheart." Adam issued the warning even though he could tell she was doing her best to handle it delicately. "It's beautiful." He was initially looking at the bulb but soon found his gaze traveling to Taylor.

For a few moments Taylor stared back at him but then she switched her attention back to Brooke. "Go ahead, put it on the tree."

When all the popcorn had been strung and hung on the Balsam fir, and every bulb from Taylor's boxes also dangled from its branches, Adam figured it was time for them to leave. He could try to bring up dinner or some other reason to stay, but in the time that he'd been with Taylor today he'd felt an overload of emotions that he'd thought long buried.

"Thank you so much for everything," Taylor said to him when they were all standing back admiring the finished tree. "Oh and um, Adam, I wasn't entirely truthful when I said I wasn't missing a traditional Christmas at home. 'Cause all of this...is pretty amazing."

She said exactly what he was thinking, but he refrained from saying those words as she smiled warmly at him.

"Let's grab our coats, honey," Adam told Brooke.

"I'll get them!" Brooke ran into the dining room where they'd hung their coats on the backs of the chairs.

"I love this tree," Taylor said when they were alone. She wasn't just smiling at this point, but practically beaming as she spoke. "And I really love that you and Brooke were here to decorate it with me."

Adam stepped closer to her. He pushed the strands of hair that were brushing against her cheek away. Her skin was so soft, her brown eyes even prettier up close than he'd imagined.

"I'm more pleased with the smile that tree has put on your face," he admitted.

Brooke returned with their coats at that moment and Adam stepped away from Taylor. After getting her coat on, Brooke hugged Taylor. "We'll see you tomorrow," she said happily.

Adam waved at her as they walked out the door, moving down her driveway already thinking about exactly what Brooke had just said— seeing Taylor tomorrow.

Chapter Twelve

THE NEXT DAY, IT WAS back to work on the gingerbread house. Everything was going according to the plan Taylor had mapped out. As she looked at how far they'd come with the frame matching her plans and all the gingerbread baked and cut into the precise size sheets they needed, she felt like happy-dancing around the exhibit stage. Of course she didn't do that. It would not be appropriate for her team to see their manager goofing off in that way. But she was humming Christmas carols as she moved around checking all their supplies for today's work.

A loud thump caught her attention and she looked around to see if someone on her team had fallen or broken something. Thankfully it wasn't their team, but someone on the teachers' team. The frame they'd cut and nailed together for their chimney had fallen to the floor. One of the teachers—the one with the long braids and great boots who usually came early in the morning and in the evenings to work—stomped her foot and groaned as she looked down at the mess.

Even though they were the competition, Taylor felt a tinge of sadness, because she would be livid if something like that happened to them. Ready to resume her work, she glanced over to the other side of the stage and saw that Bradford and Annabelle had watched what happened as well. The look on their faces wasn't nearly as sympathetic as Taylor felt and she immediately frowned.

She had no idea when Bradford had changed, but since going over to Crestford, he hadn't been the same cheerful and helpful guy she'd gone to school with. Truth be told, there'd always been a spark of friendly competition between the two of them. That spark just ignited into a full-blown flame once he switched companies. But this was a competition and everyone entered was here to win.

"Careful," she said to Adam while holding sketches of what the final house would look like in her hand. "A sugar plum dropped from that height could put someone in a sugar coma."

She was keeping things light with him now. After last night when they'd been standing by the tree he and Brooke had bought for her and she'd sworn he wanted to kiss her—a kiss she would've definitely welcomed—Taylor knew she had to take a step back. Not only were they working together, which could cause all kinds of problems if they were to become romantically involved, but she'd given up on long-term relationships.

She'd told him that over sandwiches in his dining room a few days ago. And she'd reminded herself more than once a day since then.

"Good point," Adam replied. "I'll be careful. Royal icing works like glue."

Josephine and David were watching and doing the same thing as Adam—painting the royal icing onto the beams where they would be hanging the gingerbread.

"How come they call it royal icing? Did a king invent it?" Josephine asked.

"Not exactly, but when the bakers were making Queen Victoria's wedding cake they used icing and confection sugar. That's when they found out how strong this stuff really is," Adam told them.

While they talked, Taylor glanced again toward Annabelle and Bradford's team. They hadn't begun hanging their gingerbread yet, but this time she was thinking more about the man she'd seen with Annabelle a few days ago. The man that Adam had watched so intently. Adam hadn't said anything about it and she hadn't asked, but today she was wondering.

"All right, guys, we gotta pick up the pace so we can start decorating," she said by way of getting herself back on track.

"Hey, Taylor," Bradford called to her. "Never thought we'd be doing something like this back in architecture school."

He was right. She never would've guessed she'd design a giant gingerbread house.

"That makes two of us. And just like in architecture school, we're still competing."

"Well," Bradford said with a shrug. "May the best team win!"

Adam began talking, drawing Taylor's attention back to him and their project.

"There's two things we need before we start decorating," he said while walking over to her.

"What?"

He smiled. "Inspiration and Brooke."

Taylor wasn't totally sure how they were going to find inspiration about their decorating, but she was game for seeing Brooke again. It seemed the little girl had become as much a part of this project as Adam had...and she wasn't complaining. Not one bit.

Taylor rode in Adam's truck—something she was getting quite used to doing. They picked up Brooke from the after-school program and then drove to a residential neighborhood bustling with people. Again, she wasn't sure what was going on, but she'd been trying hard to relax, as Adam was always suggesting. When he parked the truck and stepped out and Brooke followed, Taylor did the same. She immediately put on her gloves and thanked the heavens she'd worn her beret again today. "Why are we here? Are we visiting someone?"

"We come every year," Brooke offered.

"Lots of people in the city like to visit this neighborhood because they have the biggest and most creative light displays," Adam explained as they walked across the street with several of those people.

"Wow, that sounds serious." She'd never heard of this but as she looked around she noticed all the cars pulling up and parking across the street. There were already groups of people walking along the sidewalk of the cul-de-sac, which confirmed that it really was a big deal.

They stepped up onto the sidewalk and began at the end looking at houses on the right side.

"This year's theme was Vintage Christmas," Adam said as they walked. "They announced it on the news a couple weeks ago and there were flyers in the local newspaper."

"Wow. I can't believe this. Oh look, they have a horse and carriage covered in Christmas lights." She pointed at the display in one of the large front yards just as the little boy in the group ahead of them did. She let her arm fall back to her side but continued to stare in awe at the cool display.

Brooke pointed to the next house. "And all of those Santas!"

There must have been at least three dozen vintage Santa light-up statues in the next yard. There was even a Santa in his sleigh with the reindeer on top of a roof.

"Amazing, huh?" Brooke asked while they continued walking.

"Or, the perfect idea to get inspiration. All these lights." Adam's tone sounded just as excited as Brooke's.

Just as excited as Taylor felt. She could not contain her grin and admitted, if only to herself, that she had not experienced this level of happiness and anticipation in a very long time. Way back when she was a young girl, before her parents began moving around. While they hadn't walked around any neighborhoods looking at the Christmas lights, they had gone caroling with their church. Singing those great Christmas carols while families stood in their doorways and listened had always made Taylor happy.

"Well, what do you see that you would like to add to our gingerbread house?" Adam asked when they'd walked by the next four houses commenting on the different parts of the themes they saw.

Brooke pointed again. "Window boxes."

"Oh, I like those too," Taylor replied to Brooke.

"So maybe we give the gingerbread house window boxes but with candy canes instead of flowers."

Brooke happily nodded. "And for lights we string together colored lollipops."

"You are a natural," Taylor said. "So how about inside the house?"

"A gingerbread house inside of a gingerbread house," was Brooke's quick reply.

Adam agreed. "And a welcome mat, that says 'Home Very Sweet Home.'"

Taylor glanced at him and whispered, "Perfect."

All the warning bells against liking him, which had been on a low buzz in her head up until this moment, were now chiming loudly.

"So, who organizes all this?" Switching the subject was always a good defense.

"The people that live on this street. It's been going on for years. Every Christmas gets more and more spectacular. Families move out, new families move in, but the tradition carries on. They even have a committee that meets throughout the year to plan when they'll all decorate their homes each year and if there's a theme, stuff like that," Adam explained.

"How do you know all this?" His lovely single family home was in a development at least five miles from here.

"He knows because the house he grew up in is just three blocks away," Brooke answered.

Adam smiled down at his daughter. "Until

Grandma and Grandpop retired and sold the house to move back to their hometown in North Carolina."

The house Adam grew up in with his parents and his younger sister. The home where his mother taught him to bake. That was the type of home Taylor had once dreamed of having. She loved her parents, respected them immensely and was even grateful for all the opportunities they afforded her, but a part of her used to wish she'd had this type of home with these Christmas traditions and now these memories. Tonight, she realized that part of her still did.

Allowing herself to think about that house she'd once dreamed of, another idea for the gingerbread house came to her. "Oh! A fireplace would be great. I've always wanted a home with one." Where she could hang her stocking every year.

"A fireplace?" Adam asked. "Well, how would we make flames out of candy?"

"I'm not sure, but we do need to make a candy run for more decorations, so we will try and find out," she said.

They all chuckled and continued to make their way around the cul-de-sac. Brooke had been walking between them, but when she saw the life-size figures of girls on ice skates, she ran along the sidewalk to get a closer look.

"Daddy, look they're skating in the yard!"

Brooke yelled and posed just like one of the decorations.

Taylor hurriedly took out her cell phone and snapped a picture.

"Send that to me?" Adam asked before she put her phone away.

She looked at him and nodded. "Sure."

After she slipped the phone back into her pocket, Adam took her hand in his and they began walking again. Brooke caught up but walked in front of them now, still in awe of all the decorations. Taylor, on the other hand was much more focused on the strangely warm feeling of having her hand in Adam's as they moved along like a picture-perfect family.

The bulk candy store at the mall was a wonderland for anyone with a sweet tooth. Taylor wasn't a big candy person. Aside from her favored peppermint bark, cakes and cookies were her favorite indulgence. Still, she could feel the energy of every child who walked through the doors and into the oasis of barrels filled with colorful and tasty candy treats. White shelves lined all the side walls and clear jars set on the shelves filled with hard candy, licorices, and gummies. There was a section for chocolate covered everything, another section for retro candy and then another for gourmet jelly beans. She was certain they would find everything they needed to decorate the gingerbread house in here.

Brooke was once again walking right in front of Adam and Taylor. She was in charge of decorations, after all. Today her mass of hair was pulled into one afro puff sitting cutely near the top of her head. Adam looked at Taylor and smiled as they both watched Brooke go from barrel to barrel peeking inside, sometimes picking things up and really thinking about whether or not they could use them on the house.

He had one hand pushed into his front pants pocket, and his coat—which he'd decided to wear today—was zipped, but he'd taken off his hat when they'd stepped inside the store. Taylor clenched the small purse she carried in front of her to resist the urge of reaching for his hand again. Walking hand-in-hand with him while they looked at the final house decorations had felt nice and...special.

"Nah, red licorice doesn't look like flames," Taylor said when Brooke picked up the long, individually wrapped strands from a table and showed them to her.

They passed a white table filled with the type of rainbow hard candy that was always sold at amusement parks. Jumbo rainbow swirl lollipops were in one large crystal vase and long rainbow twisty pops were in another. The next table used white ceramic cake tiers to display colorfully wrapped boxes of taffy, while more clear jars were filled with individually wrapped pieces, separated by flavor. Brooke stopped at the next table and pointed.

"Maybe orange slices?" She was directing all her questions to Taylor and Adam was standing by with an amused look on his face.

Taylor shook her head. "I don't think so. Getting warmer though."

The next display was of all types and sizes of colorful hard candy.

"I got it! Glass candy can look like flames for the fireplace," Brooke announced, her eyes open wider.

Coming to stand beside her, Taylor couldn't help but agree. "That's brilliant! With reds, yellow, orange...let's get a case of it. Oh and we should get loads of the gumdrops for decorating."

"You two are really good at this," Adam said with a shake of his head.

"We are," Brooke agreed and hurried to the counter to speak to the sales clerk.

"How can I help you?" the clerk asked Brooke.

"We'll take all the orange and red glass candy that you've got. And can I get some gumdrops too?" Brooke spoke like a seasoned shopper.

The clerk's bright smile never wavered. "Sure, how many would you like?"

Brooke contemplated a moment before replying, "Um, maybe five thousand." She thought again and shook her head. "No. Ten thousand."

Taylor looked at Adam with a mixture of pride and amusement before they both shook their heads.

"You sure about that, young lady?" The clerk teasingly asked Brooke.

While Brooke nodded, Taylor chuckled and removed the credit card from her wallet to hand to the clerk. "Yeah, she's sure. She's the chief decorating officer, after all."

The clerk accepted the card. "Well, all right, then."

After signing the purchase order and giving the address to where she wanted the candy delivered, Taylor turned to join Adam and Brooke at the store's entrance. They walked out of the store together.

"So, where to next?" It hit her rather quickly that she wasn't ready for her time with them to end.

That seemed to happen more and more frequently. What usually started out as work days were turning out to be wonderfully relaxing and enjoyable times with them. It was an unexpected joy, but one that Taylor was finding she enjoyed immensely.

"We were going to look for a new dress for the Winter Concert, right, Daddy?" Brooke looked up to Adam and he nodded.

"She's singing in the concert at school tomorrow, and I did promise her that after we finished working on the gingerbread house today we would find time to make it to the mall to shop for a new dress," Adam said.

Then he leaned over and whispered to Taylor. "I usually try to have Jenny help her with shopping because I'm really not good at it. You think you could give us a hand? I mean, since we're already at the mall."

"Yes!" Brooke yelled and danced around to take Taylor's hand. "We can go dress shopping. Your clothes are always so pretty, Taylor. Can you help me find the perfect dress?"

Taylor laughed at Adam as he realized his attempt at whispering hadn't worked at all. But that laughter died quickly when she watched Adam's expression go from happy to sad. She followed his gaze and saw Annabelle coming out of a restaurant on the other side of the mall. Annabelle was with that same man who'd come to the marketplace a couple of days ago.

Taylor stepped closer to Adam. "Who is that with Annabelle?"

He hesitated as if he wasn't going to reply, but then said, "Nick Brexley. He's one of the investors I met with six months ago. The one who told me he didn't want to invest in a culinary school dropout."

"Oh." That was all she could manage because she wasn't sure what seeing the investor with Annabelle meant.

"Guess I won't be going back to him to ask if he changed his mind about investing in my bakery. Looks like he's already found a baker to invest in," Adam stated flatly.

But Annabelle already had a restaurant. Before Taylor could say that, Brooke spoke up.

"Dress shopping?" She asked the question while looking from Taylor to Adam and back to Taylor again.

Suspecting this was the last thing Adam wanted to discuss in front of Brooke Taylor replied, "I'd love to help you pick out a dress, Brooke."

Now, Brooke took Taylor's hand. "Yes! We can go to the store over there."

The store over there turned into four different stores until eventually, they struck gold.

Brooke stepped out of the dressing room wearing the cutest dress Taylor had ever seen. It was fitted black velvet at the top with long sleeves and a scooped neck, at the waist was a red bow that tied in the back, and the red, green and white plaid skirt was full falling mid-calf. She spun around in front of Taylor and Adam as if she were on a miniature runway.

"What do you think of this one?" she asked.

Taylor waited. Adam was growing weary of this little shopping spree, but he was trying desperately not to show it. In fact, he was at this moment looking at her with great consideration.

He lifted a finger and made a twisting motion. "Turn around one more time," he told her.

Brooke happily obliged.

"Hmmmm," he said, bringing that finger to rest on his chin in a great contemplative look. "What do you think, Taylor? I mean, I liked the previous one, the one with the emerald green but there's something about this one." He gave Taylor a quick, knowing glance and she went with his cue.

Taylor walked over to Brooke. "Let's see," she said and touched the material of the skirt. "The thin lines of gold weaved through this plaid design give it pizazz and hint at a celebratory mood."

Brooke nodded. She ran her hand down the material in the same way that Taylor was doing. "I agree," she told Taylor.

"But the black breaks up the color so that you're not overdoing the holiday theme," Taylor continued.

Brooke shook her head. "We don't want to overdo it."

Adam stifled a grin.

Taylor stood back and gave Brooke one long look. Then she turned to Adam and nodded. "I think this one might be it."

"Precisely what I was thinking," he said and then grinned at his daughter. "Get this one, honey. You look great."

Watching Brooke run to her father and hug him made a lump form in Taylor's throat.

"You're going to look so pretty at the concert tomorrow," Taylor told her when they were finally leaving the store, only a few minutes before it was time for the mall to close.

"I can't wait to show Jordan my new dress. Oh, and my project," Brooke said once they were through the doors and walking in the parking lot toward the car. "They're going to be judging all the class projects tomorrow at the concert. You should come, Taylor, because you helped with the project too. Please, please can you come?"

Looking into Brooke's pretty hazel brown eyes, Taylor's heart ached and also wept with joy. She recalled always wanting her parents to come to school events with her. Sometimes they could and other times it wasn't possible, either due to their work schedules or because there just simply *weren't* any school activities, depending on where they were in the world. But she did have plans to work on some final reports for her last project at work in the morning. She and Adam had already talked about meeting up later in the day to work on the gingerbread house.

"I believe Taylor may have some work to do at her office tomorrow, honey. But Aunt Jenny is coming and I'll be there," Adam said.

Brooke looked crestfallen, even though she nodded as if she agreed. Taylor stopped walking and turned to kneel down in front of Brooke. Touching a hand to the little girl's chin and tilting it up so she could once again see her pretty eyes, she said, "I would be honored to come to your concert tomorrow, Brooke."

The light was instantly back in Brooke's eyes, and the girl's arms flew around Taylor's neck for a hug that almost knocked Taylor off her feet. Taylor accepted the hug, holding on tight to the feeling of making someone happy. Someone, who at one time, she'd been just like.

Chapter Thirteen

Wᴇᴀʀɪɴɢ ᴀ Sᴀɴᴛᴀ ʜᴀᴛ ᴀɴᴅ a jingle bell necklace and earring combo that perfectly matched her red turtleneck sweater and red and green skirt, Josephine stopped at Taylor's cubicle after going for her fourth cup of coffee today.

"Ugh, I'm still so sleepy today. Went over to my dad's assisted living center to help him decorate his tree and door for the building-wide contest and ended up staying for dinner. Beef stew, those canned flaky biscuits he loves, and holiday punch. Four of the women on his floor joined us, and it turned into a mini-holiday party in apartment 6B," she said with a roll of her eyes and a groan.

Taylor chuckled. She'd just finished her last report and only had one more email she needed to send before she could leave for Brooke's concert. She had come into the office early to get everything done in time.

"Sounds like you had a good time, though," she said to Josephine who had entered the cubicle and was now in her favorite position, leaning against the edge of Taylor's desk.

"It was fun and festive, but I knew I needed to get in here on time or Linda would kill me." She took a sip of her coffee. "What time are we meeting at the marketplace this evening?"

Taylor continued typing her email. She'd heard Josephine talking but she was really trying to get the email finished.

"Yoohoo? Taylor? You there?" Josephine said this time tapping Taylor on her shoulder.

"Huh? Oh yeah, I'm sorry. Just trying to hurry up and get this done. I have to be at Brooke's school by four. So we're not going to meet at the marketplace tonight," Taylor said. She looked at Josephine and then quickly back to her screen.

"Ooooooh," Josephine said.

Taylor glanced at her again. Josephine had a knowing smirk on her face. One arm was folded over her chest while she held her coffee mug—which was a giant snowman's face—in her hand, poised just a few inches from her mouth.

"What's that look mean?"

"A few days ago you left to go bake dough at Adam's house because Brooke was sick. Last night when I texted you, you said you were going for an inspiration trip with Adam and Brooke. A day or two *before* the dough baking at his house, you were shopping for baking items with Adam. Oh, and Wendy told me when we were working on the gingerbread house yesterday that she met Adam's sister Jenny and Brooke at your house the day before. They were putting up Christmas lights." Josephine wiggled her eyebrows and continued to stare at Taylor.

"Okay, you've got my itinerary committed to memory. So what?"

Taylor returned her attention to her screen.

"Soooooo," Josephine exaggerated the word. "Now you're going to Brooke's school?"

Taylor sighed. "It's a Christmas concert and she invited me last night after we went shopping for the candy to decorate the gingerbread house. Work," Taylor said. "We were *working* last night." Taylor could exaggerate words too.

"I see," Josephine said. Out of the corner of her eye, Taylor could see her nodding. "So how exactly does a Christmas concert work with decorating a gingerbread house?"

Taylor sat back in her chair. She should've known Josephine wasn't going to let this go.

"She asked me to come, Josephine. What was I supposed to do, tell her no?"

Josephine vehemently shook her head. "Of course not, Taylor, the girl is adorable. And even though she has an aunt, I'm sure she misses having a mother. I know I did when my mom passed away when I was ten. So you should definitely go. It's a really nice thing you're doing for her."

"I'm just going to see how her project does in the contest. I helped her with a few parts of it, so I guess I'm invested," Taylor said.

"If you helped her, then I'm sure it's going to do well. Besides, I'd much rather spend time with a very cute and very talented baker than stay cooped up in here."

Josephine was a lot of things, but subtle was not one of them. Even though she'd resumed sipping her coffee, Taylor knew what she was really trying to do.

"We're working on this competition together," Taylor insisted. "That's. All."

Josephine pulled her mug slowly away from her mouth and nodded. "Right. You're just working with him." She pushed away from Taylor's desk and walked out of the cubicle. But before going to her seat she looked back at Taylor. "Have fun at the concert, where you *won't* be working."

Taylor had to turn in her chair just to see Josephine once again waggling her eyebrows and this time giving her a huge knowing grin. Taylor could only shake her head and laugh.

She couldn't have told Brooke no if she'd wanted to; the girl had looked way too sad at that possibility. And she hadn't *wanted* to tell her no. Taylor wanted to go to the concert. She wanted to see Brooke on that stage singing the

Christmas carols that Taylor already knew she could sing all the words to because she'd done so in her house before. Taylor also wanted to see Brooke's diorama win the contest, because she was certain it would, even without seeing the competition. She wanted to do all those things with Brooke because she liked the little girl. She liked her a lot.

And if she didn't hurry up she was going to be late for the girl-she-liked-so-much's concert.

Taylor whirled around in her chair and hurriedly typed and sent the memo. She was out of the building and outside hailing a cab about fifteen minutes past her planned time to leave, but she was on her way. In just a short time she would walk into school looking for the little girl that made her smile. The little girl who did not have a mother.

It had been a long time since Taylor had been in an elementary school building. Everything seemed so tiny: the lockers, the chairs and desks she peeped inside each classroom, and even the students. That thought made her chuckle as she walked down the hallway toward the auditorium. The nice secretary in the office had given her directions, but Taylor was too engrossed in the artwork taped to the walls, the colorful lockers, and a particularly intense conversation between a group of girls who looked to be no more than seven or eight about which dollhouse was the absolute best for Santa to leave under the tree.

Each little girl wore a lovely holiday dress, which meant they were probably in the concert with Brooke. She wondered why they were in the hallway instead of the auditorium and prayed she hadn't missed the entire event. With a worried look at her watch she saw that it was only a little after eleven. Adam told her it started at eleven, so she couldn't have missed it.

"Are you lost?" one of the girls asked her.

"Ah, no. Well, I don't know," Taylor told her. "I'm trying to find the concert taking place in the auditorium."

The little girl nodded knowingly. "It's this way. We're going there now. You can follow us."

This was said in such a mature and matter-of-fact way that Taylor almost felt chastised.

"Oh, okay. Thank you," she said and did what she was told.

Taylor walked happily behind the four little girls who continued their chat about doll houses and everything else they were getting for Christmas. It was a cheerful conversation that sparked a memory of when she'd been in elementary school and had a group of friends. That was before the first move. Eva and Melinda were their names; the two girls that Taylor spent time with either playing at their houses or having them come over to hers. In the years that followed she never let herself connect with other classmates, because she wasn't sure when she would be leaving them too.

As soon as Taylor walked into the auditorium the lights dimmed and a woman dressed in a gorgeous red gown stepped up to the microphone to announce that they were about to begin. Taylor picked up her step and tried to find a seat before the children came on stage. She spotted a few seats close to the front and walked in that direction.

"Psssst! Psssst!"

Taylor turned at the sound and immediately smiled when Adam stood and waved her back to the row she'd just passed. She excused herself as she eased down the row to the seat he'd saved next to him.

"You made it," he said as soon as she sat down.

"Of course," she told him when her purse was settled in her lap. "I told Brooke I would be here. I wouldn't let her down."

He looked like he was about to say something else, but the curtain opened and on the stage were about forty of the cutest children she'd ever seen. Their first song was "Frosty the Snowman." Before the show was over, Taylor and many of the parents in the audience were rocking and singing along quietly with the children.

"I think you're having more fun than the children," Adam said when it was over and they stood.

She shrugged. "It's been a long time, but I still remember school plays and concerts. They weren't always the best for me, but this was really nice. They sang so well."

He walked beside her as they headed to the back of the auditorium. "Yes, they did, and Brooke really likes to sing. Her mother sang in the church choir, so I guess Brooke gets that from her."

"Oh really? Is she in any other choirs? Maybe she should get formal lessons," she suggested. "When she sang her solo part in "Silent Night" I almost cried she was so good."

And Taylor was talking way too much. Yes, she was telling the truth but she'd tried to be covert and act as if she were fixing her hair when really she'd used a finger to staunch the tears in the corner of her eyes before they could fall.

"No. Her mother and I talked about them before...but now, I'd have to coordinate that with Jenny's schedule and I don't want to impose on her too much. She has her own life to live," Adam said.

"Oh." For a minute Taylor had forgotten that working at the bakery most likely had pretty demanding and unusual hours, especially early morning hours. It was a shame because she really thought Brooke would be fantastic with formal training. And she hadn't missed the hint of sadness in Adam's tone that he hadn't been able to let her do it.

"Taylor!" Brooke yelled as she ran up the aisle toward her. "You came!"

"I sure did," Taylor said catching the girl in her arms and hugging her close. "I wouldn't have missed this for the world. And it's a good thing, because you were fantastic!"

Brooke beamed when they ended the embrace and she looked up at Taylor. "You think so?"

"Absolutely. You were the best soloist in that choir."

"She's right, honey, you were really good." Adam leaned down and kissed her forehead.

He loved her so much. It was so easy to see in everything that he did, every sacrifice he made for her benefit. Taylor felt like she might cry again. It was the oddest thing. She'd never been prone to overactive emotions.

"Oh, Mrs. Jones is going to announce the winners of the contest right after the concert, so we have to get to her classroom right away," Brooke said. She took Taylor's hand and pulled her along. "Grab Daddy's hand so he won't get lost, Taylor."

Taylor looked at Adam, unsure about whether they wanted to do the hand-holding thing again. They'd done it on their walk after viewing the houses last night, but neither of them had spoken a word about that.

"C'mon!" Brooke insisted.

Taylor grabbed Adam's hand without another thought and they were on the move. They arrived in the classroom with time to spare and Brooke walked them over to the table where her diorama had been set up. Then they waited patiently while Mrs. Jones made the announcement.

"And first place in this year's Heart of Christmas project is Brooke Dale!"

Adam lifted Brooke into his arms and hugged her while Taylor clapped until her palms felt sore. A few parents were looking at her strangely. She didn't care. Her daughter had won—

She stopped mid-clap and let her hands fall to her side. Brooke wasn't her daughter. She looked over at Adam. He'd put Brooke down and was now taking a picture of her standing next to her project, holding the 1st Place ribbon in her hand.

This wasn't her family. The thought made her sad, but it was true. They weren't hers to keep.

"Come on, Taylor, you take a picture with me because you helped," Brooke said and once again pulled Taylor by the arm.

Taylor couldn't pull away from her, but she wanted to. She wanted to run from this room and this school because this right here was the dream she'd put aside, the one she'd decided she could never have. And as excited as that thought made her, the burning in her chest signaled what the reality was: she still couldn't.

Because the gingerbread competition and the job in Paris were waiting.

Adam didn't know what to do. Brooke was very excited that Taylor was here. She was ecstatic that she'd just won this competition for a project that Taylor had worked on with her. And he knew that Brooke was becoming attached to Taylor. He'd known it the moment he'd stood in her doorway last night, listening to her saying her prayers.

"Thank you for sending Taylor to us. She's nice and pretty and I think you picked the right one. She'll make a great mom."

Brooke had climbed up into her bed at that moment and Adam had stepped inside.

"Ready for a story?" he asked. It was their normal nightly ritual.

"Not tonight, Daddy. I want to talk."

His baby was only ten, but she sounded like an adult.

"Okay," he told her and sat on the edge of her bed. Taylor had sat in this same spot days ago as she'd nursed Brooke through the stomach virus. "What do you want to talk about?"

"You and Taylor."

"Me and Taylor working in the gingerbread competition."

She lay on a stack of pillows covered in lavender polka dot pillowcases. Her head moved from side to side in response. "You and Taylor as a couple."

"We're not a couple, Brooke."

"You could be."

Hope resonated through her soft tone and wrapped tightly around his heart.

"You should get some rest. You've got a big day tomorrow."

"Promise you'll think about it," she said before he could stand.

Adam didn't know how to say he'd thought of little else in the past days.

"Go to sleep," he'd said and leaned down to kiss her cheek. "Sleep tight."

Brooke had smiled up at him. "All night."

Adam had woken up that morning with that scene playing in his mind. And now, combined with the way he'd just seen Taylor acting with her, he was more conflicted than ever.

"Hey! I know I'm late but I finished up at school and then had to run over to the store to answer some questions about a project," Jenny said as she came up behind him and tapped him on the shoulder.

"Hey," he said looking back at her.

"Oh boy, what's wrong?"

"Nothing." He ran a hand down the back of his neck. "Brooke just won first place for her project. She's over there celebrating."

Jenny followed his gaze to where Brooke and Taylor were talking to Jordan and Jordan's mother. They looked like mothers and daughters talking about possibly going to lunch together, or maybe to the park. Adam looked away.

"So when are you going to tell her?" Jenny asked.

"When am I going to tell who what?" he asked.

Jenny shook her head. "You're always a day late and a dollar short," she joked. "You like Taylor."

"I work with Taylor."

Nodding Jenny said, "And you like Taylor."

"I like working with Taylor, yes. There's no question about that. And there's also nothing else to it." He told her sternly what he hadn't been able to say to Brooke last night.

Jenny took a step back. "Okay, don't bite my head off about it. I'm just sharing my observation because I don't see you going over to Ray's house to put up Christmas lights for him."

Before Adam could respond Jenny walked across the room to join Taylor and Brooke. Adam watched them, his family and Taylor. With a heavy sigh, he let the truth sink in. He liked Taylor.

Chapter Fourteen

Four Days Until Judging

"I COULD HAVE DONE THAT, YOU know," Adam said a few seconds after Taylor had bent down to reach into the bucket of icing.

She shook her head and took the spatula out of his hand. "Nope. I can do it. You're not the only one who can stir."

He gave her that look that said she was being over the top. He'd been giving her that look most of the morning while they'd worked transporting the gingerbread sheets from the bakery to the Marketplace.

"Okay, guys, you can start bringing out the gingerbread now," she told the volunteers.

There were tables lined across the back area of the exhibit stage. That's where they'd stored the gingerbread and the volunteers were going to bring it up to the frame so they could start attaching it.

"Whoa, that's a lot of icing," Brooke said.

She'd been there all day helping too and had been sticking pretty close to Taylor.

Taylor agreed with her. "Well, we've got a lot of gingerbread."

David rolled out a cart with a few slabs of gingerbread on it. He took one and so did Wendy and Josephine. Taylor stood and pushed the tub of icing closer to them so they could attach it to the frame. She remained on the side watching the process and Adam stepped in to supervise.

Taylor was just about to see if Brooke wanted to go and get a snack, but before she could she saw Linda coming toward the stage.

"Good morning, I'm just stopping by with treats for this hard-working team," Linda said as she stepped up onto the stage carrying a tray of coffee and a box of donuts. She set them down. "And I just thought I would check in and see how things are going with the project."

"Excellent!" Taylor replied in a tone that may have been a little too exuberant. "The gingerbread's baked and will be up by the end of the day."

They were right on schedule, and Taylor was glad about that. She wasn't rushing the process, but after yesterday she was starting to feel like the sooner this was over with, the better for all of them.

"Oh, and ahead of the competition from the looks of it," Linda said looking over to the other teams' platforms and then back to Taylor. "Good work, Taylor."

Taylor had seen that as well, and was feeling pretty proud of it, too.

"Oh, no," David said.

Taylor turned to look at where he was crouched down inside the frame of the house, staring at a sheet of gingerbread. "Oh, no?"

Adam kneeled down and examined the gingerbread from the outside. "It's cracking," he stated and looked up at her.

Taylor stepped closer. "No!"

"This is what I was worried about. These thin sheets of gingerbread are too fragile," Adam insisted.

"And I told you that thin sheets are what works best with my design, remember?"

Taylor did not want to go through this again with him. She thought they'd already hashed out all their issues with the gingerbread.

"And remember I told you if it's too thin they're gonna crack," he countered.

Linda stepped between them. "Well it looks like we've got a problem," she said and looked pointedly at Taylor. "You better figure that out. Because the clock is ticking. Not much time until Christmas Eve. But I know you're up to the task."

Taylor met Linda's smile and quiet demand

with a smile of her own and a nod of confidence she definitely wasn't feeling right now. But when Linda walked away, Taylor's smile faltered and she turned back to Adam. He was staring at her but not saying anything, which meant he'd pretty much said what he needed to already. And as if that weren't bad enough, when Taylor looked in the other direction Annabelle was also watching her. Had she been listening this whole time? Of course she had. Taylor frowned.

"Come with me for a second." Adam touched her arm as he spoke.

She looked back at him and gave a curt nod. Then she followed him off the stage and over to where the Santa was taking pictures with the children.

"I think we need to bake the gingerbread thicker, more like bricks," he told her once they were alone.

"Look, I know you warned me about this, but big bricks won't work with my design." She knew she'd designed a great house—a house that could win.

"Well Taylor, maybe your design needs to change," he replied.

"We have to build on what we've done, not start over from scratch." She huffed and looked back at the frame just as another piece of gingerbread cracked and fell to the floor.

"Look," Adam said from behind her. "My sister is coming to pick Brooke up and she'll have her for the rest of the day. My mom always taught me, if you can't solve a problem right away, you go and do something else because that's when you figure it out."

Taylor's instinct was to work through her problems, not run away from them. That's how things had always worked for her in the past.

"Do you know how much work we have to do? We don't have time to just 'go and do something else,'" she insisted.

She lifted a hand to rub her temples as she definitely felt a headache coming on. They couldn't start over and they couldn't go forward if all the gingerbread was going to crack and fall. What was she going to do?

Adam took her hand. He laced his fingers through hers and said softly, "Come on."

Taylor wanted to say no. She wanted to stay and figure this out. Try to maybe double the gingerbread or...she sighed. "Okay."

After they'd waited for Jenny to pick up Brooke and sent the volunteers home, Taylor and Adam got into his truck and went for a short drive. When they arrived at an ice skating rink Taylor frowned at him.

"Ice skating? Really, Adam? We do not have

time for frolicking. We've got a lot of things to figure out," she told him.

But Adam wasn't listening. What he was doing was leading her across the parking lot, similar to the way Brooke had led her around at the school yesterday.

"Remember I told you that you needed to learn how to have fun?"

She opened her mouth to answer but he touched a finger to her lips. The action both shocked and warmed her at the same time.

"For just a little while we're going to relax and focus on something other than cracked gingerbread houses. Trust me."

He was waiting for her answer. Even though he'd brought her all the way over here to go ice skating, apparently, if she said no, she wanted to get back, Taylor knew that he would take her. But he was offering to help, and even though she didn't think it was going to work, she figured the least she could do for his effort was to try.

They entered the skating rink and went to the front desk to rent skates.

"You've never had on a pair of ice skates?" Adam asked when they were still sitting on the bench while Taylor fought to get her skates on.

"I got a pair of ice skates for Christmas when I was eight, but then we moved to Hawaii before I could use them. Years later, I needed another pair of skates, of course. I put them on, but it wasn't a successful event."

"Well, today's your lucky day. Brooke and I love to go ice skating. Come on, let's go," he said.

But when Taylor didn't move, he chuckled and stood up. Instead, he moved to stand in front of her as if maneuvering himself on those blades was the easiest thing in the world. He extended both his hands to her. Taylor moved slowly, skeptically, but eventually put her hands in his. Adam pulled her up off the bench. Her legs wobbled and he wrapped one arm around her waist.

"I got you," he said. "You're steadier on this floor mat than you'll be on the ice, so get acclimated to the skates right here."

Again, easier said than done. But Taylor gave it a good, honest try. She didn't fall because Adam had his arm tightly around her, and after a few steps she did feel steadier. That is, until they stepped onto the ice.

"Seriously, I can't believe you've never skated," he said when she stood perfectly still on the ice.

"Let's just say it's been a couple of decades. If I'm trying to forget about cracking gingerbread, the last thing I should be doing is skating on thin ice," Taylor quipped.

What she needed to focus on was not falling and cracking some important body parts.

"It's not thin, it's normal ice."

"Oh and I should trust you on this?"

He gave her an offended look.

"Okay. Fine! Fine. Let's do it!"

She really could trust him because Adam was not letting her go. He had one arm at her waist and another held her arm while she wobbled and took a half-step at a time.

"You want to push up with each foot," he instructed.

Taylor took a deep breath and did as he said. When she didn't immediately fall on her face, she tried again. Her ankle wobbled.

"Oooh, I don't know. This might be a bit too advanced for me."

He wasn't wobbling at all. He moved and talked and held her up as easily as if he were walking in the park.

"How are you so good at this?"

"We had a skating rink in our backyard as kids," he answered while they eased a few inches further toward the center of the rink.

It looked safer for her there. People didn't seem to be skating as fast in that area. Around the sides they were whizzing past her every few seconds.

"And every winter we'd lay out the 4x4 and a liner and turn the hose on. The next morning, bingo! Mini ice skating rink. Although—"

"Although what?"

"Ah, one winter I left the hose on."

Taylor cringed at the thought. "Oh no, your poor parents."

Adam shrugged. "My mom took it in stride.

But um, she invited all the kids in the neighbor-hood down to our winter wonderland. She even made gingerbread cookies."

"Aww, your mom sounds like a lot of fun." His childhood sounded like fun, and he was giving Brooke the same experience. He was such a great dad. An awesome baker. And now, a good teacher.

"What about you? What did you do for fun when you were growing up?"

He must have thought if he kept talking and kept easing her over this ice that Taylor would stop being scared to death that she was going to face-plant on the cold hard surface. It was kinda working.

"I always liked to draw," she told him. "I guess because I was an only child and moving around meant making new friends in each new location, I got used to entertaining myself."

"That makes sense. But don't tell me all you enjoyed doing was designing houses way back then too? " He laughed at the thought.

She didn't tell him how close to being right he really was.

"I drew people too," she admitted. "And I'd always draw a picture of me and my parents wherever we were located at the time. I guess you could say I made my own postcards."

Adam laughed. "Always about business, Taylor."

She chuckled too. "Well, it's in my blood."

They'd been easing along the ice and she just noticed she hadn't wobbled in a few minutes.

"So, if I let go, are you gonna be okay?" Adam asked.

"Ah, no, no, no. Nope. I don't think I'm ready." She was talking but she knew she was still moving. His hand was still on her back and her arm.

"Really? Then why are you doing it?" One minute she was listening to his words and the next she realized his hands really had eased away from her body.

"What?" She hadn't stopped moving. Her feet were still gliding—albeit it very slowly—over the ice. Was it really possible she was doing this on her own? Triumph pulsed through her encouraging more tentative movements.

"You're skating! Look!"

Taylor peeked over her shoulder to see that he was a couple steps behind her and she was still inching her feet along the ice.

"Oh my gosh, I'm doing it!"

With confidence brewing she tried to go just a little faster so she didn't look like a total newbie. Excitement bubbled in the pit of her stomach when she still remained upright.

"And don't think about it too much," he warned.

"Okay." She tried to continue but of course since he'd said that she couldn't help but think about the possibility of fall—

One of her feet slipped in the wrong direction and bumped into the other. She stumbled and... Adam was right there to catch her.

His arms went around her, tighter than before, and her arms found their way around his neck. To keep from falling she reminded herself. But the embrace felt...good.

"Okay," he whispered after a prolonged few seconds.

"Yeah, um, I'm okay," she replied. The way her heart was hammering in her chest was a clear indication she was anything but okay. But Taylor knew that had nothing to do with the ice or these dang skates.

Adam stood her up straight and went back to having his stabilizing arm around her waist. Even that felt different now. Taylor cleared her throat and focused on moving her feet in the right direction this time.

"So, ah, did the skating make you come up with any new ideas?" Adam asked.

She frowned. Skating with Adam had actually brought on more ideas that Taylor knew were bad. For her. For him and for Brooke.

"Um, I'm still stumped about my design, but this was fun. And I did forget about our problems for a while," she admitted.

"I know your boss wants you to come up with this cutting-edge idea, but maybe the new cutting edge could be tradition."

Adam was tradition. At first she'd simply

thought he was a broken record, but after spending these last few days with him and Brooke, she knew it was embedded in him. From his parents and now to his child, Christmas traditions meant everything to him.

"Hmmm, I hate to admit it, but I think you might be on to something," Taylor told him. "You've been talking about tradition since day one, and I was starting to think you were a broken record. But after spending these last few days with you and Brooke, I realize tradition has been bred into you by your parents and all they did for you and your siblings while you were growing up. And now, you're doing the same for Brooke. It's a great thing to see."

There were a few quiet moments where he just looked at her and she looked at him. A cool breeze from the other skaters moving quickly around them touched her cheeks that remained flushed from Adam's intense gaze. What was happening to her?

"Score one for me!" He announced after the silence threatened to fill with longings she'd been trying valiantly to keep at bay.

Later that night, Taylor still hadn't found the time to go to the grocery store. But after Adam's remark about her cup of noodles the other day, she'd decided to improvise. It had taken her twenty minutes to familiarize herself with an app and put in an order for groceries. She'd done that this morning before she'd gone to the Marketplace, and they'd been delivered ten minutes after Adam dropped her off from the skating rink.

She'd been thinking about what Adam said, that maybe the new cutting edge was actually traditional. With that in mind Taylor turned on the Christmas music but this time she'd specifically searched for traditional Christmas carols. Nat King Cole's "O Tannenbaum" was playing. When she'd stored the groceries in the cabinets she'd put on a pot of milk and turned the stove on low so that it would warm. She walked back into the kitchen and was just in time to add the cocoa, a bit of sugar and vanilla. When the mixture was smoking, she poured it into a German beer mug she'd picked up while she was in Frankfurt. She didn't drink beer but she'd liked the colors on the mug. Now, she was putting it to good use.

Walking back into the living room with her mug and a plate full of store-bought chocolate chip cookies, Taylor sat on the couch and put her dinner/dessert on the coffee table in front of her. She'd already gathered her trace paper and the pilot point pen she preferred to draw with and set them on the table. Now she sat back on the couch to think.

How could she build a modern, cutting-edge gingerbread house that wouldn't crack under pressure?

Or...

How could she blend Adam's traditional style with the modern, cutting-edge design to use the thicker gingerbread he suggested?

She ate a cookie, then two, and thought some more. Bing Crosby's *White Christmas* came on, and she sang along thinking of snow falling on the gingerbread house just like it did at the end of the *White Christmas* movie. Picking up her pen she sketched the thought forming in her mind, snow on the roof of the house. Adam's traditional roof? Hmmmm, she ate another cookie, took a sip of hot chocolate and sketched some more.

When her phone rang she frowned because she'd planned to spend the night thinking this through. She didn't have a lot of time for anything else.

Taylor picked up the phone and looked down at the screen. "Hi, Josephine," she answered.

"Hi, Taylor. Just checking on you. Any new ideas?"

Taylor sighed. "Not really. And I am so stressed out," she admitted. The music, hot cocoa and the lights from her tree were relaxing her though.

"But I thought things were going great," Josephine said.

Taylor tapped her pen on the table while she talked. "Well, I'm not so sure that the modern design is the way to go. Time is running out and we're back to the drawing board. I'm afraid Linda won't be happy."

"Stop thinking about Linda and Paris and just do what you do," Josephine said.

"How am I supposed to do that when those are the two driving forces behind this project. I mean, without Paris this project would not be an issue for me," Taylor admitted.

"And without this project you wouldn't have met the handsome baker and his cutie-pie daughter."

That was very true. "Adam is very handsome and Brooke is very cute. I like them both. But right now I need to focus."

"Maybe you're focusing on the wrong thing."

Taylor rolled her eyes and was glad nobody was there with her to see her doing it. "I'm focusing on the job at hand. What do you suggest I focus on?"

"How about what Christmas means to you or, no, because you'll take it back to work. What does Christmas mean for Adam and Brooke?"

"This isn't about them, Jos. It's about winning this competition."

"The competition that they're a part of," Josephine told her. "Look, you're in charge so I know you'll figure it out. You're you."

That was a nice thing for her to say in the

midst of her trying to insinuate that there was something more between Taylor and Adam. Jos had been on that kick for a few days now, and Taylor didn't want to hear any more of it. Especially since there was a tiny part of her that knew it was true.

"Thanks for checking on me, Jos. I'll see ya tomorrow."

"Bye."

When Taylor put the phone down Josephine's words played in her mind. They layered everything Taylor had already been thinking and more importantly feeling. This project started off being about Ogilvy's public image, Linda impressing the mayor and Taylor impressing the board so she could get a promotion. But it had quickly morphed into something else.

Standing from the couch, she went with those thoughts, letting the truth of every word settle in. This gingerbread house was now about Adam and the dough he'd lovingly prepared from a mixture of his talent, schooling and his mother's kind heart. Every decoration that they'd purchased for the gingerbread house was about Brooke and the twinkle in her eyes when she'd put this very bulb on Taylor's tree.

Without realizing it she'd moved to her tree, touching that white frosted bulb that Brooke had found so beautiful. Taylor recalled being around Brooke's age and admiring a bulb in the same way. Reaching out a hand she touched the bulb not really remembering the last time she'd hung it on a tree herself. She'd also never strung popcorn to hang on the tree, but looking at the festive strands now she knew she'd never have another tree without it. They'd created a tradition—her, Adam and Brooke.

Sentiment filled her heart and in a flash a picture came to her mind.

With that thought Taylor went into her dining room stopping at the antique wood cabinet her parents had given her three years ago. Pullling out the top drawer she fished out her old scrapbook and sat down to open it. Her mother had started the book when she was just a little girl, adding photos of Taylor in all the places they traveled. After a while Taylor began adding the pictures she drew of her parents and the scenery to the album as well. She turned one page after another smiling with the memories that came flooding back.

Surfing in Hawaii. It had been her first time and in the picture her father held onto her and the board so she wouldn't fall. They both grinned at her mother who'd snapped the picture. They'd spent the whole day together and each part of the day had made Taylor feel cherished and loved. That same feeling swelled in her now, filling her until tears brimmed her eyes.

Taylor flipped to another page tickled by the thick coats with fur hoods she and her parents wore in the picture taken in Alaska. She grinned at the huge birthday cake with twelve purple candles, a photo taken on the patio of the villa where they'd stayed while in Sicily. The warm hug of nostalgia hesitated when she turned the next page.

Her fingers moved slowly over the edges of the picture in the center. It was a drawing of a house with a shingled roof and Santa on top, a snowman doorknocker and a Christmas tree visible through the window. Standing in front of that house was a father, mother and daughter. Warmth, happiness, comfort and excitement all swirled like a funnel cloud inside her and Taylor smiled.

This was it!

She went back to the table, carrying the picture with her, and sipped her now lukewarm hot chocolate. She'd forgotten the marshmallows but that didn't matter, she had a great idea!

After working for she didn't know how long, Taylor picked up her phone and sent a text message.

Got an idea! Think you'll love it. Includes thicker brick-like gingerbread. She added a smiley emoji.

She hit send before noticing how late it was and sat back on the couch with the phone in her hand. Music was still playing and the lights on her tree were still twinkling but Taylor felt so much better than she had when she'd first come home.

The sound of her phone dinging with a new text message startled her. She hadn't really expected Adam to be awake this late.

Adam's text read, *Why are you up this time of night thinking about gingerbread?*

She grinned and answered. *What else would I be thinking about?*

Perhaps what Santa's going to bring you for Christmas. He punctuated this with a Christmas tree emoji.

I don't want anything.

Sure you do, Adam countered. *If you could ask him for one thing, what would it be?*

Taylor immediately thought of Paris, then as if it was calling to her, her gaze moved past the phone in her hand to the picture she'd propped up against her mug on the table. That house she'd drawn so many years ago now made her think of Brooke and Adam.

She answered, *Ice skates!*

He responded with a laughing emoji. *I've created a monster.*

Meet you at the bakery early tomorrow morning, Taylor typed.

He replied, *I'll be there.*

And he would be there. Adam would be at the bakery doing what he loved to do most in this world. And where would Taylor be? Where could she do what she loved most and be the happiest she'd ever been?

Chapter Fifteen

Three Days Until Judging

ADAM WAS AT THE BAKERY by 4 a.m. It hadn't been any hardship to him, because he hadn't been able to sleep, anyway.

After putting Brooke to bed, he'd gone to his room and thought about the gingerbread house and, of course, Taylor. He wondered what she'd been thinking—modern, cutting edge. Of course.

Even though he disagreed with the idea, the thought made Adam smile as he lay in his bed staring up at the ceiling. Everything about her made him smile.

He couldn't believe she didn't know how to ice skate or how good teaching her had made him feel. Fearless, that's what she was. Whatever she decided to do, she did it. She traveled the world doing the job that made her feel alive and successful. He worked at a bakery and hadn't been farther than North Carolina where they used to go for a week every summer for his father's family reunion. That thought sobered him.

What was he doing with his life?

Sure, he was taking care of his daughter that was his job, but was that all he was meant to do? Brooke and Jenny would give a resounding "no" to that question. Even Taylor had told him it wasn't too late to go for his dream. Maybe she was right. Maybe they'd all been right.

Just when he'd decided it was time to at least try and get some sleep, his phone buzzed with a message. His first instinct was to think something was wrong with Jenny. So he was relieved to see it was a text from Taylor. Relieved and surprised. The message made him smile and so did the rest of the conversation, so that by the time it was over he'd been wide awake and ready to get started.

An hour and a half later he was standing in the bakery's kitchen sliding in his first batch of new, thicker, gingerbread. By seven-thirty he had more batches finished and cooling on the racks when he heard Taylor tapping on the front door.

He greeted her with a smile. "Good morning, Future Ice Skating champ."

She chuckled. "Good morning, Future Bakery Owner."

Adam's smile grew wider at those words, and when he closed and locked the door behind her he thought again of the idea regarding his future he'd had earlier. He would find some time to implement it later today.

"I made some hot cocoa. Let me get you a cup," he told her and moved to the kitchen.

She took off her coat and followed him back.

"I finally bought something else besides cup of noodles from the grocery store and actually made myself a cup of cocoa last night." She sounded very proud of herself.

But when Adam turned to her with the two glasses of the hot frothy drink she grinned while shaking her head.

"Mine didn't look like that."

"And I bet it didn't taste as good either. This is made with the best cocoa powder and fresh vanilla, plus the extra whipped cream on top makes it divine," he said.

They walked back out to the front of the shop and sat at one of the tables. Taylor grabbed her designs and spread them out. He didn't waste a minute, but pulled the pencil from his apron pocket and began looking at them. Taylor picked up her cup and sipped.

She groaned, and Adam looked up at her to see her close her eyes while savoring the taste.

"This is magnificent," she told him with her tiny whipped cream mustache.

He didn't tell her it was there mainly because he liked how cute she looked with it. Instead he returned his attention to the design.

"I think it's totally doable. And it won't take a lot of work to redesign the frame. All we need to do is change up the booth, add the flower boxes and go with bricks. What do you think?" she asked after a few more sips of cocoa.

"I like it," he said while checking out the lines and angles of the roof. "How did you come up with the very traditional and Christmassy design?"

The quick knowing look followed by her warm smile said she recalled him saying those same words to her the first day they'd looked at her sketches. "Actually, I dug up a sketch I made when I was little and kind of went from there. Call it inspiration."

"Really? You still have your old sketches?"

She nodded. "My mom started this scrapbook for me so that I'd remember all our travels together. There are photos of me everywhere doing all kinds of things. The pictures I drew are peppered in. I found one that I'd drawn when I was eight. I'd given it to my mom when we moved into our new house, and she'd kept it hanging on the refrigerator for a while. We were only there for ten months before we moved again, but that very next Christmas she pulled the picture out and put it on the refrigerator in our next house.

And then every year after that, no matter where we were, I would hang my stocking and my mom would hang my picture on the refrigerator."

Adam smiled because she was smiling, a sharp contrast from the worried look she'd been wearing yesterday.

"Seems like your family traditions and the holiday spirit are coming back to you," he said.

"I guess so," she replied. "So what do you think?"

"I love it." There wasn't a moment of hesitation or doubt. "But I thought you were committed to doing something cutting edge?"

"Well, it won't be the design Linda asked for. But she'll be cheering the loudest when we win."

"Then we'd better get to work. I've already started a few batches but we're gonna need a lot more."

Hours later they were still at the bakery. Ray and a few other staff members had come in and they were doing the normal business of the day. Adam had just put four more trays up to cool and Taylor was in the kitchen working at the table wearing a bakery apron just like the rest of the staff.

"All right, I will get this rolled out and cut it into bricks," she told Adam just as Ray came in.

Adam nodded his agreement and went to stand by Ray to see what he wanted.

"She caught on to baking pretty quick," he

whispered to Ray who had been watching Taylor from the doorway until he finally decided to come in.

Now Ray turned his back to where Taylor was working. Adam did the same. "And how are things going outside of the kitchen?" Ray asked.

"Well, we had a big setback, but we have a new plan for the house," Adam replied.

"I wasn't talking about the gingerbread house. I mean how are things going with Taylor?"

Adam didn't want to answer that question. Instead, he shook his head and elbowed Ray playfully. Ray laughed and walked away.

Adam went back to do what he did best. He and Taylor worked with the practiced rhythm they'd developed over the past few days, moving around each other and doing exactly what needed to be done when it needed to be done. He wasn't joking when he said she'd caught on quickly. She knew how to mix the batter, roll out the dough and cut it exactly the way they needed it cut. She'd mastered the timing so that they had no more burned batches as well. And by four o'clock that afternoon they had enough bricks cooled to get started putting up the frame and decorating.

When they took the last batch out of the oven Adam caught Taylor doing a happy dance move. He joined her and they laughed together like long lost friends or possibly something more.

Later that afternoon, 11 of their volunteers were finally gathered on the exhibit stage again, and they began assembling the new gingerbread bricks. Ray even agreed to have another staff member from the bakery bring over the remaining bricks that were still baking and cooling so that Adam and Taylor would not have to run back and forth.

"David and I will start with the roof," Adam announced. "You work on the icing while Josephine and Wendy get the bricks up for the walls."

Taylor gave a mock salute and turned to see Brooke right beside her.

"I'm ready to get to work so we can start decorating," she said.

Taylor smiled. "I am too."

"Okay, there are some pastry bags over there. You two fill them up and bring them over to us," Adam instructed them.

When neither responded he looked back to see that Taylor had begun stirring one of the tubs of icing and Brooke had poked a finger into the tub bringing it up to her mouth to taste. His little girl rubbed her belly and said, "Yum!"

Taylor grinned and mimicked Brooke's action, but she wasn't as fast and as she brought her finger to her mouth icing dripped onto her chin and down the front of her sweater. The two of them laughed, but the sight made Adam think of the first day he and Taylor met at her office when he'd smudged icing on her plans and that same icing had somehow ended up on her face. The memory warmed him as much as seeing her and his daughter so easily bonding.

"This is going to be a great contest," David said to Adam when they were close to each other lining the bricks up in preparation for the icing. "Have you done them before?"

"No, this isn't usually my type of event, but I have to admit I'm having fun."

"Me too. I thought I'd be trapped in the office for the next few weeks making coffee or running errands, but this is so much better." The guy sounded so young and enthusiastic.

Adam recalled his meeting with Nick Brexley months ago—the meeting that hadn't gone the way he had planned—and wondered if he'd sounded young and enthusiastic like David. In the midst of everything else going on, he'd tried not to think too much about seeing Nick and Annabelle together, but in the back of his mind it felt as if that union meant the door was permanently closed as far as getting Nick to invest in him again.

"And Taylor's so good. I was happy when I found out I'd be working with her. The way she turned this design around so fast is miraculous," David continued.

"Yeah." Giving himself a mental shake, Adam agreed. "She is pretty fabulous."

He looked over his shoulder again and saw Taylor and Brooke carrying three pastry bags full of icing. Brooke delivered her bag to the side where Josephine and Wendy were working while Taylor walked toward him. The way his stomach went all jittery watching her coming toward him, Adam would have thought he was watching her walk down the aisle with a bouquet in hand on her way to take her wedding vows. The thought made him a little lightheaded, and when he turned to step down off the ladder, he did a little wobble.

"Oh, wait a minute, I got you," Taylor said coming up beside him and wrapping her free hand around his waist.

Adam steadied himself and avoided putting all of his weight on her, but he did look into her face and consider if this wasn't some type of fate in play.

Whatever it was left him feeling extremely embarrassed. "Sorry about that."

She shook her head. "Oh no, it's the least I could do for as many times as I fell all over you yesterday at the ice skating rink."

He nodded. "Yeah, I forgot about that."

"Here's your icing," she told him. "I can stand here to be on guard just in case you get wobbly again."

She was joking. He could see that twinkle that appeared in her eyes when she was amused.

"I think I'm better now," he announced and with the pastry bag in hand turned back to the ladder.

"Okay, well, don't say I didn't offer my help."

"Your help is getting more of those pastry bags filled. We're going to need lots of icing to get this house set up."

Taylor went back to work, and Adam did his very best to focus on the building of this ginger-bread house and not the feelings for Taylor that were slowly, but surely, taking hold of him.

A few hours later they had the entire front half of the house up, icing was piped through the crease of each brick, the white mixing with the dark red bricks of the roof. Taylor and Brooke had even started piping some of the white icing decorations onto the front of the house and assembling the window boxes.

"What number should it be?" Adam asked when he held the address block that Brooke had glued green and white gumdrops around.

"What's the number of the house you grew up in?" Taylor asked in reply.

"Twenty-seven."

She nodded. "Then that's the address."

"Cool."

Adam went to the back of the house where the tables holding their extra bricks and other decorations were set up. He cut out the numbers 2 and 7 and used more icing to stick them to the address block. Taylor was still working at the front of the house when he returned and she stood back to watch him assemble it.

"All right," she said when he was done. "We may have missed half a day, but we are almost on track. Tomorrow we're going to have to pick up the pace."

Adam nodded. "Works for me. Brooke, honey, it's time to go. We're going to give Taylor a lift home." Adam looked back at Taylor. "And there's something we want to show you on the way."

It was an impromptu idea, but it was something he was certain she would like.

"You have to cover your eyes," Brooke said the moment Taylor stepped out of the truck.

"What? Is she for real?" she asked Adam.

He was coming around from the driver's side of the truck. "Yes. Totally for real. Cover your eyes." He reiterated that direction as if he thought his words were even more convincing. And when she didn't immediately comply, he lifted her gloved hands up, positioning them in front of her eyes.

Her laughter did nothing to decrease the nervous curiosity now bubbling inside. There was a call for snow tonight and her plan had been to get home before it started. Now, she was standing outside with her hands covering her eyes in a place that had looked like a park or some kind of gathering place when they pulled up.

"Now come on, we'll help you."

He held onto one of her arms, while Brooke took the other.

"Okay, if you say so." Taylor decided to trust them and took the first tentative steps.

It was bitterly cold—perfect for any snowfall to stick and accumulate. Wouldn't it be wonderful if this year there was a white Christmas in Philadelphia?

"I don't know what you two have up your sleeves this time." She had to say something because she was feeling pretty anxious right now, and she really wanted them to hurry up and tell her what was going on.

When the only response that came was a giggle from Brooke, Taylor really didn't know what to expect.

"All right, don't tell me. I guess I'll find out soon enough."

A few steps later they stopped walking and Brooke said, "Okay. Open."

Taylor let her hands fall from her face and was amazed by what she saw. Snow from the previous snowfall seemed almost untouched here, except for the pathway in front of them. The white blanket stretched along the sides where only a few leafless trees now stood with twinkle lights hugging their branches. Lanterns lined the pathway that stretched another twenty or so feet ahead and at the end was a structure that looked like the frame of a chapel. More lights hung all around the frame with a huge wreath in its center. Six different size trees stood in the front of the structure, two of them decorated in all gold, two decorated in all red and the biggest two decorated in red, gold and green. There was a bench inside of the structure and outside to the left were life-size wire reindeers covered in more lights.

"What is this?" Taylor asked unable to mask the awe in her voice.

"It's a landing strip for Santa's reindeer and sleigh," Brooke replied.

Adam chimed in. "Each year the city uses this part of the park as its way of making sure that even if there's a blizzard Santa can find us. It's one of our biggest holiday attractions."

"And it always works. I've even seen a reindeer's print in the snow when we come here on Christmas Day," Brooke added.

"Is that so?" Taylor had never seen anything like this before. It was such a unique and pleasant idea.

"Come on. I'll show you where you can leave a snack for the reindeer in case they get hungry." Brooke walked ahead of them and Taylor looked at Adam.

"Okay," she agreed when he didn't say anything.

He did reach for her hand, and she accepted
it before stepping up onto the walkway. They
moved gingerly down the path just as they had
when she was on the ice skates last night.

Before they could get to the framed area,
Brooke turned to Taylor.

"Let's go over here to see if anyone has left
any snacks yet. Sometimes they start to leave
them well before Christmas. But Jordan said
that other people might take them if you put
them down too early and then the reindeer might
starve. So let's just check and see," she said as
she walked to the left.

Taylor and Adam followed Brooke to a trough
made of cinderblocks that had been built right
beside a tree behind the lighted reindeer.

"Nope, no snacks yet," Brooke reported.

Taylor moved in closer to see that she was
right. There was nothing in the trough except a
thin layer of leftover snow.

"Well, we don't have long for Christmas now,
so I guess that means we'd better come back in
a couple of days to leave some snacks," she said.

Brooke nodded enthusiastically. "Right!"

"When I was a little girl I used to leave cookies and milk for Santa to eat while he was at the
house. And then I'd also draw him a picture of
me playing with all the gifts I'd asked him for to
take with him because I wanted him to always

be reminded of how happy his gifts made me." The memory came clearly, leaving her breathless with that giddy excitement children held at Christmastime.

"I used to wonder if Santa would be able to find me since we moved around so much," she continued. "But each time I left the cookies and milk I woke up in the morning and saw that not only had he found me but that he'd also taken the picture I left for him."

"Santa loooves Daddy's cookies, but this year we're going to leave him brownies too. With lots of walnuts." Brooke giggled as she glanced at Adam. "There are never any cookies left when I get up on Christmas morning, so this year we'll see if he likes the brownies, too."

Taylor also looked at Adam, who grinned mischievously.

"So what do you think?" he asked her.

"I think this is pretty amazing," she replied honestly, knowing deep in her heart that she wasn't only talking about Santa's Landing. As if on cue, fluffy flakes of snow began to fall.

"It's snowing! Yay, it's snowing!" Brooke said and tilted her head back before sticking out her tongue to catch the flakes. She was twirling around catching all the snowflakes she could while Adam and Taylor stood there alone.

Was she watching a movie? How could this feel so perfect? The words tumbled out as her chest constricted and pleasure pulsed through her veins.

"Adam, I just want to thank you."

"For what?"

She was staring up at him now, unable to hide the smile that seemed so natural whenever they were together. "For the first time in a while, I feel like I'm home for Christmas."

He closed the space between them reaching out a hand to brush snowflakes from her hair. "I'm glad," he whispered.

When his other hand came up to frame her face, Taylor moved in to him and Adam leaned in touching his lips ever so lightly to hers.

"It's snowing! It's snowing!"

Brooke continued to say, the sound of her voice like a warning beacon in Taylor's head. She stepped back from Adam but continued to smile up at him. She'd liked the kiss, and a big part of her hoped there would be more.

"Let's get her home before she eats all the snow," Adam said and then moved away from Taylor to grab Brooke up into his arms.

When Taylor turned around she saw Adam spinning his daughter in the air. She smiled and wondered, *what if...*

Fifteen minutes later they were once again in Adam's truck, this time singing as loud as they could, "Five golden rings!"

Taylor knew most of the words to the song, but the swans a-swimming and geese a-laying tripped her up every time. Adam swore he knew all the words, but she and Brooke had caught him singing the wrong lyrics a time or two. The song seemed to last forever as they drove along and Taylor didn't even care. She was having the best time. They were singing about the Grinch by the time Adam pulled up in front of her house and she resisted the urge to sigh with disappointment.

"Well, thanks for the ride," she said when it was beginning to feel awkward with them sitting in front of her house and her remaining in the truck.

For what it was worth, Adam hadn't said anything or made any motion to kick her out of the truck.

"Tomorrow's December 21st—just three days left to decorate," she continued.

"We'll be ready," Brooke announced.

"Okay, great!" Taylor said and then looked back at Brooke. "Get a good night's sleep snow princess."

"I will. You too, gingerbread queen."

Taylor loved this little girl. It was as simple as that. She opened the door and stepped out of the truck before waving to Adam and walking quickly to her door. Still giddy from the day and evening she'd had, Taylor unlocked her door and stepped inside her house. She'd just closed and locked the door behind her when her phone rang.

She answered while she was still in the hall-way. "Hello?"

"Sorry for calling so late, Taylor," Linda said the moment she answered.

"Oh, no. That's fine. Is everything okay?" Of course it was fine that her boss called her. What wasn't fine was if her boss were calling to tell her about another problem.

"More than okay," Linda continued. "Listen, I appreciate you taking the reins with the competition."

"Thank you."

"Clearly, you've held up your end of our little deal. So, I have an early Christmas present for you."

Taylor was still on alert because she had no idea what this call was about.

"Can you say *Joyeux Noël*?" Linda asked.

"What do you mean?"

"Well, I had dinner with a few of our board members tonight, and you're their top pick for Paris. Of course, they have to wait for the official vote in the next few days. Which means if all goes well with the competition, you'll be heading out on Christmas Eve!"

Taylor's heart dropped and all the Christmas spirit that she'd just been sharing with Adam and Brooke fizzled. "Christmas Eve?"

"I know you don't have plans for Christmas, so this new opportunity is kind of like I made some for you! I mean, a chance to celebrate

Christmas in the City of Lights. Oh, and I'm even working on getting you an invite for a Christmas party at the Minister of Culture's chateau."

Within seconds Taylor was lightheaded. Nausea quickly followed as sorrow pierced her chest. She blinked back instant tears that sprung with the thought of not being here with Brooke on Christmas. "Oh wow. That's so soon." She inhaled slowly, her fingers shaking as she continued to hold the phone to her ear.

"I thought you'd be more excited," Linda said. "I mean, isn't this what you've been pushing for?"

"Of course, of course. Thank you so much. I can't wait." She said those words because that's what she would have said two weeks ago. "Um, let me know what the board decides."

Linda seemed fine with that response and continued, "Okay. Bye, Taylor."

Disconnecting the call was easy. Moving from the spot where she stood in the foyer was not.

Paris.

Everything she'd ever wanted in a job and to live in Paris again! It would be a dream come true.

But which dream was it that she wanted now? The one where she was a huge success, or the one where her heart was filled with love?

Chapter Sixteen

Three Days Until Judging, Continued

TAYLOR NEEDED SOME AIR. SHE needed time to think and clear her head of all the things that had troubled her throughout the night. Instead of going into the office where she knew she would see Linda—who would definitely want to talk more about the Paris position—she went to the mall. That was the perfect place to walk around and keep warm.

Of course, this close to Christmas, it was packed. If walking was what she wanted to do, she probably should have chosen another location, one where she wouldn't bump into someone every couple of steps.

She was just about to duck into a coffee shop to grab a very caffeinated beverage to deal with the mall traffic when she bumped right into Jenny.

"Oh! I'm sorry." She touched Jenny's arm and made sure she hadn't knocked any of the boxes out of her hands.

"Hi, Taylor! What are you doing here? I thought you would be decorating the gingerbread house by now."

"Yeah, I'm headed there as soon as I leave here, just had to make a stop first."

Saying *I have to figure out how I feel about your brother and this job and everything else before I can face anybody* probably wouldn't go over so well.

"Oh, last-minute shopping to take care of? I completely understand. I just had a few more things to pick up for Brooke and then I have to get to work. We're having our ornament decorating contest today."

What was it about Christmas that brought on so many contests?

Taylor recalled Adam mentioning Jenny was a marketing student and she'd been late coming to Brooke's concert because she had to work. So maybe she worked in the mall? Christmas was a great time of year for a marketing student to gain in-store experience.

"The winner gets a fully decorated Christmas tree from the store next year," Jenny continued.

Bublicity. Taylor chuckled as she thought of the word Brooke had trouble pronouncing. An ornament decorating contest would definitely bring potential customers into the store. A com-

pletely decorated tree up for grabs would probably make them wander around the store wanting to look at what might possibly be featured
on the tree they could win. Publicity was always
a good reason to have a contest.

"That sounds like fun." She didn't think she
sounded as excited as Jenny did, but then she
had a lot on her mind.

"You wanna walk with me? I have to be back
at the store before the contest starts," Jenny
said with a smile.

It was similar to Adam's smile, but different,
which made Taylor think of family. Connections
and putting down roots, building foundations,
all things Taylor had stopped believing in a long
time ago.

"Sure." Taylor fell in step beside her and
they walked in silence for a few minutes. "Adam
didn't say you worked at the mall."

"I don't. I'm a marketing student, but I work
part-time for an international toy company with
a branch here in Philly. I'm hoping to make it a
full-time position once I graduate."

"That's great. When will you graduate?"

"In May, thankfully," Jenny said with a sigh.
"I'm so ready to be done with school I could
scream. I told Adam that after I graduate I'd
have more time to help him with Brooke, and
he could go back to culinary school and finish
or just open his own bakery. I'm leaning toward
the latter because he's gained so much business

experience from working with Ray. And I know I could work up a good marketing plan to really set his business apart from all the other bakeries in the city."

Jenny sounded very excited, and Taylor couldn't help but think along those lines too. She also thought again about the investor Adam had seen with Annabelle. Maybe she should look into that and find out what was going on.

"He's very talented. I believe he would do a fantastic job owning his own bakery. I wonder if my boss knows of any other investors he could approach. I mean, since the other ones turned him down."

"He told you about that?" Jenny asked but shook her head before Taylor could answer. "Of course he did. He likes to use that as an excuse now, but I think they were silly for turning him down."

"I agree," Taylor replied. Her mind was already buzzing with people she could ask about investors—Linda, her parents, maybe even Bradford.

"Hopefully he'll get a lot of exposure from the gingerbread contest to help push him along," she said.

"That's exactly why I told him he should join you in the competition. It would be great if people knew how good he was."

Taylor knew. Adam was a terrific guy, a wonderful father and a talented baker. He could have been everything she ever hoped for in a man, if she'd actually been thinking about finding a man. But she hadn't. Not in a very long time. Not since Paris, coincidentally. How could the place where she'd been dumped by her college sweetheart still be a place where she wanted so badly to live? Because she hadn't loved Randall the way she loved that city. Paris was supposed to be the pinnacle of a career she'd worked so hard to build. And now she was so close, Paris was almost in the palm of her hand.

"We're here," Jenny said when they were in front of the department store. "Why don't you come in and join the fun?"

Taylor wanted to say yes. What better way to clear her mind than to sit down and decorate a Christmas tree ornament? But she couldn't hide forever. They had a tight schedule to meet and she didn't want to keep the team waiting.

"No, thanks. I'm going to head over to the Marketplace and get to work on the decorating. It was good seeing you, Jenny."

Jenny smiled and tilted her head as if she was hearing something that Taylor wasn't saying.

"You like him, don't you?" she asked Taylor.

"Like who?" Because answering a question with a question always worked.

When Jenny only raised a brow, Taylor sighed.

"We're just working on this competition together. That's all," she said and was about to walk away.

Jenny made a face that said she didn't believe any part of Taylor's statement. "That's the same thing he told me when I asked him about you. You two make a perfect couple because I don't know anybody else who can't see what is so obvious."

Taylor politely brushed Jenny's comment off with a smile and a wave. She was on her way out of the mall when she thought the thing that was so obvious was that she'd made a colossal mistake.

"Not bad. Just a little more decorating."

Taylor turned to see Adam standing behind her. She'd been working on more details to the decorating around one of the windows. They'd used red foil-wrapped chocolate roses to put in the window boxes, but she'd wanted to add a little more flair around the boxes and the surrounding area.

"Where did everyone go?" Taylor asked when she turned around.

He chuckled. "You must have really been in a zone. I let the rest of the team go. Holidays and such, and they were tired."

Taylor really hadn't been paying attention.

She'd been so focused on getting as much done as possible she hadn't even spent as much time talking to everyone today. That may have been on purpose, but she didn't want to dwell on it now.

"Well, I don't blame them. I'm kind of tired, too," she admitted.

"So, have a seat," he replied.

"Okay."

Adam took her hand and led her down the stairs at the front of the exhibit stage. They sat on the side right next to the gift boxes they'd thought would be a nice touch in front of their house.

"Thank you."

"Look at us," he said while looking around. "Just a couple of folks sitting on our stoop watching the world go by."

Taylor nodded. "Nice little place we got here."

"Our own little chalet," he said with a chuckle.

"You know, I have to admit, the traditional roof is nice. But we do have some competition from our neighbors who've built quite the skyscraper."

"Winning would be the icing on the cake, but I only entered this crazy competition to show Brooke her dad could dream big."

Taylor could not resist the opportunity to say what she was feeling in this regard. "And why just dreaming? Why not make your bakery dream a reality?"

He shrugged. "Ask the investors who turned me down."

"Well, you didn't have your glorious gingerbread win under your belt then."

"Well, fingers crossed." He actually crossed his fingers and they both chuckled.

"You could always look for new investors. I mean, I know you're thinking the guy you met with before may be working with Annabelle now. And that might be true, but he's not the only investor in the world."

"I've been giving it some thought," he said. "Actually, I've been giving lots of things some very serious thought."

"Well good for you." She wouldn't tell him about the people she planned to ask about potential investors yet. Just in case they didn't pan out, the last thing she wanted was to discourage him again.

"You know this takes me back to sitting at the front of the house with the family. A little music playing—something to dance to because my parents both love to dance."

"I have an idea, do you think we could use music for our gingerbread house?"

"That's a great idea. I mean, we already have four of the five senses. Sight. Smell. Tastes." He leaned in a little nudging her until she smiled.

"Touch and ah, hearing. Awesome. That'd be great."

Taylor nodded her agreement, pleased with how easily they seemed to come up with ideas together. While that hadn't always been the case, she could look back now and see the natural progression of their relationship. Their *working* relationship, that is.

"How about a doorbell that plays music? Or isn't that traditional enough for you?"

He did this whole sarcastic thing with his face and shoulders and she nudged his shoulder because he thought he was so funny, but really he was just being charming, as usual.

"I'll allow it. What kind of music?"

"Um, a carol maybe? Something up-tempo."

He pulled out his phone and scrolled through an app to find the right music. After skipping through two or three songs, he landed on one that sounded strange but then familiar as the lyrics began a very upbeat "Jingle Bells."

"This one?" she asked skeptically.

"It's a good song to dance to," he replied before getting up. "Here, let me show you."

"Huh?"

"What? Can't dance?" He started to move.

"Oh, I can dance, all right," she replied, but decided she'd rather watch him.

He fell into the rhythm easily, snapping his fingers as he moved. This man could bake, cook a fantastic pizza, ice skate, and now dance.

It's no wonder I'm in love.

What? Did she just think...

Adam did another dance move that ended with some type of flourish, and Taylor could not help but laugh.

"What?" she asked when he pointed at her.

When he danced his way over to her and took her hands, she figured this was definitely better than overanalyzing what she'd just been thinking. "Okay," she said and joined him while he danced in the aisle.

They moved to the music together as if they'd been dancing like this for years. They did a little flourish together this time and a move that Taylor only recalled seeing on those reality TV dance competitions—not the one where the guy lifts the woman into the air, thank goodness, but he held one of her hands and they both reached out the other hand as if they were going to take a bow. She was laughing and enjoying herself when he pulled her back to him and they danced up close. She was never going to listen to "Jingle Bells" and not think of this moment again.

When Adam held her arm up for a spin, Taylor thought this was so much more than she'd bargained for...and then that spin turned into an embrace which led to him dipping her over his knee and leaning so close that...

Yes, Taylor wanted to kiss him. She absolutely did.

But a light flashed in the distance and the spell was broken.

"What's going on over here?" A security officer asked while continuing to point the flashlight at them.

Adam brought Taylor up until they were both standing.

"Just working on our house," he told the guard.

"This place yours?" the guard asked skeptically.

"Yup, all of it," Taylor said with a nod as if she thought that would make him believe her.

Adam added, "Wait until you see it finished."

"Looks good," the guard replied. "But you can't really be here right now. I've got this place on lockdown like Fort Knox. Anything happens to these houses, it's on me."

"We're about to head out, but ah, you want a taste?"

The guard looked like he was taking his job of watching the gingerbread houses very seriously, but Taylor doubted he'd turn down the offer of a piece of gingerbread.

"I'm on duty." He shook his head like he was going to refuse, but continued, "I suppose a little taste wouldn't hurt."

Adam walked back to the stage and picked up a tray of gingerbread. He returned to where Taylor and the guard were standing and extended the tray to the guard.

"Baked fresh this morning," Adam stated proudly.

The guard took a piece and bit into it. He chewed for a few seconds and then nodded.

Taylor and Adam smiled at each other and then at the guard.

"Not bad. Not bad at all." He took another bite and chewed some more. "Well, carry on. Merry Christmas!"

When he walked away they both sighed with relief. Adam leaned into her and said, "So ends our dancing."

"Okay. We have a big day tomorrow," she said.

"Yes, we do," Adam agreed. "But ah, I mean, about before—"

Taylor wanted to act like she didn't know what he was trying to say, she really did. But she couldn't because it had been on her mind too.

She nodded. "We're working on this project together," was what came out of her mouth first. "A project that's very important to both of us."

"I understand," he told her. "But there's also something else. I think we both know that."

"I agree." There was definitely something else. "But I haven't figured that out yet. I think it's best if we just stay focused on the competition. Right?"

He looked at her for long seconds that made her feel like a complete jerk. Why couldn't she just wrap her arms around his neck and kiss him? Couldn't they have a long distance relationship? She knew others who did. And failed. No, it was better they just think about the competition.

He didn't agree. She could tell by the way he was looking at her. He wanted to say more. He wouldn't because he was too nice and too much of a gentlemen to push her. She was both grateful for that and a little disappointed.

"Right," he replied. "Come on, I'll give you a ride home."

Chapter Seventeen

Two Days Until Judging

𝒯HERE WAS STILL A LOT of work to do, and Adam had a couple more gifts to get for Brooke and the audio book to order for Jenny. He hadn't been able to do as much of his Christmas shopping because he'd been spending so much time working on the gingerbread house with Taylor. And when he wasn't working with Taylor he was at the bakery making some of the decorations and still helping Ray. He'd been more than a little preoccupied lately. So much so that he hadn't realized how many signs he'd missed over the last few days.

With his mind full of thoughts, Adam moved methodically through the kitchen at Ray's. He was making the last few sets of decorations for the gingerbread house. They were meeting at the marketplace today at noon because Taylor thought it was a good idea to give the team some additional time off to shop.

"Working overtime?" Ray asked when he walked into the kitchen.

Adam hadn't heard him come in because he'd been so focused on what he was doing.

"Yeah, we're down to the last two days of decorating," he replied without looking up.

"Doing this part by yourself?" Ray asked.

At this point in his career, Ray rarely did any baking. He was the owner and general manager of the bakery, but he kept his eye on everything and knew all of his repeat customers by name. Ray's Bakery was a staple in this neighborhood; hence the reason Ray had been so resistant to any type of change to what they offered. Adam could understand that even if it stifled his creative energy somewhat.

"It's a special project I wanted to handle to make sure I got it just right," he said. It had been the first time he'd spoken that aloud. Taylor had given him the idea a few days ago, and he'd done at least half a dozen sketches in his bedroom at night after Brooke had gone to bed. Not that he'd been undecided on the design or the materials, but he hadn't been totally sure he was going to do it, not until this morning. They didn't need it in the gingerbread house, but Adam needed to make it.

"Because you want it to be special," Ray said.

He was standing on the side of the table a few steps from where Adam was working.

Adam nodded. "Yep."

"Because this is a very special project," Ray continued. "Something you really like doing."

With his fingers pressed against a green gumdrop, Adam held it in place waiting for the icing to dry.

"It's making Brooke extremely happy," Adam replied when he glanced at Ray.

The older man had turned to lean against the table. He'd folded his arms across his chest, glasses that he did not like wearing hung on a chain around his neck.

"And that's important," Ray said. "Doing things for our children. Making sure they're healthy and happy. I know; that's why I worked so hard building this bakery. So my boys could have everything they needed."

"It's called responsibility. That's what my father taught me. I make sure she has a roof over her head, food on the table, clean clothes and a stable home environment." He picked up another gumdrop and repeated the process of sticking it into the spot where he wanted it. "But that's not all, because children need more from their parents than just what money can provide. I'm always careful to make time for her, to do things that I know she likes to do, like ice skate and watch movies. My hours here at the bakery get a little crazy sometimes, but I make it happen."

"You certainly do," Ray added with a nod.

"And there's no skimping on our traditions, either. We still wake up on Christmas morning and open presents. After breakfast we get dressed, check out Santa's Landing to see if the reindeer enjoyed the snacks that were left, and then head to the skating rink. All the things that Cheryl started with us."

"You're a good father, no doubt about that. And Brooke knows it. She thinks the world of you."

"She misses her mom." That was something Adam thought of frequently, but didn't verbalize often because he'd never felt there was anything he could do about it. He missed Cheryl too, but missing her wouldn't bring her back. "And she likes Taylor very much."

"And this right here," Ray said pointing toward the table. "This says you like Taylor very much, too."

Two seconds after hearing Ray's words, Adam realized what he'd just done. Every thought he'd been having this morning, every revelation he'd come to had just spilled out while he worked on items for a gingerbread house.

Ray was already wearing a knowing smirk.

"You're not funny, Ray," Adam said but couldn't help but chuckle when he saw that Ray was barely holding back a smile.

"No. No. This is very serious. What you've made here is nice. Taylor will like it. But what the three of you—Taylor, you and Brooke—have built together in this time is something, too. It's something you should stop running from and maybe consider is a good thing."

Ray didn't wait for a response, but moved away from the table and walked out of the bakery as quietly as he'd come in.

Adam looked down at what he'd just created and felt a swell of pride blooming in his chest. He thought about Brooke and all the things he wanted for her, the things he could and should give her. That pride shifted to yearning and as a comfortable warmth flowed like water in his veins, the conclusion he'd tried to escape took root: he wanted to be with Taylor.

The thought had been bubbling around in his mind since the night she'd burned that gingerbread in his kitchen, and with each day they were together it grew. Not that he'd done anything to cultivate it. He hadn't. In fact, at one point he'd been totally on board with denial. But now he wanted more. Last night she'd said they should focus on the competition, but that was almost over. So what would happen after Christmas Eve? Adam knew what he wanted to happen and he planned to let Taylor know too. Just as soon as he finished with this special project.

"Our fireplace looks amazing! Glass candy flames, who would have thought it?" Adam asked and looked down at Brooke.

Taylor looked at her as well, loving the blue jumper she wore today with the tiny white flower print and white shirt. Her hair was pulled up to a puff and her brown eyes sparkled with happiness. That happiness poured into Taylor's heart, making her feel even more conflicted about leaving for Paris.

"Our chief decorating officer, that's who," she said wanting to be sure she gave Brooke all the credit she deserved for her creative contributions to this project.

They were standing in front of the house looking over all the decorations they'd added, admiring their hard work. Taylor had to admit it looked really good. And when she glanced at their main competition, while Crestford had a cool, sleek design—similar to what Linda was requesting of her—Taylor felt comfortable with what they'd come up with. In fact, she loved it.

Adam stood with his hands thrust into the front pockets of his pants.

"So how does dusting the window with icing powder and grated coconut sound, to give it that morning frost look?" he asked.

"I love a morning frost," she admitted. "Or a fresh snowfall? Could we do that?"

"Yeah. Of course," he replied. "There's just one more thing." He bent down to pick up a box. "Here's a little project I've been working on."

He pulled it out of the box and Taylor's eyes grew wide. Butterflies danced in her stomach so fast and quick she couldn't instantly speak. It was the prettiest, most thoughtful thing anyone had ever done for her.

"A candy chandelier? All in your spare time? Adam it's wonderful," she said and tried not to completely fall apart.

"And I have one more idea," Brooke added. "We need pictures on the wall of a family."

Adam nodded his agreement. "Good point. It is a home after all, so it needs that lived-in look."

"We could always put up some pictures on the mantel," Taylor suggested while keeping a loose hold on her emotions.

"I have a better idea," Brooke offered. Taylor loved when she got that look in her eye, the one that said she had an idea and she couldn't wait to share it.

"What's that?" she asked.

"Why don't we take a photo of the three of us? That way it'll be a picture of the family that lives in the house, or, I guess the family that built the house, but it's the same thing, right?" Brooke's idea seemed simple enough, and yet there was nothing simple about the question she was asking.

Were they a family?

In Taylor's dreams last night, they had been. In those moments that she sat on the side of Brooke's bed wishing she could take the sickness away from her while Adam watched them with concern, they had been. As she'd sat at the concert next to Adam, both of them brimming with pride at how good Brooke had done, Taylor had felt just like they were family. *Her* family.

Taylor looked up from Brooke to see that Adam was staring at her. Their gazes held as it seemed they were both trying to figure out what to say.

Brooke continued, "Daddy can use his phone to take the picture and then we can print it out. They have printers at Santa's Workshop because that's where they print Santa's pictures."

"Um." Taylor cleared her throat when it seemed apparent that Brooke was moving forward with her idea. "Sure."

"Come on." Brooke walked around Taylor, clearly expecting her to follow.

Taylor looked at Adam once more, hoping he could save her— or rather them— from this. Taking a picture as a family was sending a definite message to Brooke. A message that they both needed to consider before it was too late.

"I'm ready," Adam said after slipping his

phone out of his pocket and wiggling it in his hand.

"Great, come on, stand by me, Taylor," Brooke insisted.

Now that it was clear whose side he was on, Taylor turned and walked over to stand where Brooke had directed. They were right in front of the door of the house. Adam joined them on the other side of Brooke and held the phone at arm's length away to take the selfie. Taylor smiled already seeing in her mind how domestic and quaint this photo was going to look. Part of her, that part she'd long ago buried, that felt this was absolutely right. It was absolutely perfect.

Adam snapped the picture.

"Yay! Can I take your phone over to Santa's Workshop to see if they can print the picture, Daddy?"

"Ah, sure," Adam said and let Brooke take the phone and dash off.

"I love how this place is coming together," Taylor couldn't help but admit when just the two of them were left. It was the simple truth and she really wasn't in the habit of lying. With-holding information, maybe, but never lying.

"It just proves that anything is possible. Like you and I working as a team," he told her.

A team. That's exactly what they started out as. Now, Taylor wasn't certain what they were.

"So, what happens if you win, anyway?" he asked. "Linda giving you a big corner office?"

This was the first time he'd asked that question. And in all honesty, Taylor had never thought it necessary to go into details about what she would get if she won the competition. In her original offer to him, she'd told him that this was part of her job, which it was. Again, she never lied to him. So why did she feel like she'd betrayed him and Brooke somehow?

"Kind of," she replied. "Um, actually, I've been meaning to mention something. If all goes well, I might have some news of my own."

She paused because the look on his face was of genuine interest. He wanted to know how this competition was going to help her at work. Like if it were something fantastic, he was ready to celebrate with her. Taylor wondered what his reaction was going to be when he found out the reward was her moving out of the country.

Someone close by cleared their throat.

"Ah, Annabelle," Adam said and Taylor turned to see her walking up to them.

"*Bonsoir*," Annabelle spoke with a tentative wave. "Look, I just wanted to say I'm impressed. I've been watching you two. You had an enormous setback but you really bounced back. Your gingerbread house is really quite good."

"I'm glad you like it," Taylor replied proudly. "But it's mostly thanks to our talented baker here." She looked at Adam and then back to Annabelle.

Annabelle looked at Adam too. "Well, if there's anything I can appreciate, it's talent and hard work."

Annabelle walked away after making her comment and Taylor wondered what had just happened. She leaned closer to Adam and whispered, "A warm word from Annabelle? Did I hear that right?"

"It's a Christmas miracle," he said looking down at her with a smile.

Taylor returned the smile knowing exactly how Christmas miracles felt for once in her life.

"By the way, what is it you wanted to tell me?"

His question came about two seconds before Brooke ran back onto the platform. Adam held a finger to his lips signaling her to be quiet while he looked at Taylor expectantly.

He was waiting for her to tell him something. Taylor looked down at Brooke to see that now, she was waiting to hear what Taylor had to say too. And Taylor didn't know what to say. She didn't know how to say it, where to begin or what to expect when the words did come tumbling out.

She needed to tell them because Christmas Eve was right around the corner. There was no point in keeping it a secret any longer. But she couldn't. Holding on to the happiness they'd felt moments ago while finishing the gingerbread house was crucial to her.

"Nothing important," she said with a shrug and decided to hate herself for chickening out later.

Chapter Eighteen

One Day Until Judging

"Let the last day of decorating begin!" Mayor Arnold announced with gusto.

Taylor had watched him on television last night talking excitedly about the competition and the upcoming re-development project he planned for the city. Word around the office was that this project would be the coup of Linda's career, but Linda hadn't mentioned it to Taylor again since the day she told her about the competition.

"It's the final stretch for teams here at the Giant Gingerbread House Competition," the same reporter from the broadcast last night took over from where she stood in front of the exhibit stage.

The mayor's press conference was just about over and they had to get to their final decorations before tomorrow's judging. But while the reporter continued to speak, Taylor took a moment to look around at the people who had come out to attend the festival. There had been a steady crowd coming inside the Marketplace and walking outside in LOVE Park enjoying the good food, shopping for gifts and bringing the children to see Santa. Of all the places in all the world Taylor had been during Christmas, this year, in this place, felt like the best. Just as she'd told Adam when they were at Santa's Landing, it felt like home.

When the press conference was officially over the music was turned up louder and Christmas carols blasted through the space once again.

Taylor, Adam and Brooke moved around the gingerbread house adding final details. At one point, Taylor looked up to see Annabelle and Bradford stealing glances at what they were doing. A huge part of her felt like gloating. But the bigger part just wanted to enjoy the time she had left with Adam and Brooke. With that in mind, she'd decided on another detail last night and she needed to get to her bag.

She walked around to the back of the house and pulled the stocking from her bag. When she came back Bing Crosby's "I'll Be Home for Christmas" had started to play. Taylor smiled as she walked inside the gingerbread house and hung her stocking on one of the hooks they'd put on the mantel. For a few seconds she just stood there, looking at her name on the stocking, and remembering all the years she'd been sure to hang it somewhere. This year was special, this place was special and that's why she'd known her stocking needed to go here for this gingerbread house to be complete. She stepped out of the house to see Adam and Brooke standing on the stage looking at her.

"Only a few minutes left," she said to Adam and looked back at the house.

"We literally have nothing left to decorate. I'd say we're done here."

She wished there were a few more days in the competition...or weeks. That was silly; more time wouldn't stop the inevitable.

"I saw one of the other houses has a name, so what's the name of our house?" Brooke asked.

"Good question," Taylor replied. "Um, maybe something with "home" in it?"

Adam peeked through the window. "I saw you hang your stocking on the mantel."

Taylor shrugged. "I thought it was pretty fitting." That was the best way she could explain how she'd felt about adding that small detail to the house.

"We've got something else for the mantel," Brooke lifted a frame up to show Taylor.

Taylor smiled and her heart wept. The picture frame was made like a gingerbread house and inside was the picture the three of them took yesterday. It looked just like she'd known it would when they took it—like the perfect family. She wanted to cry and then she wanted to hug Brooke to her and never let her go.

"I love it. That's perfect," Taylor told her while trying to hold on to every bit of the sadness boiling around inside of her.

"I'll go put it inside," Brooke announced before walking inside the house.

Taylor watched her go before turning to Adam to say, "Traditional. Bold and new." Such a change from the sophisticated cutting-edge house she'd originally planned.

"Maybe I need to try something bold and new myself." Adam stood just a few steps away from her. He was wearing a red sweater and jeans and managed to look festive and handsome at the same time.

"Maybe another try at your own bakery," she suggested, because that was a much safer project than her thinking of how handsome he was.

"I was thinking the same thing. In fact, after we talked briefly about it a few nights ago, I thought you were right and put in another call to Nick Brexley." He shrugged. "I invited him to the judging tomorrow and he said he already had plans to be here. I guess he was coming to see Annabelle's entry. Either way, I figured I had nothing to lose and if he says no again, I'll look for other investors. So, thanks for the push."

Well, her heart was just taking all kinds of hits today. She was brimming with pride at the step Adam had taken toward his future. She'd planned to speak to Linda right after the judging, but he'd already made his own plan. Taylor prayed for only the best things for him. "My pleasure."

He continued talking, saving Taylor from completely breaking down in tears.

"Taylor, I know you can't be with your mom and dad this Christmas, but if you wanted... Brooke and I...we're hoping you would spend Christmas with us."

Nope, tears still wanted to fall. Taylor could not believe this. How had she come to be in this position? None of this was supposed to happen. Yet, she could not be upset that it had.

"That's the best invitation I've ever gotten," she told him honestly.

"Well, everyone needs a place for the holidays," he said.

"That's it!" Adam's words and the song that just finished playing had an idea sprouting in her head.

"What?" he asked.

"The name of the house...A Home for the Holidays."

Adam smiled and Taylor barely resisted the urge to amend that to *Our* Home for the Holidays.

"It's perfect," he said and smiled.

Yeah, it was perfect.

"Hey," Linda said as she stepped up onto the

stage. "Just had to come and see it for myself," she continued and looked at the house.

"That...is not the plan we discussed," she told Taylor.

Taylor hadn't discussed the change in plans with Linda. For one, because Linda hadn't specifically asked her about them and two, because she'd been so excited about the idea she'd just wanted to surprise Linda. And while she'd hoped that Linda would like the house in the end, Taylor was more proud of the fact that she, Adam and Brooke loved the house they'd created.

Adam raised his hand as if to take responsibility for the house, but Taylor had also opened her mouth ready to defend the changes as well.

Linda interrupted them both. "But I love it! Great job!" she squealed.

Taylor grinned with relief and Adam nodded proudly. Linda turned to walk off the stage, but stopped and looked back at Taylor.

"Oh and Taylor, I'm gonna be sorry to see you go. But a couple members of the board are heading out of town for the holidays so they took the vote last night. The formal announcement will go out tomorrow. You're on your way!" Linda grinned and pointed at Taylor. "*Au revoir!*" She walked away as quickly as she'd appeared, taking the air out of Taylor's lungs with her.

Every part of Taylor tensed after Linda's words. She stared out at the atrium, at Linda's retreat, and all the people moving throughout. Looking at anyone but Adam because she knew, unfortunately, the time was now.

"What does she mean?" he asked while Taylor was still trying to reconcile the piercing regret building in the pit of her stomach.

"Adam, I was gonna tell you." It was important to her that he knew she really hadn't tried to keep this from him.

"Tell me what?"

"We need to talk," she said simply knowing those were four words every man hated to hear. Well, today, Taylor hated having to say them.

"I will be running the Paris office of Ogilvy & Associates Architecture," Taylor said. "When Linda first told me about this competition, she said it might be a possibility that the Board would consider me for the position. Now, they've made their decision."

They were walking through the marketplace while she talked. He was actually glad that they'd left Brooke at the gingerbread house with Josephine because he didn't know how he was going to break this to her. He was still trying to figure out how he was going to digest it himself.

"Wow. Paris. Pretty hard to compete with that." The words stuck in his throat and came out a little huskier than he would have liked. But her announcement had landed like a punch in his gut and every breath he took now was ebbed with pain.

"Well, it's the dream job I've wanted for years," she said. "But I thought I'd have more time to decide."

But if she'd wanted this job for years, wasn't her decision already made?

"You dreamed of going back to the place where you and your ex broke up?" Raw, unwanted turmoil, bristled against his normal laid-back personality.

She looked startled by his words, but he couldn't find an apology to offer her.

"This isn't about him. Paris was in my heart before him and long after he was gone. This job is everything I've been working for these past seven years. I'll be running the entire office, overseeing the most unique international projects in the company's history. It's a big deal."

"There are things bigger than a job, Taylor. There's family, traditions, togetherness, standing still and making connections," he countered.

She blinked rapidly, her lips going into a straight line before she replied. "I don't know how to do those things, Adam. That's not the life I've led. It's not the life...not the way I decided to live my life."

His nostrils flared as he pushed out the breath that had been burning his lungs. "Well, I guess I'm the opposite. I stand where I'm rooted, holding on to the things I've committed to. It's the way I decided to live."

They were standing only a few feet away from each other but it might as well have been thousands of miles separating them already.

"So I guess you won't be joining us for Christmas this year."

Taylor stopped walking. She touched a hand to his arm and he stood still too. He wanted to lash out at the warmth that was still in her touch and the way his traitorous heart still skipped a beat when she stared up at him with those reddish-brown eyes.

"Adam, believe me, I want to spend Christmas with you and Brooke, it's just..."

"It's just this is your job and it's what you live for. Your work is your life; I get it. And this was just a competition. Isn't that what you said yesterday, that we should focus on the competition?"

She nodded. "I did. But I know that...I mean I feel like..."

He interrupted her because he knew this wasn't fair, for either of them. "Hey, don't worry. I'll explain it to Brooke. After all, Santa's got a lot of places to visit this year, right?"

He looked at her for a few moments but before she could reply he decided it was enough. The torture he'd been feeling hearing her say she was leaving the country forever was much more than he'd imagined going through again. Adam walked away from her knowing that there could have been more words said, but what good would they have done? Taylor had to take this position, if she didn't and it was because of him, she would hate him. Adam would rather her leave like this, than know that one day she would wish she had.

Chapter Nineteen

Christmas Eve

TAYLOR WAS DRESSED AND READY to head to the marketplace for the final judging. But she really didn't want to go. She didn't want this to be the last time she saw Adam and Brooke. Since when did she ever get what she wanted?

Well, she'd gotten the job in Paris.

Her tablet on the dining room table pinged with an alert. She sat down and accepted the call from her mother.

"Sweetheart, my friend Diana emailed that she saw a news report about you and some giant gingerbread house," Carol immediately began.

Taylor nodded and gave her mother a weak smile. This was not what she wanted to talk about right now, not after last night. "Well, you know the expression, truth is stranger than fiction. That's pretty much the case here."

Her mother was instantly intrigued. "Really? Tell me how this happened. Is this the new assignment you were talking about?"

Taylor sighed heavily. In addition to the calls she and her mother shared, they also emailed a few times a week. "Sort of. It's a charity competition that my job wanted to win. So I teamed up with this baker and we created a fantastic house." That was at least something Taylor could be proud about. The house was great and she'd had a wonderful time creating it—a fun, warm and memorable time.

Carol smiled. "That's great, honey. Well, you know now that Diana's retired, she decided to sell some of the stuff she knits, so she has a stall at the Marketplace this year. She also mentioned something about you working pretty closely with a handsome young man. Is he the baker?"

He was so much more than a baker, but there was really no way to explain that to her mother.

"That's Adam. And yes, he's the baker doing the project with me. He's nice," she said as nonchalantly as possible.

"Nice, huh? I can see you blushing." That was probably true, but Taylor was certain her mother could not see her heart breaking.

"It's just...it's just, I don't know," she tried to explain.

"What's wrong, honey?"

"I got offered the job in Paris."

"That's great! Isn't it?"

Taylor wanted to bang her head on the table because yeah, Paris was great, and then again, it wasn't.

"Yes...it's just that Philadelphia has been growing on me. There's such a feeling of Christmas here. I went ice skating and there's this place called Santa's Landing. It's so cute with the decorations all over the place and the music. It's kind of starting to feel like..."

"Like, home?" Carol asked with a knowing smile. "I've always told you that home is wherever you hang your Christmas stocking. You'll know in your heart when you've found the right place, or the right person."

She groaned with those words and used her hands to cover her face.

"Have you found the right person?"

That question. Six little words. One simple answer.

She let her hands fall to her lap. "It's complicated."

"Why? Because you want it to be complicated?"

Taylor was shaking her head even before her mother finished the question. "No. This isn't what I wanted. None of it is, or was." She took a deep breath and released it slowly because this was the first time she'd ever admitted this out loud. "I wanted everything we didn't have. The house where I could grow up year after year with the same friends in my neighborhood growing up with me. The connections to people who shared memories with me and the traditions a family creates."

"We had traditions, Taylor. While we did do things in different places, we still did them. Birthdays were always celebrated with parties whether we were the only guests at the party or not. You drew pictures and we put them in a book as a way of recording our history."

Carol spoke slow and precisely as if she were presenting a case in a courtroom.

"You're right. But I wanted something else. I longed for it—that's why I drew that picture. But after a while I decided I could be happy without it. You and dad were."

"Oh honey, your father and I are happy because this is the life we chose for ourselves. Now it's time for you to choose. If you want something else, Taylor, it's okay to change your previous plan and go for what will make you happy."

But that was just it: her job made her happy, too.

It was getting late, and Taylor really needed to get to the Marketplace.

"Thanks, Mom. I love you. I'll call you and Dad tomorrow on Christmas Day," Taylor said.

"Looking forward to it. Love you!" Carol blew Taylor a kiss and Taylor did the same.

Taylor left the call and minimized the screen only to sigh at the background photo she'd added to her tablet. It was the picture of her, Brooke and Adam. Each of them were smiling at the camera with their glorious gingerbread house in the background. They were happy in that picture. Now, Taylor had to go to this competition that had once meant so much to her, feeling as if it was the worst thing that could have possibly happened to her.

"Santa's coming tonight, Daddy," Brooke announced when they were in the living room wrapping the last of the gifts he'd finally purchased for Jenny.

"I know, honey," Adam said. After spending the night replaying the conversation with Taylor in his mind, nursing the ache for which he had no cure, he knew it was time to tell Brooke. He had no plans for what words he would say; he just wanted to get it out without both of them breaking down.

"Did you wrap the gift for Mr. Ray?" she asked after placing a box under the tree.

Adam turned to look at her and saw that she was now on her hands and knees lifting every box and checking the names. She did this every year and Adam found it funny each time. On Christmas morning, there would be several boxes with Brooke's name on them, all from

Santa. She would hug and kiss him after opening them and he would feel flanked by her love, covered and supported. That was a feeling Adam longed to feel right now.

She sat back on her knees. "We didn't get Taylor anything."

Leave it to his daughter to give him the best opening to tell her the bad news.

"Honey, Taylor won't be joining us for Christmas," Adam told her. His father had always said it was best to just rip the bandage off.

Her shoulders immediately drooped, hands falling into her lap as she stared down at them. He crossed the room and sat down on the floor beside her, lifting her onto his lap.

"I thought she liked us."

She spoke the words quietly and they still pelted Adam like shards of glass.

"You know that Taylor has a very important job. She designs great buildings. And because she did so well with the gingerbread house, she now has to go to Paris and design more wonderful buildings there." He hoped the explanation was a good one even though it had done nothing to stop him from feeling so awful about it.

Brooke pouted—something she didn't do often. "I've seen pictures of Paris in the books at school and on TV. They have enough buildings there, they don't need Taylor to build more. She can stay here with us because Philly could always use new buildings."

If a heart could fill to the point of bursting, his did in that moment. Brooke deserved the best of everything, and Adam wished with all that he had that he could give her this. He'd even spent a portion of his sleepless night trying to come up with scenarios for Taylor to stay. But in the end, Adam had known this was how it had to be. Nobody was going to be happy if they always wondered if she should have taken this position. It was unfair, but that was life. Hadn't his mother told him about making plans? Life always happened on its own terms.

"I thought she was gonna stay here with us," Brooke said.

Adam hugged her to him, resting his chin on top of her head. "I know, honey. I was kind of hoping she would stay with us too."

"Did you tell her we wanted her to stay, Daddy?"

No.

"It's not that simple, Brooke. Taylor has things she wants to do in her life, and we can't stand in her way."

"Those things don't include us?" she asked. "Because I thought she liked coming to my concert and helping me with my homework. I know she didn't really like baking in the kitchen with you at first, but since the gingerbread house came out so nice, I thought she might have changed her mind."

They'd both changed their minds. Neither Taylor

nor Adam had particularly cared for each other when they first met. But that had changed. So much was different now, but none of that mattered. This was how it had to be.

"I'm sure she loved doing all of those things with you, Brooke. If she didn't, she wouldn't have done them. This decision has nothing to do with your or me, this is about Taylor. She has a job to do and her new home is going to be in Paris while she does it," he said.

"No. 'Home is where you hang your stocking.' Taylor's mother told her that and Taylor told me. Plus, she hung her stocking in the gingerbread house we all built together. Her home is right here with us."

Adam nodded sadly and kissed Brooke on the forehead. "I wish that were true, honey. I really do. But life has been known to happen in good and bad ways. So let's get this finished up and head down to the Marketplace for the judging. Tonight's a big night and you have to get to bed to wait for Santa!"

Adam had tried to add more enthusiasm about the holiday than he'd felt at the moment. And to her credit, Brooke did too.

"Okay, Daddy," she said and eased off his lap. "Let's go to the gingerbread competition."

Adam smiled and stood up. Through heavy hearts and sadness, just like before, they would move on, together.

Taylor arrived at the Marketplace with Wendy, her son and daughter. As one of the volunteers, who coincidentally was also her neighbor and friend, Wendy had given Taylor a ride today. They walked toward the exhibit stage with the kids wandering over to different stands every now and then.

"My kids have been asking me every day for the past week when this day would come," Wendy said after she'd wrangled the kids up one more time.

She positioned them between her and Taylor this time so they wouldn't wander off again. Taylor had smiled down at them and recalled the time she'd walked through the Marketplace with Brooke. No matter how many times they'd come to the marketplace Brooke had always wanted to see another stand and another, even if she'd already seen them all before.

"Well, I promise, we won't disappoint." She tried to sound optimistic and unbothered and hoped it was working.

"I never thought you would. You and Adam made a great team."

Past tense. As in, it was over. She walked with slower steps, the lack of energy she felt either from tossing and turning all night or the deep turmoil still ripping through her.

"I know. It was the best of luck that he baked the cake for the office party. If he hadn't, then we would never have met and I probably wouldn't have gone to him with my crazy request."

"Exactly! That was definitely amazing luck or fate. Either way we're about to find out how that'll all play out." Wendy signaled for her children when they arrived at the atrium in front of the exhibit state.

She put on a bright smile and forced her tone to a more cheerful level. "Well, I guess it's showtime."

"I know," Wendy clapped her hands together. "I'm so excited! You designed a great house that actually tastes good too. I'm sure you're going to win."

This had started out with winning being the priority, but that had definitely changed. "Thanks, Wendy, for all your help. I really appreciate it."

Before she left, Taylor looked down at the children. "Hey guys, you know what? After the competition is over there'll be lots of gingerbread and other goodies that we had leftover that you can have."

"Yes!"

"Cool!"

The kids yelled and Taylor smiled at them. "See you in a bit," she said to Wendy and walked over to where she saw Adam and Brooke standing.

"Hey," she said when she was close to them.

"Hey," he replied.

"Hi, Taylor," Brooke's tone was softer than it had ever been with Taylor, even during the time when she was sick. And she hadn't looked at her when she spoke which meant that Adam had told her she was leaving.

"Hi, Brooke." Taylor spoke with an upbeat tone and tried to give her a smile, but Brooke only stepped back to stand closer to Jenny. Stricken with guilt, she held back a gasp and looked at Adam. "About yesterday, Adam, I'm sorry I didn't mention it."

He shrugged. "Don't worry about it. I'm happy for you."

"It's starting!" Brooke said and pointed to Mayor Arnold as he stood on the stage behind that same green podium where he'd first announced the contest.

"Glad we made it on time," Jenny said when she walked up to join them with Ray right behind her.

Jenny waved to Taylor and Taylor waved back. Ray winked at her and Taylor smiled at him in return.

"Happy Holidays, everybody, and welcome to the judging of our first-ever Giant Gingerbread Competition!" Mayor Arnold announced.

The stage had been decorated even more since the houses were now complete. There were life-size gingerbread people standing between each house and gift boxes along the edge of the stage. Lights blinked on the sign with the name of the competition that was stretched over the stage.

A huge crowd had showed up for the judging and they clapped with the mayor's announcement. Taylor stood and nervously stuck her hands into the pockets of her coat.

"Can I please have our teams approach the stage?" Mayor Arnold asked. "Come on up!"

Adam, Taylor and Brooke walked up and stood at the front of the stage. Taylor looked to her side to see Bradford and Annabelle taking their position. To her other side the two other teams stood as well.

"Now it's the moment we've all been waiting for," the mayor continued. "May I present our first gingerbread house, Snowman Sanctuary." The mayor pointed toward the house built by the teachers from the high school who called themselves Design Collective. It was a blend of modern and traditional, with huge gumdrops around the perimeter of the house and a candy cane pathway leading to the front door.

After applause from the crowd, the mayor continued. "Our second entry, the Elf Castle."

This one was impressive as well. Taylor had watched with interest as team Excelsior—the culinary students—had put together the castle-shaped house. She'd thought the idea was unique, and really liked the execution with the snow-topped turrets and glazed sugar windows.

"Next we have the Northern Tower," Mayor Arnold announced Bradford and Annabelle's house and Taylor looked to Adam.

"This is gonna be tough," she whispered.

"No worries," he said and when she looked at him, he smiled.

The instant clench in her chest seemed like her heart was smiling in return. She was going to miss seeing Adam like this—relaxed, calm, confident in his element.

The crowd clapped even more and Taylor looked around to see a very proud—and rightfully so—Bradford and Annabelle. Nick Brexley, the investor, was also standing with them.

"My goodness, that can go in a museum someplace, am I right?" the mayor asked the crowd as he pointed to Bradford and Annabelle's house.

A few cheers and a couple of chuckles came from the crowd.

"And now, may I present our final gingerbread house, A Home for the Holidays!" For the first time today excitement bubbled inside her upon hearing the name of their house being announced. Her lips spread into a wide grin as she clapped and looked to Adam, Brooke and the rest of their team who were doing the same.

She thought there was louder clapping coming from the crowd. Ray, Jenny, Josephine,

David, Wendy and her kids were definitely enthusiastic, adding hoots and whistles to their applause. When she saw Jenny give Adam and Brooke a thumbs up, her heart melted.

Brooke began counting, "Three, Two, One!" and the special effect that Adam rigged to the chimney of the house exploded into the hair. Confetti drizzled over the house and onto the stage and the crowd stared in awe, clapping even louder.

As confetti rained down over the house, happiness felt like snowflakes falling over her. "Told you I love fresh snowfall." Everyone was clapping now and staring at the still-falling confetti, even Bradford and Annabelle.

"Well, to say all of our entries exceeded expectations would be an understatement. But, this is a contest, so unfortunately, we have to pick a winner. Judges, your results, please."

A lady walked up to the podium and handed the mayor a slip of paper.

"And the winner of our first Giant Gingerbread Contest is..." Mayor Arnold paused to open the envelope and Taylor held her breath.

She released it slowly when Brooke reached up to grab her hand. That clinching that started in her chest a few minutes ago exploded, spreading warmth all over her and she happily wrapped her fingers around Brooke's. When she looked up it was to see Adam smiling at both of them.

"A Home for the Holidays!" the mayor announced and the crowd erupted with loud cheering.

Taylor clapped and Brooke yelled, "Yay!" Adam clapped and shared a high-five with Taylor.

Jenny hugged Ray and the rest of their volunteers all exchanged hugs.

Taylor was very proud of their accomplishment and she was excited for the win, but the very best part of the moment was when Brooke turned to hug her and seconds later Adam pulled them both into a big hug. This was it, every spark of joy, happiness and love pouring through her at this moment, was everything she was going to give up. She inhaled deeply trying to absorb every feeling, memorizing it so she would never forget.

"You did it," he said when their hug broke.

"*We* did it," Taylor corrected him. "And I bet your investors are pretty impressed. Speaking of which, I saw him over there with Annabelle."

Adam shook his head. "I did too. And it's okay. I'll come up with something else."

"Oh, I'm sorry," she said.

"Don't be." He shook his head. "It doesn't matter. What matters is we won."

"Congratulations," Annabelle said when she walked up to them.

"Yeah," Bradford added. "That was really something." He pointed to the house and the still-falling snow.

"Ah, thank you. I mean, your house is spectacular," Taylor told them.

"Yeah, we're pretty proud of it," Bradford said.

"Adam, your flair for design is quite exceptional," Annabelle told him.

"Thank you. And you're impressive as always," he replied.

"I understand you've already met Nick Brexley."

Nick, a tall slim man with crystalline blue eyes smiled and extended his hand to Adam.

"Nice to see you again, Adam," Nick said when Adam accepted and shook his hand.

"You too, Nick. How did you enjoy the competition?"

Adam didn't seem irritated or uncomfortable at all, and Taylor admired him for that. There were so many things she admired about this man.

"I enjoyed it very much. So much so that Annabelle and I have come up with a proposition for you." Nick looked to Annabelle, and Taylor held her breath.

What was happening here?

"Yes, well, as you may or may not have heard, I am looking to expand, with two more restaurants throughout the state and with a possibility of eventually opening more throughout the country. I would need to train a new baker to help run one of the locations." Annabelle stated while keeping her gaze on Adam.

This was fantastic. Taylor resisted the urge to begin clapping again. If Adam went to work with Annabelle, it would allow him to use his own designs, and the fact that Nick Brexley was standing there offering his approval with a smile meant the investor also knew how much talent Adam had. Still, Adam wouldn't own his own shop.

"Thank you, both, but I already have a job." Adam gave his answer just as Ray and Jenny came up to join them.

The slight wavering of her smile signaled Annabelle's disappointment, while Nick only nodded at Adam. "Fine. But if you ever do open your own place, please do invite me to the opening," Annabelle said.

"And me too," Nick added.

"I certainly will," Adam replied.

"Great job, you two. Congratulations again on the win. Taylor, I'll be seeing you around." Bradford said before he and Annabelle walked away.

"We're gonna go over to the food court to get something to celebrate. We'll see you guys over there," Jenny said before walking away with Ray.

Taylor, Adam and Brooke remained standing in front of their winning house. There was so much to say and then nothing left to say.

"So, when are you leaving?" he asked her.

"I fly out tonight," she said hating the sound of the words.

"Thank you for believing in me. I'm glad we made it happen."

"Me too," she replied.

"Are you really leaving on Christmas Eve?" Brooke asked.

Taylor leaned down to look at her. "Aww, sweetie, I have to. But I had a great time."

"I did too." Brooke hurried to swipe away a tear that had fallen. "Bye, Taylor."

"Bye, Brooke," Taylor whispered and hugged the little girl so tightly she thought she might crush her.

When she released Brooke, Taylor stood, blinking rapidly in order to hold back her tears. This was too hard. Leaving had never been this hard before. Adam took Brooke's hand and they started to walk away. Taylor shouldn't have stood there watching them. She should have turned away and left.

Adam looked back and said, "Merry Christmas."

"Merry Christmas," Taylor replied.

Chapter Twenty

TWO HOURS LATER TAYLOR ZIPPED her last suitcase. She rolled it close to the door and came back into the living room to look around. The tree that Adam and Brooke had brought for her was still decorated, the lights flashing in the corner. Wendy had insisted she leave it up and said she would take it down the day after Christmas when she took hers down.

"Wendy, thank you so much for doing this," Taylor said when she turned to see Wendy carrying one of her boxes from the dining room and sitting it down on the floor.

"Are you kidding? It's the least I could do," Wendy said. "My kids are so excited about all those snacks you sent them home with. I had to hide them, or they would have eaten them all tonight."

"They're wonderful children," Taylor said, her voice a little more wistful than she'd intended.

"Thanks," Wendy said and then tilted her head to stare at Taylor. "Are you sure about this? I mean, are you really choosing work over what you had with Adam and Brooke?"

Taylor shook her head adamantly. "It's the wrong time. Or maybe I was right when I was younger and decided that I wasn't meant to have the family and house. I don't know. I just know that this job in Paris was my goal, so I've gotta go."

Wendy nodded. "You're beautiful, Taylor, and you're good at what you do. But I think you'd also be good at doing your job and being a mom. You were terrific with Brooke. I saw that and so did Adam."

And Taylor had felt it. But it wasn't enough. She'd made her decision. There was no turning back now.

"The movers said they'd come the day after Christmas. Much of everything was boxed up. If you could just give them the keys." Her quick change of subject was all Taylor could do at this point. She'd been over and over all of this in her mind and this was what had to happen. It was the way it had to be.

Wendy smiled. "Consider it done. We'll miss you. But Paris for Christmas, I guess you'll be calling the City of Light your new home."

"Yes," Taylor said with another sigh. "Home."

A horn sounded outside.

"That must be your shuttle," Wendy said.

"Yeah. Merry Christmas, Wendy." Taylor hugged her and thought that not only was she leaving Adam and Brooke, but she was leaving a friend, or rather two. She'd said her goodbyes to Josephine before she'd left the Marketplace, even though she was certain she would speak to her over the phone frequently whether for business or personal.

"Have a good flight," Wendy continued when they pulled away from each other.

"Thank you." Taylor walked to the door. She grabbed her coat and the suitcase she'd put there moments ago.

She opened the door and started to walk out, but then she stopped and looked back at Wendy because leaving felt all too familiar to her. Wendy gave her a hesitant smile.

Taylor turned and kept going. She climbed into the back of the shuttle and she stared forward. Always moving forward, never looking back. That's what she used to tell herself when she was younger and they were moving. There was nothing in the past to look back on.

But that had been then, and this, unfortunately, was now.

"Christmas is tomorrow. You think I can order a gingerbread house?" a customer asked Adam.

After they'd had a slice of pizza as their celebration meal, Adam told Ray he would come
back to the bakery and work the rest of the day.
Jenny was taking Brooke to the mall with her for
last-minute shopping, and Adam hadn't wanted
to sit in his house alone. He would have just
thought about Taylor if he did.

"I'm afraid I don't have the time. I'm so sorry.
Would you take a pound cake as a Christmas
present?" he offered.

She smiled happily. "You're a lifesaver,
Adam!"

He turned around and selected a boxed cake
out of the display case and handed it to her.

"Merry Christmas!" she said.

Adam replied, "Merry Christmas." Even though
the last thing he was feeling at this moment was
merry.

"Well, that's another one," Ray said from behind
him. "You're turning away customers, Adam, by
not giving them what they really want."

Adam stepped away from the register and
walked closer to where Ray was standing.

"You know I don't have time to do those
custom orders. We're behind on ginger snaps.
The sugar cookies are running low."

Ray held up both hands. "Adam, slow down,
I can get help for all of that." He turned and
leaned against one of the tables in the back.
"We're a neighborhood bakery, selling to people
what they expect. Now, all of a sudden we have

people coming in here every five minutes asking for your cakes. This line is outside the door." He pointed outside.

"Ray," Adam began. "Is this your roundabout way of saying you're firing me?"

"Firing you?" Ray asked and shook his head. "I'm talking about making you a partner."

Adam couldn't believe what he'd just heard. "Are you serious?"

"Yes! Look, I know I've been a stubborn old fool trying to stick to what's always worked around here. But now we have people banging down our doors to get to your cakes. I heard that big-time pastry chef offer you a job at one of her new restaurants."

"And you also heard me turn down Annabelle's offer."

"Yes, I did. But I know you've always wanted to open your own bakery, so I've been thinking, why not open it right here?"

"I don't follow," Adam said, afraid to get too excited.

"I'm talking about your own display case, building your own customer following for your specialty cakes. Your name out front so that all of Philly will know where to find you. What do you say, partner?"

This was unbelievable and unexpected. But that didn't mean it wasn't fantastic. "Sounds pretty good to me," he told Ray before shaking his hand.

"Okay then. We'll get all the legal stuff done after the holidays." Ray clapped his hands together after their handshake.

Feeling as if a weight had been lifted from his shoulders, Adam couldn't help but grin. "Wait 'til Brooke hears about this."

"And Taylor, what about her?" Ray asked. "You know, ever since you found out she was leaving, you haven't smiled much. So why don't you go tell her how you feel," he suggested. "And let her decide if she wants to leave or not."

"Ray," Adam said and then turned so that he was leaning against the table right beside Ray. "I don't want to stop Taylor from living her life."

Ray nodded. "All I'm saying is, Taylor is the one who walked in here and asked you to partner up. She came to you, cap in hand. Now maybe it's your turn to do the same."

Adam could have continued to argue but something told him that would be futile. "Is it that obvious how I feel?" he asked Ray.

"Is Christmas tomorrow?" Ray replied. "Please, I can tell you don't want Taylor to go. So go tell her."

"What if she leaves, anyway?" Which had been Adam's fear all along. He'd thought long and hard about just pouring his heart out to Taylor and asking her to stay here with him and Brooke, but the thought of her saying no and still walking away was something Adam did not want to experience.

"Well, then she leaves. At least she'll know how you feel." Put so plainly in Ray's way, it didn't sound so bad. Still a little scary, but wasn't that what change was? Taking the risk, doing the thing that frightened you, to get what you wanted the most?

Adam could spend more time contemplating this, or he could do what he'd wanted to do all along. "Thanks, Ray," he said and clapped his boss, now partner, on the shoulder before running out the door.

Adam drove as fast as legally possible to Taylor's house, praying the whole time that she would still be there. He had no idea what time her flight was leaving; she'd just said tonight. So he had a chance. He didn't know what he was going to say to her, but he would figure that out when he got there.

He parked his truck crooked in the spot in front of her house and then got out to run up the walkway. He rang the bell, waited about two seconds, and then rang it again. Another second or so ticked by and he lifted his hand to knock, but the door opened and he breathed a sigh of relief.

"Thank goodness I thought I'd missed—"

Adam's words halted when he saw Wendy on the other side of the door.

"Wendy? Is Taylor here?" he asked.

"Sorry, Adam, I was just taking care of a few things. She was in a hurry and she left for the airport a couple hours ago. Her flight's taking off any minute."

Adam thanked Wendy and walked back to the truck, deflated. He'd been too late. She was gone and so was his second chance at love.

Chapter Twenty-One

$\mathcal{T}$AYLOR SAT AT THE AIRPORT holding her plane ticket. A few seats down from her was a family—mother, father and daughter. The little girl was looking down at the tablet in her hands. Taylor smiled because the entire scene reminded her of herself when she was younger. Drawing while they waited for a plane. Boarding with her parents and starting over in a new place, again and again. She wondered if that little girl felt sad about going to Paris. Was this a move for them? Or just a vacation?

Instrumental Christmas music played overhead and a Christmas tree stood in one of the corners of this section of the airport. Other people waited to board the same flight. It felt like business as usual, even though it was Christmas Eve. Taylor wondered what Brooke was doing. Was she baking the cookies to leave for

Santa's snack? Or maybe she had more gifts to wrap? No, she was probably watching a Christmas movie. Taylor smiled at the thought. She would have loved to sit and watch that movie with Brooke.

"This is the pre-boarding call for flight 714 bound for Paris. At this time, anyone requiring assistance or traveling with children, please check in," the attendant announced.

Families had pre-boarding privileges, and since she was not part of a family, Taylor remained seated, waiting for her turn. But as the family walked through the door to board the plane, Taylor noticed the little girl had left her tablet. She hurried to pick it up, intending to take it to the attendant, but she looked down at the screen first. Everything went completely still as Taylor saw the picture the girl had been drawing using an app on her tablet. It was a father, mother, a little girl and a Christmas tree.

Taylor held the tablet in her hand but did not move. Memories flashed through her mind like a movie trailer of her life, so fast she was instantly out of breath. She'd drawn a picture of the house she'd dreamed of living in and packed it to take with her when she moved. Everywhere she went she drew another picture of another dream, another family. Her family. The one she wanted in a place where they decided to live. One place, one family, forever.

She hurried over to the desk.

"Excuse me, a family that just boarded forgot this," she said and handed the tablet to the flight attendant.

"Oh. I'll make sure they get it," the flight attendant replied.

Every ounce of sadness that Taylor had been feeling was now replaced by nervous energy. Her heart thumped as she went back to her seat and grabbed her phone out of her purse. She started pressing numbers on the phone with shaking fingers and spoke the moment the call connected, "Linda? This is Taylor. We need to talk."

Christmas Morning

Brooke was on gift number four. She'd ripped through the first three so fast, Adam was just getting a chance to gather up the wrapping paper and put it into a bag.

"Look, Dad, new skates! Santa even remembered I was wishing for pink skate guards!" She lifted the skates out of the box and showed him.

There was nothing better than seeing his child happy, and Adam knew he needed to cherish these moments.

He put the bag aside and knelt down on the floor next to her. "Santa doesn't usually drop the ball," he told her with a grin.

"I know! I'm so ready to go out and skate with them. It's just too bad Taylor's not here. We could have all gone skating together."

Adam thought about Taylor's text message to him several days ago. She'd said she wanted ice skates for Christmas. The thought made him smile in spite of how sad he still felt about her leaving.

"It's okay. You and I will go. But first, we've gotta check out Santa's Landing, so go get dressed and grab your coat."

"You're right. We can open the other gifts when we come back. That way Jenny'll be here with us."

Adam nodded. Jenny was coming over at noon and they were going to have lunch and then watch movies all day until dinner. That was their grand Christmas plan.

"Right. Now go on and get dressed while I finish cleaning up your mess," he told her.

"Okay. I'll be right back." Brooke was only gone for a few seconds when Adam began picking up after her.

She'd gone through her stocking and left everything that was in there on the couch. Adam put it all away. He went to hang her stocking up again and paused. Brooke's stocking would hang next to his. What would it have been like to have Taylor's hanging there too? If he closed his eyes, he could still see it hanging in the gingerbread house, and he could hear Brooke saying "home is where you hang your stocking."

With a shake of his head, he promised himself he would not spend his entire day thinking about her.

Adam was just about to take the bag of trash out to the garage when there was a knock at the door. He went to answer it, expecting to see one of his neighbors. Mrs. Riley, maybe; she always baked fudge for the holidays and she hadn't brought them a pan yet. Adam really liked Mrs. Riley's fudge. But when he opened the door he decided he liked who was standing there much more.

"Taylor? What are you doing here?" He was unable to mask the surprise and the happy tinge to his voice.

"I'm sorry. I hope I'm not interrupting anything," she said.

"Not at all. I thought you'd left. Come in." He moved and let her step inside, because the last thing he wanted was for her to leave again.

She looked great in a red sweater and beige coat. He'd missed seeing her, and it had only been one day.

"Well, I was on my way last night, but then I realized I forgot something." She came inside and stopped just in front of the stairs.

"What'd you forget?"

She sighed. "I've been traveling for so long, I

forgot what home felt like. And since I found it again this week, why would I want to leave?"

Adam was afraid to get excited. "But what about your job?"

Taylor smiled, a light in her eyes.

"My firm got the downtown re-development project. The mayor confirmed it, which meant that Linda would need someone to manage it. I met with Linda last night and we had a long talk before conferencing with the Board. Linda is now taking the Paris position, and I'm going to stay here as director of special projects, starting with the re-development project. Josephine will take my position and be on hand should I need any support staff. This will be the biggest job I've ever done."

His pulse quickened as he struggled to make sure this was all really happening. "But what about Paris? Your dream?"

She shook her head. "I thought that was my new dream, but then I realized that I've got everything I used to dream of right here."

"So you're staying?"

"I am."

Adam resisted the urge to yell with joy, or to pick her up and spin her around to show how happy he was. Instead, he decided to share some news he had.

"Great! Then you can come to my grand opening, or re-opening I should say."

"Excuse me?"

"Ray's Bakery is having a grand re-opening as Ray & Adam's Bakery. I'll be handling the specialty pastries only. I'm so glad you came into the bakery that day, Taylor. This wouldn't have happened without you."

Taylor grinned. "Are you kidding?"

He shook his head.

"Adam, that's great! This calls for a celebration!"

"Then we better get you some skates because in this house on Christmas Day, after we go to Santa's Landing, we hit the ice."

Adam stepped closer to her then because he'd fought it long enough.

"But, before we go this year, I think there's another tradition we should start." He was standing right in front of her now, so close he could smell the floral fragrance of her perfume.

"Oh, no, I'm afraid to ask what that is," Taylor said.

Instead of saying it, Adam looked up at the mistletoe hanging from the ceiling.

Taylor followed his gaze and when he eased his arms around her waist, she lifted hers and looped them around his neck.

Adam lowered his head and kissed her the way he'd been dreaming of doing since the day they met.

"If I'd written a list for Santa, he couldn't have brought me a better gift. Merry Christmas,

Taylor," he whispered when he finally pulled back.

"I'm glad I finally found somewhere to hang my stocking. Merry Christmas, Adam."

"Dad, who are you talking to?" Brooke asked as she came running down the stairs.

She stopped at the bottom and exclaimed, "Taylor! You're here?"

"Yes, I'm here," Taylor began, but before she could finish Brooke came over and hugged her.

Adam watched their embrace with barely restrained joy.

"And I couldn't be happier!" Taylor said looking over Brooke's head.

He knew he was wearing a wide, goofy grin that at this moment he had no intention of changing.

"Me too!" Brooke said.

Taylor broke the hug. "Now, how about we go check out those new skates I see under the tree."

Adam followed them into the living room. He stood back watching the two of them talking about the skates. Brooke knew exactly which store they could go to after the holidays to find Taylor a pair just like hers, and Taylor suggested she take some formal lessons.

With his arms folded over his chest, Adam wondered what his mother would have to say about this. She would most likely tell him to enjoy every minute of it.

Epilogue

One Year Later

"EVERYTHING'S BETTER WITH BUTTER," GLORIA Dale said as she eased a Pyrex dish out of the oven. "It's definitely the key ingredient to my baked macaroni and cheese."

As if to prove her point to Taylor, Carol, and Jenny, who were all standing in the kitchen preparing for some part of the huge dinner they were having, Gloria peeled back the aluminum foil covering the dish.

"Mmmmmm," Jenny immediately moaned.

"Oh yes, Gloria, that looks absolutely scrumptious," Carol added.

Taylor made a sound and rubbed her stomach, her gaze catching on the glare of the princess-cut diamond wedding ring on her finger. "It tastes as good as it looks," she told her mother. "I've had it a few times this year, and I personally went to the grocery store to get everything she needed to make it for tonight."

"We had to have everything just perfect for this dinner," Jenny chimed in. She was using a knife to smear butter over the dinner rolls that had come out of the oven just a few minutes ago.

Jenny was right, tonight did have to be perfect. It had to be everything Taylor had dreamed it would be—her first family holiday dinner.

"Would have been even more perfect if your friend could have joined us," Gloria said.

Jenny rolled her eyes at that statement, but only Taylor could see her because she was standing across the island from her. Jenny's back was thankfully to her mother so Gloria couldn't see her reaction to her comment.

"Oh, Jenny, I didn't know you were seeing someone," Carol said.

Taylor jumped in as she glimpsed Jenny's eyes widening with irritation. "I think we're just about ready. Jenny, why don't you go in and gather everyone? We'll bring the last dishes out to the table."

Mouthing a silent "thank you" to Taylor, Jenny made her way out of the kitchen with haste.

There was no need for thanks. Taylor understood what Jenny was going through. Break-ups could be hard, and during the holiday season they could be brutal.

In the last year Jenny had become the sister Taylor never had, and in turn, she'd become the same to Jenny. So she'd happily given her a reprieve from the mothers who could be a bit overbearing at times.

"Taylor, I didn't get a chance to tell you when we got in last night, but you did a fabulous job with this house. Your father and I are so proud of you for starting a new job and taking the time to design a bigger house for your family," Carol said. She was scooping the green beans out of the pot on the stove and putting them into one of the white china bowls that matched the themed set she'd purchased online a few months ago.

"Yes, she did. Designing it from the outside and then decorating the inside. Such a talented girl," Gloria added.

Adam's mother and Jenny were like twins with their mocha brown complexions and high cheekbones. Gloria's hair was streaked with gray and styled in neat pin curls.

"Will said the construction crew did a good job, too. You know he was concerned when he left from up here two months ago and they hadn't even finished the plumbing," her mother-in-law continued.

Warmth and pride washed over Taylor as she looked up to see her mother and mother-in-law watching her. With all the love and respect she had for them, Taylor smiled and tried to contain the tears of joy that she finally had a complete family in her home for the holidays. As if on command, the little one inside kicked and she rubbed a hand over her stomach again.

It wouldn't be long now. Excitement and anticipation filled her days, and sometimes she actually had to pinch herself to make sure it was all real.

"Thanks, but Adam and Brooke helped a lot."

"I know. Brooke told me all about the plans she had for her bedroom," Gloria said. "And when we got here two days ago she couldn't wait to show me the finished product."

"I'm really glad all of you could come and are staying here with us for the holidays," she said.

It was exactly how she'd envisioned it, her husband and daughter and all their family and friends here on Christmas Eve getting ready to share a delicious dinner.

"Babe, can you ladies come on, they're getting restless out here." Adam stepped into the kitchen with a panicked look on his face.

"Oh tell your father to cool his britches. I know he's the one who's making a fuss. That man likes to eat at the exact time you say you're having dinner," Gloria said. She grabbed the macaroni and cheese and headed out to the dining room.

"I've got these beans," Carol said. "Adam, you get those sweet potatoes from Taylor. That pan is hot and heavy. And Taylor, you carry those rolls in."

Carol was gone before Taylor could say she was perfectly capable of carrying the pan into the dining room.

"I don't care what you're thinking, I'm grabbing this pan like my mother-in-law instructed me to do. And if you know what's best for you, you'll grab those rolls." He slid the pan from where it sat in front of her on the island, but before picking it up he leaned in to drop a kiss on her lips.

"Merry Christmas, Mrs. Dale."

If she'd been feeling any type of way about her mother's comment, that feeling dissipated at the sound of those words. "Merry Christmas to you, Mr. Dale."

She would never tire of hearing him call her his wife.

They headed out to the dining room, and Taylor stopped just a few steps from the massive glossed, cherry wood table that one of Adam's bowling teammates made for them as a wedding present. It sat ten people on each side and two at the heads, perfectly. Tonight, on their first Christmas Eve as a married couple and in this new house, both of Adam's brothers, Jenny, Josephine and her father, Wendy and her family, Ray, Brooke and their parents sat waiting for dinner to start.

Taylor's dream had come true. Tears filled her eyes as she stared out to her family and friends and vowed that this was only the first in what would be many more family holidays in this house.

"Come on, Momma, so Pop can say the grace. I'm ready to eat that mac 'n cheese." Brooke was wearing her hair straight today. She'd been begging Taylor to let her have it down instead of in ponytails for weeks because she was getting older.

Taylor had been reluctant but she knew growing up was inevitable, besides, Brooke was still so very cute with the snowman earrings and matching headband that Josephine had given her for Christmas.

"I'm coming," Taylor said, but the moment she took a step she paused.

The streak of pain came quickly, taking her breath away in the process. She stood still for another second thinking that it would go away, but instead it strengthened. Her entire body tensed and she dropped the pan she'd been holding to grab her stomach.

Groaning, Taylor bent over. "Oh no!"

"'Oh no' is right, you dropped all the rolls. Hope there's more in the kitchen," Will Dale grumbled.

Taylor moaned, a long guttural sound that did absolutely nothing to stop the pain now seizing her body.

"The baby's coming!" Adam yelled.

"The baby's coming?" Brooke jumped out of her chair following Adam to stand beside Taylor.

"She's not due until New Year's Eve," Jenny said, panic lacing her tone.

Gloria and Carol were both out of their seats.

"Babies go by their own clock," Gloria said.

"Yes they do," Carol added. "Taylor was three days late."

Gloria shook her head. "Adam was late too. Now I guess their baby's gonna show them how to get here early."

"The baby's coming!" Brooke yelled.

Taylor nodded at the chaos that had begun. Adam had one of her arms and was guiding her to the door. Brooke was on the other side of her.

"I'll call your doctor and tell him you're on the way to the hospital," Josephine yelled out from wherever she was now.

Taylor closed her eyes with each pain.

"I'll get the truck," she heard Ray yell.

"I'll go get the bag you packed," Wendy said.

Taylor just kept moving. She tried to recall those breathing exercises they taught her in Lamaze class, but gave up when the pain rendered them futile.

"Here, she needs a coat on, it's cold out there."

Taylor's eyes popped open at her mother's words.

"Brooke get your coat on too. And Will you come on. We're going to the hospital."

Ray ran back inside. "Forgot my keys."

"Ohmygoodness the baby's coming!" Brooke yelled again.

"This baby's gonna be born right here in the middle of my new house if we don't hurry," Taylor wailed.

Two hours and twenty-three minutes later, Aiden Dale lay sleeping in his mother's arms. Adam sat on the side of the bed, his arm draped around Taylor, his gaze set on his son. Brooke sat on the other side of the bed leaning over to touch her baby brother's hand.

"I can't believe you have two children now, Adam," Jenny said from where she stood at the end of the bed.

"Building a family," Ray said with a nod. "That's what he's doing. He's building himself a strong, beautiful family."

Adam smiled at Ray and the new grandparents who were standing behind Ray beaming.

"I think you're right," Adam told them.

"Christmas is tomorrow," a very tired Taylor said. "We have to get Aiden's stocking hung up with ours."

"Right," Brooke said with a curt nod. "So Santa can find him because home is where you hang your stocking, right, Momma?"

Taylor smiled at Brooke. She lifted a hand and rubbed it over her hair. "No, sweetie, home is where your family is. And my family, my beautiful loving family is right here."

The End

Gingerbread Cake With Lemon Butter Sauce

A Hallmark Original Recipe

In *A Gingerbread Romance*, Taylor just wants the gingerbread to be sturdy enough to build a life-size house. But Adam insists on making sure it doesn't only look good, but *tastes* good. His commitment to quality ingredients and preparation inspired this recipe. You can't build a house out of it, of course; its only purpose is to be absolutely delicious.

Yield: 12 servings
Prep Time: 15 minutes
Cook Time: 45 minutes
Total Time: 1 hour

INGREDIENTS

Gingerbread Cake
- ½ cup (1 stick) unsalted butter, softened
- ½ cup brown sugar, packed
- 1 large egg
- 1 teaspoon vanilla extract
- 2 cups all-purpose flour
- 2 teaspoons ground cinnamon
- 2 teaspoons ground ginger
- 1 teaspoon baking soda
- ¼ teaspoon ground nutmeg
- ¼ teaspoon kosher salt
- ¾ cup unsulfured mild molasses
- ¾ cup hot water

Lemon Butter Sauce
- ½ cup granulated sugar
- ¼ cup unsalted butter
- 3 tablespoons fresh squeezed lemon juice
- 1 teaspoon fresh lemon zest (optional)
- 1 teaspoon vanilla extract
- whipped cream as needed

DIRECTIONS

1. To prepare gingerbread cake: preheat oven to 325°F. Butter a 9-inch spring-form pan; set aside.

2. Combine butter and brown sugar in bowl

of a stand mixer fitted with a paddle attachment; beat at medium speed until light and fluffy.

3. Add egg and vanilla extract and mix until well combined.

4. In a separate bowl, combine flour, cinnamon, ginger, baking soda, nutmeg and salt; stir to blend. In a separate bowl, combine molasses and water; stir to blend.

5. Alternately add about 1/3 dry and wet ingredients to mixing bowl and mix until just combined. Scrape down sides of bowl; pour batter into pan.

6. Bake for 40 minutes or until a toothpick inserted in center of cake comes out clean. Cool cake in pan on rack. Serve slightly warm or at room temperature.

7. To prepare sauce: combine all ingredients in saucepan. Bring to a boil, reduce heat, and simmer over low heat for 3 minutes, stirring frequently, until sauce thickens.

8. Slice cake into wedges; top each with warm lemon sauce and whipped cream.

Thanks so much for reading *A Gingerbread Romance*. We hope you enjoyed it!

For information about our new releases and exclusive offers, sign up for our free newsletter at hallmarkchannel.com/hallmark-publishing-newsletter

You can also connect with us here:

Facebook.com/HallmarkPublishing

Twitter.com/HallmarkPublish

About The Author

Lacey Baker, a Maryland native, lives with her husband, three children, grandson and an English Bulldog in what most would call suburban America--a townhouse development where everybody knows each other and each other's kids. Family cook-outs, reunion vacations, and growing up in church have all inspired Lacey to work towards her dreams and to write about the endurance of family and the quest to find everlasting love.

To date she has written in several genres including small town romance, YA paranormal (as Artist Arthur), a cozy mystery series titled Rumors, and adult paranormal (as A.C. Arthur).

Turn the page for a sneak peek of

An Unforgettable Christmas

Chapter One

ANGIE HURRIED PEPE OUT THE door of their modest third-floor apartment and into the chilly stairwell. He wore his coat, hat, and mittens, and had his Batman backpack slung over his shoulders. But, lunch. *Where's lunch?*

She halted midstride, calling out, "Hang on! We forgot your lunchbox."

Pepe turned his big, dark eyes in her direction. He'd been racing ahead and had already made it to the second-floor landing. "But, Mo-om, I'll miss the bus."

He was right, and she knew it. She didn't have time to drive him in to school today. She rapidly descended the steps after him, taking care with her footing in her new cranberry-colored pumps. They matched her bag as well as her necklace and earrings. When combined with her jolly Santa Claus pin, the fun accessories added a pop of color to her otherwise drab work outfit.

"Okay," Angie said, relenting. This was what her son always wanted—to purchase lunch with the cool kids in his first-grade class. "You can buy today."

Pepe fist-pumped in the air. "Ye-es!"

"But eat your lunch before the ice cream," Angie warned, knowing the tempting dessert was what he was secretly after.

She followed him down the stairs, marveling at how much taller he'd grown since September. He'd been the new kid in his class but appeared to be settling in. He'd never had trouble making new friends.

Pepe reached the building's front door as Angie stepped up behind him, shoving it open. A sharp blast of wind greeted them, and icy droplets prickled her face. She cinched the belt on her coat and tugged her hat down over her ears, shivering in the cold.

Pepe held out his hands, catching the tiny flakes in his mittens. "Woo-hoo! It's snowing!"

"Yeah. How cool is that?" Angie's gaze swept the street where she spied the school bus approaching, its windshield wipers swishing.

As she and Pepe scurried that way, Angie's mother parked her gold-colored sedan at the curb abutting their apartment building. Elena climbed from the passenger seat, and her short, layered, dark hair was instantly speckled with little white dots. Beneath her puffy blue coat, Elena's nurse's scrubs were adorned with cartoon storks carrying pink and blue baby bundles in their pointy beaks.

"Grandma!" Pepe waved his arms, as Angie escorted him toward the now-waiting school bus. "It's snowing!"

Elena grinned. "Yes, yes! I know."

Angie hugged Pepe's shoulders, giving him a quick kiss on the head. "Have a great day at school. If it closes early, don't worry. Grandma and Lita will be here," she said, mentioning Pepe's great-grandmother. When Angie was small, she'd been unable to call her maternal grandmother by her preferred name, *Abuelita*, Spanish for little grandmother. "Lita" was all toddler Angie could manage, and so the endearment had stuck. Pepe now called Alma "Lita," as well, even though she was technically his *bisabuela*.

The bus driver opened the door, and Pepe surprised Angie with a question. "Can Bobby come over?"

"What?"

"Home from school? We can play in the snow."

Angie knew Bobby was Pepe's new special first-grade buddy, but things like that needed to be arranged ahead of time. Besides, today was impossible. "I'd have to talk to his mom," Angie said apologetically. "Maybe tomorrow, all right?"

Pepe puffed out his bottom lip as Angie greeted the bus driver, "Hi, Mr. Jackson!"

"Morning, Ms. Lopez! Looks like a snowy one."

"Indeed."

Pepe climbed the school bus steps with a dour look, but moments later he was smiling again. He took a seat beside another boy, waving at Angie through the school bus window.

Kids.

Angie whirled on her heel, checking her watch. She'd need to get going in order to pick up the Christmas wreath she wanted for the shop. She caught up with her mom, who was removing a couple of reusable shopping totes from the trunk of her car.

"What's all this?" Angie asked Elena, rushing over to help her.

Elena handed Angie one of the heavy bags, and Angie spied sketch pads and paintbrushes inside it. "More art supplies for Lita."

"How nice of you. She's running low," Angie answered, surmising Elena must have stopped at the craft store yesterday evening on her way into the hospital.

Elena worked the night shift as a labor and delivery nurse, and Angie worked days as an accountant at a jewelry shop. Elena slept while Pepe was in school and also kept an ear out for Lita, who was still largely self-sufficient and could get herself around reasonably well by using a combination of her wheelchair and a walker.

Angie nodded at Elena as they climbed the apartment stairs, carting their armloads of supplies. "Today she's doing birds."

Elena smiled. Lita loved painting birds nearly as much as she adored painting butterflies. All were colorful creations and masterfully done for a woman who'd only begun painting much later in life.

Angie unlocked their apartment door, letting her mother inside. "How was your night?"

"Long, but good." Elena heaved a breath. "We had a last-minute C-section. That's why I'm running late." When Angie's brows rose in concern, Elena added, "The mom's *very* tired, but fine."

"And the baby?"

"A perfectly healthy little boy." Elena shut the door and winked. "*And* his perfectly healthy sister."

"Twins? What fun!" Angie grinned and eyed the clock on the stove. "Uh-oh. Gotta dash." She reached for the canvas bag on the kitchen table that contained her lunch and a few other personal items she carried in to work.

Angie saw Lita seated in her wheelchair at a card table in the nearby living room. The stylish older woman's chestnut-colored hair was pulled back in a bun, and she'd tucked a bright pink orchid into it. Lita's fashionable costume jewelry and her beautiful floral scarf complemented her lilac-and-turquoise outfit. The woman leaned forward, busily outlining something on the sketchpad in front of her. Lita raised her eyes to view a cardinal perched on the birdfeeder outside the living room window, its spectacular crimson plumage visible through the pelting snow.

"Bye, Lita," Angie called. "Have a great day!"

The older woman looked up and smiled softly, giving Angie a parting wave with her pencil.

"Leaving already?" Elena asked. "What's the big rush?"

"I've got to make a quick stop on the way in. Sam's big sale is today," Angie replied, referencing her boss.

"I thought that was last Friday. Black Friday?"

"That was one of them." Angie tucked her purse into her canvas tote and slung the bag over her shoulder. "The first part of Sam's one-two punch."

"His what?"

"It's a two-part sale. Beginning with Black Friday and ending on Cyber Monday."

"But it's a jewelry store," Elena complained. "Not a tech shop."

"Folks can print out discount coupons online."

Elena frowned at this. "That means you'll be working late, I suppose?"

Angie gave her mom a peck on the cheek. "Hope not!"

"You already worked extra last week," Elena

said. "You went in on Saturday too. To train the new girl."

"She's a woman, Ma. Close to your age."

"What does that mean?"

Angie wryly twisted her lips. "Mature."

"Good. Maybe she'll be able to talk some sense into him."

"Who?"

"Sam!" When Angie stared at her, Elena continued, "Help him see that there's a *world* beyond work. People have lives...commitments..."

Elena initially had been pleased by her daughter's employment at Singleton's Jewelers. But before long, she'd started questioning aloud whether the job was the right fit. Sam Singleton worked extremely hard. Those who worked for him were expected to work hard, as well. Which would have been fine, in Elena's opinion, if that didn't sometimes entail extra hours. Extra hours without extra pay, since Angie was in a salaried position. Then, there were the additional hours Angie put in processing her accounting reports at home.

Angie honestly didn't mind her demanding schedule. She slept better at night when her tasks were wrapped up for the day and not lingering overhead to be tackled tomorrow.

She sighed and buttoned her coat. "I'll try to be home by seven, okay? We can all have a nice dinner together then."

When Angie turned to go, her mother said,

"I don't know why you continue to work for that man. We don't need the money that badly. I can take on extra shifts until you find something else."

Angie knew that Elena was just being proud—and protective. The truth was, they did need the money. She and her mom were both saving up to purchase a house: some place really nice for Pepe to grow up in.

"I don't *want* another job, Ma." Angie turned from where she stood on the threshold. "'That man' is my boss. And in many ways, he's a good one."

"Ha!"

"I mean it," Angie insisted. "He pays me well, and the hours aren't bad." She winced at her amendment. "Normally."

"Maybe if you explained you have a family—"

"I can't risk being unprofessional," she countered. "Not with so much at stake." Her gaze flitted to the refrigerator crowded with magnets and a combination of Pepe and Alma's artwork. Pepe's latest report card hung there, too, and he'd received very high marks. They were all settling in here. What's more, Pepe was *thriving*.

"Besides, Sam's not really *that* awful. Not really. Not once you get to know him." Angie shrugged. "He has potential! You know, like a diamond in the rough."

Elena studied her daughter and then her tone took on a teasing lilt. "And just who do you suppose will do the shaping and polishing? You?"

Angie blushed hotly. "Me? No! That's...that's not how I look at Sam. He's my *employer*. I wouldn't dream of—" She paused and drew in a breath, surveying Elena. "Just what are you hinting at?"

Elena's mouth dropped open. "I can't believe it. You actually *like* him."

"Of course I *like* him. As a person. In a way," Angie stammered. "The way any person would like another individual. Person to person. Not that we're really that personal with each other. Sam and I, I mean."

Elena's eyebrows arched and she got that sage look in her eyes. "You never mentioned that he's handsome."

"I'm not saying that now," Angie added, feeling weirdly caught out. Naturally, she'd noticed Sam's good looks. Who wouldn't? The guy was tall and built, with short, dark hair and deep blue eyes.

That only made Angie observant, not interested. The thought of adding one more item to her already crammed to-do list, like becoming romantically involved with someone, frankly made her exhausted.

She added, "It's not like that, okay?"

Even if she *had* had time for dating these days, which she didn't, she clearly wouldn't entertain notions of going out with Sam. He was her boss, for goodness' sake.

And no matter how Angie defended him to her mom, Sam was also a little stuffy. Although he was just three years older than she was, with his firmly set jaw and that determined stance, Sam gave the impression of being much older.

Angie couldn't begin to imagine him on a date. The man appeared to have absolutely zero interest in fun, which was fine with Angie. She wasn't angling to have fun with Sam, anyhow.

"Anyway, I've got to go!" Angie tugged the door open, shaking off Elena's weird suggestion. *Me and Sam. Ha, ha.* Not *happening.* Then, she scurried down the stairs and out into the blustery cold.

Sam Singleton strolled down the sidewalk through the drifting snow, the crisp morning air adding an extra spring to his step. Holiday garlands circled the lampposts lining the road and each held an green pennant, decorated with holly sprigs and joyfully welcoming folks to Hopedale, Virginia. On each pennant, two fluttering white doves held an unfurled banner in their beaks showcasing the town's motto: *Where love springs eternal.* This was partially in reference to the thermal springs in the nearby Hopedale Valley

Springs Ski Resort. The slogan was also meant to inspire greater business among couples visiting the area on romantic getaways.

When the Hopedale Chamber of Commerce first proposed the new motto, Sam had privately considered it hokey. Nonetheless, he'd grasped its marketing potential. Since love and the sale of elegant diamond engagement rings went hand in hand, Sam had been among the first to vote in favor of the change from the old town saying: *Home of the Hopedale Honey Bee.*

Sam ambled along, passing shuttered storefronts. Only the Main Street Market had its interior lights on. He could see a few folks milling about through its big front window. The quaint grocers had a café section selling fresh-baked breads, muffins, and pastries, and offering an assortment of imported coffees to early birds. Mostly, those patrons were individuals like him: people with jobs downtown who were on their way into work. Sam prided himself on being the first to arrive at work each day and the last to leave in the evening. Although his staff was small, as the boss, it was fitting for him to set the example.

He crossed the street at the corner before reaching Harris Hardware. Pete Harris's granddaughter, Hannah, ran it now. She took over the place right around the time Sam's dad, David, retired from his long career as a clerk there. David had never aspired to a higher education than high school. He'd reserved ambition for his one and only child, Sam. Precisely why Sam had been shipped off to Ashton Academy as a boy. Those were times he preferred not to think about. What Sam enjoyed was focusing on his current goals, including his typical checkerboard trajectory to work. This customary path gave him a keen appreciation for all of Hopedale, a quaint Blue Ridge Mountain town with a high walkability score.

One could live quite well here and accomplish most daily errands getting around on foot. He did just that, as he lived in a cool condo complex beyond the historic area. Local residents had kicked up a fuss when the sleek five-story chrome and glass building had gone in, but he truly hadn't understood what the hubbub was about. The building was eco-friendly with many green initiatives in place, such as solar panels on its roof, and it didn't stand out *all that much* against the thicket of woods it bordered.

Sam traversed Main Street again before reaching the library. The red brick building with a low tin roof had been fashioned from the small train depot, which was once operational in town back in the day when westbound passenger trains still stopped there. The cozy reading area inside, comprised of a semicircular stack of carpeted steps, was positioned by a plate-glass window overlooking the tracks. When Sam was small, his dad used to take him there sometimes to pick out books and watch the trains rumble by. That was all before Ashton, when he got too grown-up for train watching anyway.

Sam passed the post office and tamped down his hat, hunching his shoulders against the wind. He hoped the weather wouldn't deter shoppers today and, as he drew nearer, he saw he had no worries. A healthy crowd had gathered outside Singleton's Jewelers with its impressive front window display and that stunning marque hanging overhead. Sam loved the way the dot in the letter "i" in Singleton's was shaped like a glistening diamond.

His new television commercials advertising Sam's Signature Diamond Collection were doing especially well. *A Singleton's Signature Diamond Says Forever.* Sam grinned to himself, envisioning the way that line rolled across the television screen: stylized gold font shimmering against a darkened background, with the diamond-shaped dot of the "i" in Singleton's giving a little twinkle. He and his advertising director had designed a total of five ads, each one featuring a touching marriage proposal.

He'd requested Angie's input on that, since he had very little idea what women considered romantic. His past relationships had been companionable rather than affectionate, as neither he nor his former partners had entertained much interest in forming a bond that was too deep. His last girlfriend, Rebecca, was a banker and no-nonsense like Sam. When they'd broken up due to her job transfer out of state, neither one had shed a tear.

Sam approached the crowd gathered outside his shop, giving a cheery wave. "Morning, folks! Thanks for coming out."

People nodded and smiled, taking cover from the pelting snow under open umbrellas. Sam gauged the crowd to number roughly thirty individuals, and he was encouraged to see so many eager shoppers anticipating the store's opening. This could be his most profitable sales event—ever.

He grinned at the expectant faces as he edged his way through the crowd. Sam recognized several patrons as regulars, but there were newcomers as well. There was a time when he knew almost everyone in Hopedale by name. Then, the fancy ski resort had gone in nearby, and the tiny mountain town had boomed. Not just during tourist season, either. People were discovering what Hopedale's residents had known all along: This was the ideal, picturesque place to settle down and raise a family. The excellent reputation of the school district served as an additional draw. Due to Hopedale's fine medical facility and its adjacent hospital, retirees were discovering Hopedale, too. All this growth had been good for business. Sam's business, in particular. He'd had to hire an additional sales associate just last week.

Sam stood under the awning outside his shop's front door and slid his key into the lock as happy anticipation skittered through him. He could just feel it. Today was going to be a memorable day.

Get the book! *An Unforgettable Christmas* is available now.